Prai~~se for~~

Murder for Choir

"Joelle Charbonneau brings a professional's eye and experience to *Murder for Choir,* and readers will enjoy her heroine Paige Marshall's take on high school show choirs. Music and drama lovers who can't get enough of Rachel, Finn, Kurt, and the gang will have enormous fun with this delightfully witty take on 'Murder, She Sang.' Encore, encore!"
—Miranda James, *New York Times* bestselling author

"Charbonneau hits all the right notes with her show choir coach sleuth."
—Denise Swanson, *New York Times* bestselling author

"An intriguing mystery . . . I'm looking forward to future entries in this series."
—Donna Andrews, *New York Times* bestselling author

"Imagine if Stephanie Plum joined the cast of *Glee*, then someone proved to be more felonious than harmonious."
—Deke Sharon, vocal producer of NBC's *The Sing-Off*

Berkley Prime Crime titles by Joelle Charbonneau

MURDER FOR CHOIR
END ME A TENOR

End Me a Tenor

JOELLE CHARBONNEAU

BERKLEY PRIME CRIME, NEW YORK

THE BERKLEY PUBLISHING GROUP
Published by the Penguin Group
Penguin Group (USA) Inc.
375 Hudson Street, New York, New York 10014, USA

USA / Canada / UK / Ireland / Australia / New Zealand / India / South Africa / China

Penguin Books Ltd., Registered Offices: 80 Strand, London WC2R 0RL, England
For more information about the Penguin Group, visit penguin.com.

END ME A TENOR

A Berkley Prime Crime Book / published by arrangement with the author

Berkley Prime Crime Books are published by The Berkley Publishing Group.
BERKLEY® PRIME CRIME and the PRIME CRIME logo are trademarks of
Penguin Group (USA) Inc.

For information, address: The Berkley Publishing Group,
a division of Penguin Group (USA) Inc.,
375 Hudson Street, New York, New York 10014.

ISBN: 978-0-425-25216-1

PUBLISHING HISTORY
Berkley Prime Crime mass-market edition / April 2013

PRINTED IN THE UNITED STATES OF AMERICA

10 9 8 7 6 5 4 3 2 1

Cover illustration by Paul Hess.
Cover design by Rita Frangie.
Interior text design by Laura K. Corless.

ALWAYS LEARNING   PEARSON

For my son, Max.

Acknowledgments

Although a writer's job is solitary, no author ever publishes a book alone. I owe countless thanks to my family, especially my mother, Jaci, my husband, Andy, and my son, Max, for their love and support. Also, I owe a great deal of thanks to my students, especially Chessie Santoro, Kristen Bock, Jacob Groth, Megan Gill, and Breanna Lucas, for the inspiration you provided. You make teaching a true joy and I am so very proud of each and every one of you.

To my agent, Stacia Decker, I'm so lucky to have you as a partner in this publishing adventure. You're the best. Much gratitude also must be extended to Donald Maass, everyone at DMLA and to the gang of Team Decker. Also, this series would not be possible without the insightful guidance and enthusiasm of my editor, Michelle Vega, the wonderful leadership of Natalee Rosenstein and the rest of the fabulous team at Berkley Prime Crime. You guys are amazing. And I would be remiss if I didn't give a shout out to Paul Hess for his amazing art and Rita Frangie for her art design. I love my covers.

I would also like to say thank you to members of the performance world whom I have been lucky enough to work with and to three specifically who allowed me to use their names in this book. To Ray Frewen, Bill Walters, and LaVon Fischer as well as the performers, directors, and production staff who have graced the stage of my life—your creative force and dedication to storytelling are an inspiration to everyone around you.

Last, but by no means least, thank you to all the booksellers, librarians, and readers out there who pick up this book. You make everything possible.

Chapter 1

Whoever invented artificial snow deserved to be shot. No matter how careful I was, iridescent flakes landed in my hair, my clothes, and my mouth. Not only did they taste bad, but the sparkly flakes made me sneeze. The label claimed they were hypoallergenic. The label lied.

Then again, none of my show choir students strategically scattering handfuls of the stuff across the stage seemed to be having a problem. They were delighted to spend their Saturday afternoon flirting, rehearsing, and decorating the auditorium for the Winter Wonderland concert. Show choir was their life. I was sorry to say that, at this very moment, it was my life, too. But not for long. I'd gotten an opera gig, and my performance next weekend was going to be my big break. My real career would take off, and I'd be done with teenage angst.

"The stage looks great, don't you think?" Prospect Glen's choir director, Larry DeWeese, walked over to me. His smile was bright, but the way he was wringing his hands spoke volumes. Clearly, the Yoga he'd been doing in his spare time hasn't helped calm his nerves.

"What's wrong?"

"Wrong, Paige?" Larry raked a hand through his disheveled brown hair as his smile widened. Not a good sign. "Why would you think anything is wrong?"

I'd only been working with Larry and the Prospect Glen show choirs for four months, but every time Larry smiled like that bad things happened. I just hoped that whatever the crisis was it wouldn't involve a dead body—like it had my first week on the job.

"Miss Marshall?"

I turned toward the sound of my name, sneezed, and then smiled at the student who patiently waited for my attention. Megan Posey was shy, but she had a fabulous soprano voice and a great work ethic, which made up for her lack of dance training. Some of the other students snickered at Megan's struggles to pick up the choreography, but she ignored them and always came to the next rehearsal prepared. I had to admire that. "What's up, Megan?"

The blonde senior frowned. "One of the snowmen lost his head. Do you want us to duct-tape it back on?"

The mere mention of the word "snow" was enough to make me sneeze and sneeze and sneeze. Both Megan and Larry took a step back as I sneezed one last time.

"Why don't I handle the snowman problem?" Larry fished a crumpled tissue out of his pocket and handed it to me. "That way, Miss Marshall can start rehearsal. We only have the theater for another two hours."

Larry headed stage left to work his magic on Frosty, leaving me in charge. Drat. While the students pushed the boundaries of good behavior around him, they always stepped back before crossing the line into detention. His having the power to fail them garnered a semblance of the teenagers' respect. As a voice teacher and extracurricular activity coach, I didn't have the power to alter their grade point average, which meant I was forced to gain their respect the old-fashioned way—through fear. While I didn't see the allure of show choir, I was grateful these kids lived in terror of losing their places on the squad.

Sneezing one last time, I yelled, "Time for warm-ups. Music in Motion will rehearse first. Then Mr. DeWeese will run the Singsations through their numbers."

A few of the boys helped me move the grand piano into place, and I tried not to cringe as my fingers touched the keys. While the keyboard had been disinfected (I knew because I had done it myself) it was hard to forget Greg Lucas's dead body that was once perched on top of it. Assuring myself that the piano didn't have death cooties, I began to play the first vocal warm-up.

Five minutes later, I was happy to leave the death piano and walked over to the CD player at the end of the stage.

"We're going to run the entire program from beginning to end. Once we've gone through all the songs, we can go back and polish. Take your places."

When everyone was in his or her starting position, I pressed play and watched my choir swing into action.

For the first three songs, the teens twirled, shimmied, and sashayed around the stage singing about reindeer, sleigh rides, and other winter topics. No mention of Christmas, Hanukkah, or other religious holidays was allowed, which in my mind eliminated some of the best music selections. But the students didn't seem to care what the music was about as long as it was upbeat and had plenty of solo opportunities. I winced as the current soloist reached for a note and missed. Sighing, I made a note to work on that along with missed dance steps, an out-of-tune harmony, and a lift that didn't quite get off the ground. None of the students looked concerned by their mistakes. They laughed and smiled and had a blast.

Then the music changed and so did their attitude. This music wasn't just for their friends and family attending the winter concert. Though these songs would also be performed at the concert, they were part of the show choir's repertoire for the competitions that would start in two months—competitions my students intended to win. But not if they danced and sang the way they just had.

When they struck their final poses, I hit the off switch and got to work. "Megan, you need to spot your turn so you don't fall out of it. Markus, keep your head up. No looking at the floor. Ethan, I need more diction. If you're singing English, I should be able to understand you. Chessie, don't push during your solo. The pitch is going flat."

"What do you mean, I'm going flat?" Chessie flipped her long dark hair behind her shoulders and gave me a look that could kill. Which I suppose I should have expected. While senior Chessie Bock was undeniably the most talented member of my choir, she was also the most difficult.

When I first started as coach, Chessie had done her best to get me ousted from the job. Not too long after school started, we came to a truce that I hoped was based on my talent and leadership. Most likely it had more to do with my willingness to keep some of Chessie's less-than-legal antics under wraps. Chessie was applying to several of the top music theater schools in the country. While most colleges looked for extracurricular activities, making license plates in the clink probably wasn't going to gain her a scholarship. Over the past couple weeks, I'd noticed her attitude reasserting itself. Clearly, the cease-fire gained by my silence had come to an end.

Hoping to avoid a meltdown, I chose my words carefully. "The solo is in the perfect range for you to show off your voice, but today you're pushing the volume. When you push, you have a tendency to go flat."

Chessie's eyes flashed. "I never go flat."

A few of the students behind Chessie rolled their eyes. Taking a deep breath, I explained, "Everyone goes flat. The best singers recognize the areas they need to improve and make adjustments."

The set of Chessie's jaw told me she still wanted to fight. Instead, she gave a sharp nod of her head and said, "Can I try the solo again?"

While Chessie hated being critiqued, she far more disliked being thought of as less than the best. Taking a seat at the death piano, I ran Chessie through her solo. While she still looked pissed, she sounded fabulous. Chalk one up for me.

Once the rest of the problems were addressed, I started the CD player and watched the choir go through its routines again. Aside from a couple slips on the snow, the team looked like it might be ready for the concert on Thursday night. Thank God!

When the last number was complete, I gave a couple more notes, reminded the kids about tomorrow's rehearsal with the Music in Motion band, and asked them to drive safely home. The thought of fourteen teenagers cruising down the icy streets made me happy I had offered to stay late and help Larry polish the second-tier show choir's routines today.

And after seeing their routines, I knew why Larry needed help. Made up mostly of underclassmen who aspired to compete in the top show choir, the thirty-four-member Singsations did their best to perform Larry's unique brand of choreography. With so many kids and only so much room to move, the dancing quickly dissolved into a human game of pinball.

Yikes.

An hour later, the dance steps had been simplified, one song had been axed from the program, and the kids looked ready to drop. But the routines were better. I hoped by the concert that they'd look better still.

While the students pulled on their coats and boots and gathered up boxes from their show choir Secret Santas, Larry yelled, "Good work, everyone. Don't forget to remind your parents that you have rehearsal every night before the concert. Miss Marshall and I expect to see each and every one of you there."

"Music in Motion is meeting after school this week," I reminded Larry. "I won't be at the evening rehearsals. Remember?"

I'd shifted the practice schedule when I was cast as the soprano in the sing-along *Messiah* starring world-renowned tenor David Richard. While David Richard wasn't expected to attend the weeklong rehearsal schedule preceding the sold-out performances, the rest of the soloists were.

"I know that was the plan, but that was before."

"Before what?"

Larry's attention shifted from me to the students walking

out the door. "I need to make sure everyone has a ride home. I'll explain everything when I come back."

Before I could protest, Larry hurried to the back of the auditorium toward the lobby, leaving me to wonder what had changed since yesterday when Larry and I last spoke about my rehearsal plans. While I wasn't interested in being a high school show choir coach for the long term, I needed the job to pay the bills until my performing career took off. This week's gig had the potential to help me take that step, but nothing in the performing world was guaranteed. Talent didn't necessarily translate into fame and fortune. Luck was a huge part of it. Until Larry's cryptic announcement, I'd hoped my luck had taken a turn for the better.

"How did rehearsal go?"

I turned toward the voice coming from the stage wings and smiled as Prospect Glen's theater teacher, Devlyn O'Shea, stepped out of the shadows. The sexy glint in his blue eyes made me think that maybe my luck wasn't all that terrible after all. Standing over six feet tall with brown hair, a slightly crooked nose, and a muscular dancer's body, Devlyn was enough to make any girl feel lucky. Until they noticed the pink sweater that coordinated perfectly with his pink and gray pinstriped pants.

That's when most girls would curse the fates that such a fantastic male specimen was gay. I should know. I'd cursed those same fates when we first met. Of course, that was before I learned his secret: At Devlyn's first job he'd seen a teacher's life destroyed after the teacher rejected a student's advances. In a fit of pique, the girl marched to the principal's office to file a report of sexual misconduct. By the time the teacher was exonerated, his career was in shreds. When

Devlyn started this job, he took to wearing pastels to protect himself and his job from high school girls' unwanted advances.

"They have a ways to go before the competitions in the spring, but they'll hold their own at the concert." Ignoring the way my heart jumped as Devlyn sauntered across the stage toward me, I asked, "What are you doing here? I thought you had a family thing today."

"Larry called and asked if I could swing by for a few minutes. I was happy to say yes since my mother was trying to talk me into a blind date with the daughter of one of her friends."

I stamped down a flicker of jealousy and asked, "What did you tell her?"

He gave me a sexy grin. "I said for the past couple of months I've had my eye on a beautiful brunette. That our schedules hadn't allowed us to pursue a relationship, but I was hopeful we'd find the time soon. What do you think?" he asked, taking a step forward. "Do you think we can find the time?"

I could feel the heat radiating off his body, and my heart skipped a beat. "Sure. I think we can make time for that."

Devlyn's eyes scanned the auditorium and then settled back on me. His head dipped and his lips brushed against mine. The kiss was light, and over before it began. But my lips were tingling and my legs weak when Devlyn said, "What do you say we catch a late dinner after—"

"Thank God you're here, Devlyn." Larry's panicked voice echoed from the back of the large auditorium. "We have a huge problem."

As Larry hurried down the center aisle to the stage, Devlyn shot me an amused smile that I couldn't help returning. Larry often referred to a hole in his sock as a huge problem.

"Did Chessie complain about my critique of her singing?" It wouldn't be the first time she'd gone running to Larry. The last was when she'd been assigned only one solo for this winter concert.

Larry shook his head as he climbed the escape stairs onto the stage. "I want you both to brace yourselves. This is the worst news possible."

The terror shining in Larry's eyes had my stomach clenching. Was someone injured? Dead?

"Buffalo Grove's and Madison's show choirs are going to be competing with one of our same songs. We're in serious trouble."

"Are you kidding?" I laughed with relief, but then stopped. Devlyn and Larry weren't laughing. "I guess I don't understand. Why does it matter if we perform one of the same songs?"

Larry let out a dramatic sigh. "The judges look for creativity as well as execution. They won't invite us to compete at nationals if they think we're taking our ideas from other teams. The choir booster president has already contacted the school board to express her concern. If we don't come up with a new song by Thursday's concert . . ." Larry swallowed hard and looked at Devlyn, who in turn looked at me.

"What?" I asked. "What's going to happen if we don't have a new song ready?"

Larry's lip trembled as his eyes met mine. "You'll be fired."

———

Being a show choir coach might not have been my life's ambition, but the idea of being fired freaked me out. Which is why I was driving through the sleet and snow to Prospect Glen High School at nine o'clock on a Sunday morning. Last night, over pepperoni pizza and warm soda, Larry, Devlyn, and I had kicked around ideas for replacement songs. I'd stayed up until midnight tweaking what I hoped was a brilliant arrangement of the chosen number. This morning, Devlyn and I would create the choreography. How the team was going to learn the music and steps before Thursday's concert was beyond me. Personally, I didn't understand why we couldn't just tell the choir boosters that we were working on a new song. Unfortunately, Larry nixed that option. The new song had to be ready and performed by Thursday. Or else.

If I didn't want to lose my source of guaranteed income, I needed to find a way to squeeze in extra practice time with the show choir in between *Messiah* rehearsals. While my aunt would be happy to let me sponge more than free rent, I was raised to pay my own way. I couldn't lose my coaching job. At least, not yet.

Wrapping my scarf around my mouth and nose, I grabbed my dance bag and climbed out of my toasty warm car into the arctic cold. My car told me the temperature outside was ten degrees, which seemed optimistic. By the time I reached the school's side door, I had barely enough sensation in my fingers to slide the key into the lock, open the door, and close out the cold behind me.

Achoo. Achoo. Achoo.

Crap. Some of the artificial snow must have gotten on my coat. It was the only explanation for the sneezing, because I was not getting sick.

Warmth was beginning to return to my appendages as I unlocked the choir room door, dumped my dance bag on a chair, and pushed the piano to the side of the room to give

Devlyn and me room to dance. I had taken off my electric blue coat and gotten down on the floor to stretch when Devlyn walked in carrying two large cups of coffee.

"I thought the caffeine might inspire us." He set the cups on the piano bench and shrugged out of his black trench coat and violet scarf. Underneath he was wearing black sweats and a fitted gray T-shirt. Between the coffee and Devlyn's biceps, I was starting to think this morning rehearsal wasn't such a bad idea after all.

Devlyn handed me a cup of coffee, walked over to the CD player, and pushed play. "I know you have to be at *Messiah* rehearsal in a couple of hours, so let's get to work."

Any ideas of a fun, flirtatious morning were quickly put to rest. The minute the music started, Devlyn danced like a man possessed. We twirled, dipped, and stomped, arguing about the best dance moves.

"The dance needs more difficulty or it won't score well."

"Well, it won't score well if the team is too winded to sing," I shot back.

"Your job is to make sure they can." Devlyn grabbed a towel out of his dance bag. "The only way the school board and the boosters will let you keep that job is if we get this number ready."

My stomach clenched in panic. Somewhere between last night and this morning, I'd half convinced myself that Larry was just being overdramatic. That my job didn't hinge on a new show choir number being ready by Thursday. By the way Devlyn was acting, it was clear he believed it did. That meant I was totally screwed.

"How can the school board fire me for doing the same song two other choirs are doing now? The competition isn't even until spring. That's not fair."

"This isn't about fair." Devlyn's eyes flashed. "This is about winning. Especially since Chessie Bock's father is on the board. If he thinks a new coach will get his daughter a better shot at landing a trophy, he'll make sure a new coach is hired."

Oh, crap. If Chessie's father was in charge of my fate, I might as well hang it up now.

My dejection must have shown because Devlyn put his arm around me. "Don't give up. We're going to show them that you're the best thing to ever happen to this program. Right?"

Taking a deep breath, I considered my options. Give up or fight?

Since giving up wasn't my style, I walked over to the CD player, hit play, and nodded. "Right. Let's get to work."

———

Every muscle in my body wept as I walked into Northwestern University's Cahn Auditorium. I'd changed into black pants and a deep green sweater, which I hoped looked casually professional. Making a good impression on both my fellow soloists and the show's conductor was important. My heart pounded with a combination of excitement and nerves as I walked through the lobby and into the historic thousand-seat theater. Four chairs were positioned on the front of the stage. Risers lined with chairs sat farther back. A blonde was flipping through music in one of the chairs up front.

As I walked down the side aisle of the theater, the blonde looked up and smiled. "You must be Paige. I'm Vanessa Moulton."

"It's nice to meet you," I said, climbing the escape stairs onto the stage. Technically we'd met before, not that Vanessa would remember. She had performed the role of Ida in *Die Fledermaus* at the Lyric Opera while I sang in the ensemble. She had a stunning voice and a demanding personality, which according to gossip, was the reason she had yet to land any major roles.

Carrying my bag filled with singer essentials—a black binder with the music score, a large water bottle, and several well-sharpened pencils—I walked across the stage to my chair. "Where is everyone?" According to my watch, rehearsal began in five minutes.

Vanessa snorted. "You don't really expect a rehearsal conducted by Magdalena Tebar to start on time, do you? She's known for making an entrance. I think Jonathan McMann is lurking downstairs in the greenroom, and our accompanist is having a smoke. If you need to freshen up, you have plenty of time."

Vanessa went back to studying her music, and I headed backstage to the stairs that led to the greenroom. I'd performed in this theater before. When school wasn't in session, like now, the university rented the facility to other performance groups. In past years, I'd done a number of professional shows here. I was hoping this performance would be the one that made critics sit up and pay attention. With talent like David Richard on the bill, how could I lose?

Wrapped up in my own thoughts, I barely registered the sound of raised voices. Until I turned the corner and saw a petite, busty brunette punch world-renowned tenor David Richard dead in the face.

Chapter 2

"How was rehearsal, dear?" My aunt Millie smiled at me from her perch on the stool at the kitchen island. On the other side of the counter, her houseguest, Aldo Mangialardi, was dropping biscuit dough onto a cookie sheet.

Aldo was a gifted pianist and a friend of Millie's. A few months ago, he'd tried to take my car for a spin only to end up in the hospital. When the doctor refused to discharge Aldo because he lived alone, Millie offered him her guest room for a few days. Only Aldo hadn't left. Instead, he cooked gourmet meals and feigned deafness when Millie suggested he move out.

Sitting at Aldo's feet, looking for handouts, was Millie's prizewinning standard poodle, Killer. The minute Killer spotted me, he started to growl. Most days I was intimidated by Killer's anger management problem and gave the dog a wide berth. Today, my need for the wine sitting on the counter trumped all.

Dumping my bag on the floor, I ignored the dog's low growl and poured myself a large glass of red, which just about matched my aunt's current hair color. "The other soloists are very talented. It should be a great show."

"With you singing, how could it not be *brillante*?" Aldo smoothed the tufts of white hair springing from the sides of his head and gave me a wink. "Millie has been telling everyone that you are singing with the famous David Richard."

"Did you see him today?" Millie's eyes twinkled behind her pink-rimmed glasses. "Is he as handsome in person as he is in his photos?"

"I didn't have the chance to meet him today." Between David clutching his nose and the brunette screaming angry threats, I'd decided it was best to make an exit before anyone noticed I was there. Which was probably a good thing since the brunette strutted into rehearsal ten minutes later with her orchestral score tucked under one arm and her conductor baton in the other. Something told me that international conductor Magdalena Tebar wouldn't be happy if she knew I'd witnessed her right hook. The last thing a singer wants to do is piss off the conductor. David Richard must not have gotten that memo. "The conductor said David would be at rehearsal tomorrow. Speaking of rehearsals, I need to go work on some new choreography Devlyn and I are putting together. I have to teach it to the choir tomorrow."

Millie's eyes narrowed. "Why do you need new choreography?"

The idea of sharing my plight was tempting. But I knew my aunt. She hadn't earned her pink Mary Kay Cadillac convertible by waiting for a problem to resolve itself. She'd end up on the school board president's doorstep, doing an impersonation of the Christmas caroler from hell.

Plastering a smile on my face, I said, "Another school is doing one of our songs and we want the option of changing routines if we need it. No big deal." Grabbing my bag, I headed up to my room and hoped I was right.

———

"Five, six, seven, eight. Step kick step prep turn turn turn. Eric, you're turning the wrong way. Let's try it again. Five, six, seven, eight."

I started the music again and watched the team as they stumbled through the dance steps. To their credit, the kids didn't whine and moan about learning a new routine. The minute Larry and I explained the problem, the team was ready and willing to work.

"Ms. Marshall." Chessie planted her hands on her hips. "You haven't assigned the solos yet. I don't see why the soloists should have to learn some of the steps when they won't be performing them."

Well, most of the team.

"For now, everyone learns everything." When Chessie opened her mouth to complain, I added, "Solo or not, I would think you'd have the biggest motivation for learning the routine. Aspiring music theater majors are expected to learn and perform dance routines in under an hour at their college auditions."

Chessie's eyes narrowed, but she stepped back in line. I counted off the routine again, trying not to let my embarrassment show. Yes, I was purposely avoiding casting the solos so I didn't have to deal with the fallout that would occur when Chessie didn't receive one. The girl didn't have the right sound for the song. It was as simple as that.

Sneezing, I glanced at the clock and hit stop on the CD

player. While the choir could use more work, I had to get going or I'd be late for my next rehearsal. "That's it for today. I expect everyone to come in tomorrow morning with the dance steps learned. Mr. O'Shea will be here for both rehearsals tomorrow to help demonstrate the two lifts we will be adding into the choreography. Get some rest, and I'll see you first thing in the morning."

I popped a zinc cough drop into my mouth and watched as the kids slowly gathered up their stuff, shrugged on their coats, and strolled toward the door. I tried not to look anxious about heading to the exit myself. If I left in the next couple minutes, I'd still have time to hit the drive-thru and get dinner before my six o'clock rehearsal.

"Ms. Marshall."

Crap.

"Yes, Chessie?"

"Can you give me any advice on what I should work on for my solo audition? My parents are hoping that I'll get another solo, and I'd like to do everything I can to make that happen." She gave me a sweet smile, but I could see the implied threat in the glimmer of her eyes. Chessie knew my job was at stake, and she was trying to leverage that into a second solo. I wanted to scream.

Instead, I gave a wide smile and said, "Make sure you keep your sound open and don't push when you get to the high notes. We'll have solo auditions on Wednesday morning. That gives you plenty of time to practice."

I glanced at the clock and grabbed my bag, hoping to make my escape, but Chessie had several more questions. By the time I shook her loose and got to my car, snow was falling. Even without stopping for dinner, I'd need a miracle to make it to rehearsal on time.

I practiced my arias as traffic crawled while trying hard not to think about Chessie's not-so-veiled threats. If I didn't give her the solo, I could kiss my job good-bye. If I caved, I'd be compromising my musical integrity and the chances of the group winning the national competition in the spring. Well, at least my day couldn't possibly get worse.

It took ten minutes to find street parking at the theater. The snow was falling harder as I slipped and slid down the sidewalk to the stage door.

The loud chatter of voices hit me the minute I stepped into the building. Today was a full run-through, which meant both the orchestra and the chorus were in attendance. The place was a madhouse. This version of the sing-along *Messiah* was getting media attention not only because of David Richard's stunning tenor voice but also because the chorus was comprised of both professional and college singers. Richard was currently a visiting faculty member at Northwestern University and had hand-selected the students who were participating in this concert. From the articles I'd read, the selected students not only got to sing in the concert, but also received private coaching sessions with David. At their age, I would have killed to have both on my résumé.

I signed my initials next to my name on the cast list on the call-board and followed the posted instructions for soloists to wait in their dressing rooms until the orchestra and chorus had been seated and warmed up. Several string players, instruments in hand, were filing into the orchestra pit as I walked through the greenroom to the soloist dressing rooms on the other side. A gorgeous and somewhat familiar-looking redhead carrying a violin case almost smacked right into me, but I ignored both the woman and the dirty look she shot me as I stared at my name listed next to one of the dressing room doors. It didn't matter how many shows I'd been in, seeing my name on a dressing room gave me chills. The fact that Vanessa Moulton was sitting in the dressing room, pushing buttons on her cell phone, didn't alter my excitement in the least.

"You're late." She glanced up at me. "Half the chorus and orchestra are late. So much for this being a professional production. I've already talked to my manager about filing a complaint."

Before I could say anything, a deep voice from behind said, "Give it a rest, Vanessa. Your manager can't control the weather." Our bass soloist, Jonathan McMann, smiled at me in the mirror. "Don't mind Vanessa. She's just testy because our star didn't remember her."

"He was simply distracted, that's all."

"Probably by his reflection in the mirror." Jonathan laughed. "Hell, if I looked half as good as he does, I'd probably be enamored with myself, too."

Vanessa gave Jonathan a weak smile. "You've always looked good to me."

Me, too. While gray threaded through Jonathan's close-cropped brown hair, the signs of age only served to set off the flecks of silver in his green eyes. With that and his six-foot-three height, Jonathan was still capturing romantic lead roles both in the smaller opera companies here in the city and no doubt in the dreams of many of the Northwestern female population he gave voice lessons to.

Hanging up my coat, I tried not to feel left out as Vanessa and Jonathan chatted like old friends. Since my water was only half full, I grabbed the bottle and my music and left the dressing room. I headed toward the water fountain at the other end of the greenroom—and ran smack into a snow-covered

David Richard. Music and water bottles hit the deck. I would have, too, if not for a pair of strong arms catching me before gravity took effect.

My heart cringed. While I wanted to make an impression, this was so not it. I started to apologize, but was cut off as David hoisted me to my feet and yelled, "What the hell do you think you're doing down here? All chorus members are supposed to be on stage. You don't belong in this business if you can't follow the simplest of instructions."

I couldn't decide whether I was embarrassed or angry that he assumed I was a member of the ensemble. Straightening my shoulders, I said, "I'm not a member of the chorus."

The chiseled face that my aunt admired sneered. "Well, if you're a fan looking for an autograph, you're going to be disappointed. I'm here to perform, not be fawned over."

Decision made. I was pissed. World-class singer or not, the man needed an attitude adjustment. "It's a good thing fawning isn't on my to-do list." I held out my hand. "Paige Marshall—soprano soloist. I would say it is nice to meet you, but neither of us would believe it."

I watched understanding bloom in David Richard's deep blue eyes. He ran a hand through his wavy dark hair, flashed the same crooked smile that appeared on every one of his CDs, and took my hand in one of his perfectly tanned ones. "I apologize for my behavior. You are so much more attractive than your photograph. I didn't recognize you."

Sure. Photography, not ego, was the problem here.

While I didn't buy his apology for a minute, I knew when to back off. "I appreciate the compliment." I stooped down and picked up my binder and bottle of water, only to have the bottle snatched out of my hand.

"That one is mine." David reached down and snagged a second bottle that had rolled under a folding chair. "This is yours."

The brand, bottle size, and quantity of liquid inside were, to me, identical. I wasn't sure how he could tell the difference. Before I had a chance to ask, our stage manager's voice rang out from the monitors. Soloists needed to report to the stage in five minutes.

David gave me another cover-model smile. "I need to warm up before we take the stage." With a wink, he disappeared into the dressing room next to mine.

I considered heading back to my own dressing room, but the warm chuckle I heard from Jonathan made me think I'd be interrupting. So I headed for the stairs. My stomach danced with nerves as I stood in the wings and waited for my fellow soloists to join me. Today was just a rehearsal. Soloists still had two more—one on Wednesday and another on Friday—before we would face the public and the critics. While mistakes didn't technically matter today, they mattered to me. I needed to prove I belonged on this stage.

Vanessa strolled up next to me. "Nervous?"

Yes. "Should I be?"

She smiled. "If I were you, I'd be terrified. This place will be teeming with critics on Saturday. I've handled that kind of pressure before. Have you?"

Okay, if Vanessa was trying to freak me out, it was totally working. Desperate to change the subject, I asked, "Where's Jonathan and David?"

"They're having a rather loud discussion behind their dressing room door."

"Why are they fighting?"

"David doesn't need a reason to have a tantrum." Vanessa

laughed. "If you hadn't already guessed, David is a lot like a toddler—both in angelic looks and irrational temperament. He also doesn't play nice with others unless he expects something in return."

"Soloists, please take the stage," a voice crackled over the monitor, making my heart trip. Showtime.

Jonathan appeared and smoothly walked onto the stage. Vanessa went next. I brought up the rear and walked to my chair near Vanessa's located downstage right. The chorus applauded. The redhead who had almost run into me started to tap her bow on the music stand in front of her. A moment later, the rest of the strings players followed her lead and tapped their bows as Maestro Tebar took her place behind the podium. As the redhead put her bow down and the others followed suit, I realized why she looked familiar. The red-haired woman was none other than Ruth Jordan, best known for her virtuosic violin playing and her equally impressive dislike of singers.

Maestro Tebar's eyes narrowed the minute they settled on David Richard's empty chair. Her hand tightened on her baton, but her voice was calm and professional as she said, "My name is Magdalena Tebar and it is my honor to work with all of you on one of my favorite pieces of music. With the talent assembled in this room, I'm certain this show will be talked about for years to come."

She paused and the expectation for greatness hung in the silence.

"We will run the entire oratorio tonight. I will only stop if there is a major issue that needs to be addressed."

Excited whispers made me turn my head in time to watch David Richard stroll across the stage, waving at the ensemble like he had just been crowned Miss America. When he reached his chair, he set his bottle of water next to it, opened his black music binder, and gave Magdalena a cocky grin. "Are we ready to begin?"

Magdalena's hands shook slightly as she opened her conductor's score, but they were steady when she raised her baton to signal the start of the overture. Personally, I was amazed at her restraint. The man deserved a baton upside the nose.

As the orchestra played the overture, I took several deep breaths and told myself to enjoy the music. There was a good thirty minutes of it before my first aria. Panicking now was pointless.

Magdalena smiled her approval as the overture came to an end, and then nodded to David. He stood and raised his black binder, and the music for his first solo began.

The man might be a jerk, but his voice was glorious. The high notes soared with hope tinged with sorrow. He navigated the passages of fast-running notes with effortless panache. The guy was a genius. And I was on stage with him.

When the final note shimmered across the hall, Magdalena waited a moment before giving the chorus its cue to rise. As the members began their number, I watched David take his seat. He looked relaxed as he listened to the ensemble sing their piece. When the song came to a close, David picked up his water bottle, uncapped it, and noticed me watching him. His smile was fast and playful, giving his classically sculpted face a boyish quality. Lifting the bottle in a silent toast, he leaned back in his chair and took a drink while Jonathan sang about the earth shaking.

And maybe the earth did shake because David's water bottle hit the floor, and David's body followed a moment later. David clutched his throat and began to convulse.

Someone shrieked. The orchestra stopped playing as Magdalena yelled for the stage manager to call 911. Jonathan knelt next to David. He began CPR as I raced over, sank to my knees near to the puddle of water left by the dropped bottle, and took David's hand. I wasn't sure if I could help, but I wanted to try.

After a few minutes it was clear: No amount of medical assistance would be of use. World-renowned tenor David Richard was dead.

Chapter 3

I'd thought stumbling across a dead body on Prospect Glen's stage would be the worst thing I'd ever see in a theater. I'd thought wrong. The flushed cheeks and empty eyes of David Richard as he stared unseeing up at the rafters of the auditorium were worse. Much worse.

Whispered voices filled with tears echoed in the hall. Holding tight to David's lifeless hand, I watched as Jonathan stood up, looked at Maestro Tebar, and shook his head. For a moment, everything went still.

"No." The word trembled on Maestro Tebar's lips. The color drained from her face, her eyes rolled back, and down she went. She, too, would have hit the ground had it not been for the quick reflexes of a violist who dove to catch her. That's when all hell broke loose. Hysterical screams mixed with shouts of despair. People sobbed. A few ensemble members ran off stage and into the wings. I couldn't move as I watched our stage manager, Bill Walters, climb onto the stage and holler for everyone to be quiet.

At least, that's what I think he said. It was hard to tell over the mass hysteria. After several tries, the stage manager finally got everyone's attention, and by the time the paramedics stormed down the center aisle, the chorus and orchestra were headed off the stage and down the stairs to the greenroom.

I placed David's hand gently on his chest and joined my fellow soloists at the edge of the stage along with our stage manager and a now conscious but still pale Magdalena Tebar. The EMTs raced up the escape stairs and checked David's pulse and eyes and even smelled his breath. Several uniformed police officers arrived as the paramedics were finishing their examination.

Vanessa buried her face in Jonathan's chest. Magdalena blinked back tears as she watched one of the uniformed cops make a call on his radio. My throat was tight, but my eyes were dry. I was too numb to cry.

Stage manager Bill pulled out his phone. "I have to send a message to the producers and find out if they want to hire a replacement or go with David's understudy." When we all stared at him, he said, "Yes, I know this is a terrible tragedy, but David Richard would be the first to say the show should go on. It's my job to make sure it does."

With a dramatic huff, Bill hurried down the escape stairs and into the theater in search of a signal and a replacement tenor. That left the rest of us to talk to the officers who were heading in our direction.

The tall mustached blond hooked a finger at Bill's back. "Where's he going?"

Magdalena brushed a tear off her cheek and stepped forward. "Bill is contacting the producers of the show. They need to be informed of David's tragic death. It must have been a heart attack, don't you think?"

The officers exchanged a look that made the back of my neck tingle. The shorter, gray-haired cop said, "We need to take your statements. If you could all wait in the lobby, we'll talk to you one by one as well as anyone else who witnessed the deceased's final moments."

Sitting on a hard, metal chair in the back corner of the lobby, I watched as Jonathan comforted Vanessa and Magdalena until they were escorted into the theater to be questioned. When someone finally came to talk to me, it wasn't one of the uniforms, but a steely-eyed, gray-and-black-haired detective dressed in jeans and a worn navy sport jacket. Instead of going into the theater, he pulled up a folding chair and sat down next to me.

"Thanks for waiting. I know it's been a long night." From the way the detective looked at me, I had a feeling it was going to get even longer. "I've already talked to the alto. You must be the soprano."

I nodded. "Paige Marshall."

"Will you be offended if I say I haven't heard of you?"

That made me laugh. "No, but I'm guessing the others were." His smile said I'd hit the target in one. "I'm still breaking into the business. Singing with David Richard was a career making opportunity for me."

"And now he's dead." The detective took a notebook out of his pocket and flipped it open. "Could you describe what happened tonight after the deceased took the stage?"

My throat ached as I walked the detective through

David's belated entrance to holding his hand after he died. Tears pricked the back of my eyes and my chest burned. Talking about David's death made it feel real.

The detective flipped a page in his book. "The others mentioned that you and David had an altercation before rehearsal began."

Hurt and embarrassment swirled in my stomach. I should have expected Vanessa and Jonathan to mention my encounter with David. "I left my dressing room and ran smack into David. He read me the riot act. I yelled back, and he apologized for his behavior. We sorted out whose water bottle was whose, and he went into his dressing room. End of story. I can't imagine two minutes of yelling at me triggered his heart attack on stage. From what I can tell, the man was always fighting with someone."

"I thought the two of you just met today."

"We did." I took a deep breath and explained. "Vanessa was upset with David when I walked into our dressing room today, and yesterday I saw our conductor smack him in the face."

The detective flipped through the pages of his book. "David Richard wasn't at rehearsal yesterday."

"David didn't sing," I agreed. "He wasn't scheduled to be at rehearsal. But he and Magdalena were having an argument in the greenroom before rehearsal. I walked into the room as her fist made contact with his nose, and backed out before either of them noticed I was there."

The detective asked a couple more questions about my fight with David and the water bottles. He then took my contact information and handed me his card. "If you think of anyone else who might have had a problem with the victim, please let me know."

I nodded as alarm bells jangled in my head. Not deceased. Victim. David Richard wasn't just dead. He had been murdered.

━━━━

"I don't see why we can't go home." Vanessa paced the greenroom like a caged bear. "They already released the chorus. At the very least, I would think we'd demand the same consideration."

A half hour earlier, the police had sent the members of the orchestra and chorus home and then moved the rest of us to the greenroom to wait. Bill, Magdalena, and our assistant stage manager/intern, Jenny Grothe, closeted themselves away in the ensemble dressing room in order to powwow on Bill's cell with the producers. I wasn't sure how much help Jenny was going to be. Not only was she twenty-one years old, but the last time I'd seen her, Jenny looked ready to throw up or pass out. Or both. Meanwhile, Jonathan was doing his best to soothe Vanessa from his perch on the worn sofa. "The police are just doing their jobs."

Vanessa rolled her eyes. "They're covering their asses. David died. It's a tragedy, but there's nothing any of us can do about it."

"I think they assume one of us may have had something to do with it." I shifted in my chair as Jonathan and Vanessa looked at me.

"Why would you say that?" Jonathan's eyes met mine.

"Well . . ."

"Don't humor her, Jonathan." Vanessa glared at me. "She's just being dramatic. You know how young performers are."

I wanted to be insulted, but I couldn't get up the energy for it. Besides, Jonathan looked insulted enough for the both of us. "Don't take your frustration out on Paige. You're upset David is dead. We all are."

Vanessa let out a bark of laughter. "Are you kidding? David's death is the best thing that could have ever happened to you. Now you don't have to worry about him taking your job."

"David wasn't interested in being a professor of music." The look on Jonathan's face, however, made me think perhaps the opposite was true.

Vanessa's smile said she thought the same. "David was interested in taking anything that didn't belong to him. I should know."

Yikes.

"People." Bill emerged from the dressing room with a wide smile. "The time for fighting is over. The show has been saved. Maestro Tebar and the producers have convinced Andre Napoletano to fly in from New York and perform with us this weekend."

Holy crap. Andre Napoletano was a rising star in the opera world. Critics tripped all over themselves comparing him to the great tenors of the past.

Bill paused to give us time to absorb his news and then continued. "Andre will not be able to make Wednesday's rehearsal and was inclined to turn us down. He has worked with Maestro Tebar before, however, and she was able to convince him that he will not need the extra rehearsal to create a spectacular performance. Which, of course, will be performed in David Richard's honor."

At the mention of her name, a red-eyed Magdalena swept out of the dressing room. "To ensure a flawless performance,

I would like all of you to set aside the constraints of your contracts and come to rehearsal early. I would also like to add a movement of Mozart's *Requiem* to our first performance to honor David's remarkable life."

Magdalena brushed a tear from her face as Bill discussed how best to deliver the music to us. Out of the corner of my eye, I saw the detective I'd spoken with earlier standing in the doorway. When Bill finished talking, the detective crossed the room to stand next to Magdalena.

"Are we free to leave, Detective?" she asked.

"If you, Mr. Walters, and Ms. Grothe could stay for a couple more minutes, I have a few things you can clear up. The rest are free to go."

Walking up the stairs to the stage door, I heard Vanessa behind me whisper, "With the publicity from David's death and Andre Napoletano singing tenor, this will be the most talked-about production of the *Messiah* ever."

I hated the zing of excitement I felt at Vanessa's prediction and had to wonder if creating the most talked-about production was exactly what the killer had intended all along.

———

Snow fell hard and fast as I turned onto Aunt Millie's street. Though I could barely see the street in front of me, there was zero chance of missing Millie's house. Astronauts on the space station couldn't miss it. Millie was serious about three things in life: her work selling Mary Kay products, her show dogs, and decorating for the holidays. While most of her Fortune 500 executive and professional sports–playing neighbors decorated their places with tasteful white lights, Millie had opted to merge her marketing plan and the holidays. Twinkling pink lights outlined the castle-like house. A row of pink and white candy canes bright enough to land planes outlined the driveway, and tree after tree was glistening with Aunt Millie's favorite color. Even Santa's suit and Rudolph's nose had been customized to go along with the theme.

I opened the garage door, steered my blue Chevy Cobalt into Millie's three-car garage, and cut the engine. Leaning my head against the steering wheel, I sat there for a moment as the emotions I'd been holding at bay threatened to overwhelm me. David Richard was dead. Murdered. Driving home, I'd pictured him in those final moments. Cocky. Proud. Toasting me from across the stage with the water bottle I'd knocked from his hands only a half hour before.

Holy crap. The bottle.

I sat up straight, and the world spun around me. David had drank from the bottle and died. The bottle I had thought was mine. If David hadn't noticed the difference, I might not be sitting here now.

My throat went dry, and I automatically reached in my bag for my water. Then I ditched the idea. I'd get a drink inside.

Leaving my boots in the laundry room, I tiptoed through the dimly lit kitchen to grab a soda. The house was quiet, and I hoped that meant Aunt Millie and Aldo had already gone to bed. Talking about tonight's events was definitely not high on my to-do list.

"Paige," Millie yelled, "is that you?" A minute later, she burst into the kitchen and wrapped her arms around me. At least, I thought it was my aunt. The lack of glasses and the green glop on her face made it hard to tell. When she stepped back she said, "We heard on the news about David Richard. Are you okay?"

No. "Yeah. I'm okay."

"I hated the idea of you being upset and driving home in all this snow. Aldo told me not to worry, but I couldn't help myself. He'll be so glad to know he was right. He's in the living room, helping me give Mary Kay opinions on some potential products."

While I desperately wanted to take a hot bath and burrow under the covers, I knew my aunt. If she wanted to reassure herself of my mental and physical well-being, she would go to any lengths to do it. Since I didn't want her camping out on the toilet while I shaved my legs, I grabbed a cookie from the Christmas assortment that had arrived yesterday from Cousin Ashley and headed for the living room.

A cheerful fire crackled in the fireplace as Bing Crosby's voice crooned about a white Christmas. The Christmas tree's silver and pink ornaments glistened from the corner of the room. An ever-growing stack of brightly wrapped presents was nestled under the evergreen boughs. Four dogs sat warming themselves in front of the fire. The scene would have looked like something out of a Currier & Ives holiday card if not for the fact that the dogs had glass eyes and permanent-press fur. Aunt Millie couldn't bear the idea of burying her pets when they died. She thought taxidermy was much more dignified. Since the dogs in question were currently accessorized with pink antlers and jingle bells, I wasn't sure the word "dignified" applied.

Since Killer was less than fond of his taxidermied counterparts—a feeling we shared—he was nowhere in sight. That allowed me to take a seat on the couch without being growled at. Which was good; after the night I'd had, I wasn't sure my nerves were up to dealing with canine intimidation tactics.

"See, Millie? I told you that you worry for nothing." Aldo's lips twitched in what was probably meant to be a smile. The blue face goop he was sporting looked as though it had hardened to the consistency of stone. "When you no come home right away, she started calling your friends."

"Devlyn said he'd be up late in case you needed to talk. Otherwise, he'll see you at rehearsal in the morning." Millie grabbed a towel and swiped some of the green glop off her face. "He also said I should tell you not to worry about losing your job. The new choir number is going to wow the school board."

Busted.

"It's not—"

Millie gave me one of her looks. "Don't tell me this isn't important. We all know that's a lie." I opened my mouth to explain, but Millie held up her hand. "We won't talk about it now because you've had a rough night, but tomorrow the two of us are going to have a heart-to-heart. If that school board thinks they can fire the best thing that ever happened to them, they have another think coming. The mayor is going to hear about this."

So much for not talking about it tonight. I was thankful the doorbell rang, saving me from whatever other phone calls Millie planned on making.

I made a mental note to steal Millie's Rolodex and took the opportunity to escape by volunteering to answer the door. Since Millie's and Aldo's friends weren't the types to visit after ten, I assumed whoever was at the door was here for me. Hoping Devlyn had decided to offer his very sexy shoulder to lean on, I flung open the door—and almost slammed it shut on the smirking face of Prospect Glen detective and all-around pain in my butt, Michael Kaiser.

"What are you doing here?" Not the most gracious greeting in the world, but sue me, I'd had a rough day. Seeing the man who'd investigated the last dead body I'd run into wasn't making my day any better.

Mike's smile widened as he scooted inside and brushed the snow off his long, navy blue coat. "Aw, I've missed you, too. And I'm here because your aunt called me."

Of course she did. "Look, I'm sorry Aunt Millie interrupted your evening. She was worried about me driving home in all this snow."

"I can see how that would upset her, although I'd think hearing her niece witnessed a man drop dead from cyanide poisoning would freak her out more."

Cyanide. In the water that I almost drank. Oh my God. Trying to get a grip, I asked, "How could you know it was cyanide poisoning? It's not your case."

"When a famous opera guy ends up dead, it makes me curious. And when I find out my favorite brunette singer is a witness . . ." He leaned against the wall and gave me a crooked smile. "I made a couple calls. The tox screens won't be in for a while, but the dead guy had seizures, his face turned red, and his breath had what the paramedics described as an almond smell. All the hallmarks of potassium cyanide. Someone really didn't like the dead guy."

"Do they have any idea who?"

His smile disappeared. "They're questioning several persons of interest. At the top of their list is the one who waves the stick at the band, but right below her was a person I found a little more interesting."

"Who?" Vanessa? Jonathan?

Mike's brown eyes met mine as his lips formed the word. "You."

Chapter 4

"Me?" Clearly the glop on Millie's face had hallucinogenic properties because I was most definitely hearing things. "I just met David Richard. Why would I kill him?"

Mike folded his arms across his chest. "That's a really good question. A question Detective Frewen has no doubt already asked himself, which is why you aren't the current focus of the investigation."

"I don't understand why they'd focus on me at all." My voice was starting to sound a little like I'd inhaled helium, but I couldn't help it.

Mike rolled his eyes. "Probably because you are the only one who admitted to touching the murder weapon. That tends to get a cop's attention."

I'd spent so much time contemplating the possibility of my own death from that bottle that I hadn't considered that my fingerprints were on the murder weapon. Yowzah. I was a murder suspect.

My legs went limp, and I leaned against the wall for support. "Now what do I do?"

"Nothing." Mike's voice was low and firm. His eyes lost their usual glint of sardonic humor. "Detective Frewen and his team might ask you to come down to the station and answer a few more questions. Your job is to do what they ask and nothing more. You don't want to stick your pretty little nose into a murder case again. You could have died last time." He pushed away from the wall and strolled over to me. "I'd hate to see you push your luck and lose."

Me, too. Facing the wrong end of a gun was not an experience I'd care to repeat. I had no intention of poking into this murder case. Still, the macho "back off and let the men handle it" attitude had me saying, "If the cops do their jobs, there won't be any need for me to poke my nose into their business. If not . . ."

If I was hoping to get a rise out of Mike, I hit the bull's-eye. His eyes narrowed, his face turned bright red, and the vein on his forehead began to dance the mambo. Yeah—score a direct hit for me.

"Are you implying that it was my fault you got nosy and almost got killed?"

Maybe. Had Mike investigated the real murderer instead of one of my students, I would never have needed to ask my own questions or face down a killer. Since I wasn't interested in watching Mike implode, however, I crossed my fingers behind my back and said, "Of course not. Look, between watching a man die and finding out I'm a potential suspect, I've had a long day. What do you say we call a truce?"

Mike's expression softened. He reached up his hand and brushed a lock of hair off my face. "Paige, the Evanston police know you didn't kill the opera guy. Do what they ask and everything will be okay. Got it?"

"Got it."

"Good." He smiled and put on his gloves. "And just in case you were wondering—the blonde I was seeing moved to Florida. I thought this might be a good time for the two of us to think about resuming our relationship."

Relationship? What relationship? Mike and I had kissed twice. The kisses were spectacular, which should have led to something more interesting. Too bad after both occasions Mike felt compelled to ruin the moment by speaking. And while Mike's rugged features and toned muscles still made me sigh, I wasn't sure going back for another round was in my best interest.

Opening the door to a burst of arctic air, I gave Mike a sweet smile and said, "Thanks for dropping by. It was nice seeing you."

Grinning, Mike strolled past me toward the door and then stopped and turned. Before I could protest, his lips brushed against mine, making my pulse leap. Then Mike stepped back, gave me a wink, and headed out the door with a promise to see me soon.

Damn. As if I didn't have enough trouble.

"Who was at the door, dear?" Millie asked as I walked back into the living room. Her eyes were wide, her face a mask of complete innocence. The Las Vegas casinos were lucky my aunt had gone into makeup sales. If ever she decided to take a whack at poker, she'd break the bank in no time.

"Detective Kaiser stopped by," I answered as though she didn't already know. "He wanted to make sure I'd gotten home safe and sound." Informing Millie about my murder-suspect status seemed like a bad idea. Between that and my job issues, Millie would freak out, which would be a waste of energy since I was freaking out enough for the both of us.

"How nice of him. You know . . ." Millie's eyes twinkled. Crap. I knew that look. "You don't have a date to the country club's Winter Ball yet. I'm sure Michael would be happy to go if you asked."

While my aunt had yet to bop down the aisle to *Here Comes the Bride*, she felt compelled to ensure I didn't escape taking that trip. While I couldn't fault her for her loving concern, I did take issue with her methods. More than once, I'd been sent on an errand only to be accosted in the store by a guy with a fistful of flowers and a dinner reservation down the block. I guess my refusal to do any more of Millie's shopping had resulted in more drastic measures.

"Mike's not the country club type." Unless I was performing, neither was I, but that wasn't the point. I wasn't going to be pressured into a relationship with Detective Mike or anyone else. Since my aunt wasn't about to agree with my point of view, I faked a wide yawn, plead exhaustion, and bolted upstairs. Did I know how to handle confrontation or what?

My sore muscles whimpered with relief as I cranked the shower to scalding. For several minutes, I just stood under the steaming water, trying to wash away the mental image of David Richard collapsing to the ground. When I was clean and dry, I pulled on a pair of worn flannel pajamas, set my alarm for the crack of dawn, and climbed into bed.

An hour later, I was still staring at the ceiling, waiting for sleep to come. No matter how fatigued my body was, my mind wouldn't hit the off switch. Tired of lying in the dark, I flipped on the light and padded over to the desk. A moment later my laptop hummed to life.

As a performer, I'd had a couple of opportunities to act out murder on the stage. My favorite was playing Rosa in the *Mystery of Edwin Drood*. The music was challenging, the humor dark, and the audience got to vote on the person they believed was responsible for the murder and watch that ending play out on stage. I was thrilled when the audience voted for my character. On stage, being an accused murderer was fun. Real life? Not so much.

Since none of the murderous shows I'd performed in involved potassium cyanide, I decided to Google it. Less than a minute had passed between David chugging his water and his becoming intimately acquainted with the stage floor. A poison that potent should be hard to acquire, right?

According to the Internet, Mike was right. The hallmarks of potassium cyanide poisoning were seizures and red cheeks. Crystals of potassium cyanide were reported to smell like bitter almonds, which explained the paramedic's report on David's breath. The small salt-like crystals were easily dissolved in water, and if I did the math right, a teaspoon of the stuff mixed in David's water would have been enough to fell a small elephant in almost no time.

My stomach clenched. Had the poison been added before or after my run-in with David? As a singer, drinking from my water bottle was a reflex, something I did without thought. At least twenty minutes passed between the time I smacked into David and the moment he took that deadly drink of water. The bottle hadn't been full when I picked it up off the floor. Like mine, the bottle had been half empty, but the bottle David Richard toasted me with had been filled to the top with water. That meant someone had refilled the bottle and added the drug sometime between the time David waltzed into his dressing room and his appearance on stage.

My stomach muscles unclenched. Even if I had ended up with the wrong bottle, I wouldn't have suffered David's fate. More important, after filling my own bottle, I had gone upstairs and waited in the wings of the stage. Several backstage techs walked by while I was there, which meant I had an alibi for the time of the poisoning. While Mike said I wasn't a serious contender for the murder-suspect title, a rock-solid alibi would take me out of the running for sure.

Phew.

Now that I had a method of proving my innocence to the cops, my mind started working. If the crystallized version of the poison smelled like bitter almonds, I doubted the drug was tasteless. Of course, according to the Internet, no one who tasted the drug actually lived. But if the poison had a strong smell, I was banking on it having some kind of flavor.

A flavor David didn't notice. If he had, I'm sure there would have been a look on his face. From our brief encounter, I suspected David wasn't the type to suffer imperfect-tasting water. His dissatisfaction would have shown. But it hadn't. I'd been looking straight at him, and he'd smiled. The water tasted as he expected it to. That had to mean something. Too bad I didn't have a clue what that something was.

Deciding the cops would have to come up with the answer to that one, I crawled back into bed and made a vow. Now that I could clear myself of any suspicion, I was going to steer clear of this murder investigation. End of story.

———

Sneaking out of the house before Millie got out of bed wasn't cowardice. It was self-preservation. The radio report told me the public works department had shattered the snow-day dreams of my students. Most days, I would have joined the students in their disappointment, but today was Tuesday. There were only two days left until the school board would pass judgment on my show choir coaching abilities. If I didn't want to find myself unemployed, my choir needed all the rehearsal time it could get.

Several students were waiting at the choir room door when I arrived. I slid the key in the lock and asked everyone to take off their wet shoes before tracking slush into the room. The way my luck was going, the combination of wet floors and complicated dance moves would land someone in the emergency room.

Dumping my coat and bag in the office, I changed my shoes, got out the music, and headed back into the choir room ready to work. A quick head count told me twelve of my fourteen singers had arrived. I heard the final two come through the door as I walked to the closet to retrieve the CD player. Voices whispered behind me. The minute I turned, everyone went quiet.

Crap. There were only two reasons for teenagers to stop whispering when you faced them: because you had an alien-looking pimple on your nose or because you were the topic of juicy gossip. For the first time in my life, I was hoping I had a zit.

"Is it true you watched a guy get murdered last night?"

Damn. So much for the pimple. "Yes, I was at rehearsal last night when David Richard died."

"Was there lots of blood?" Blonde, angelic-looking Emily Svoboda's eyes were filled with equal parts disgust and glee.

Yikes. I chewed on my bottom lip as I debated what I should say. When I'd taken this job, Larry had sat me down and given me a dissertation on the topics that were and were not acceptable when talking to students. Murder hadn't been on either list. Now what?

I could try to stall until a real teacher walked through the door. Devlyn would be here any minute. But waiting felt wimpy, so I said, "No, Emily. There wasn't any blood. David Richard was poisoned."

The boys looked fascinated. The girls were shocked. Chessie looked intrigued. Great.

Making a note to keep my water bottle with me at all times, I sat at the piano to start vocal warm-ups. Before my fingers could play the first chord, Eric asked, "Have the police arrested anyone yet?"

"Not that I know of, Eric." But I was hoping they'd have it wrapped up soon. Being on the potential suspect list, even if I was at the very bottom, wasn't any fun. "I'm sure the police are working hard to track down the person behind David's murder."

My fingers moved toward the piano keys.

But Eric wasn't ready to sing. "Are you going to help the cops solve the murder?"

"I think the police are more than capable of solving the murder themselves."

"They weren't last time."

I met Eric's serious eyes and could see the concern behind them. No doubt he was thinking about the time the police questioned and almost arrested him for murder of choir director Greg Lucas. I was the one who had gotten him off the hook. "I'm sure this investigation will go more smoothly. Now, if you guys don't mind, we have work to do."

Devlyn arrived in the middle of vocal warm-ups. His smile was bright as he strode into the room wearing vibrantly hued purple workout pants and a purple and lime green shirt, but I could see the question in his eyes when he looked at me. Nodding, I let him know I was okay, and we got down to business.

Out of the three disciplines of stage performing—acting, singing, and dancing—dancing was the hardest for me. I'd taken all the classes and knew the technique. I could do time steps and execute a triple turn without falling flat on my face. But for some reason no matter how much I practiced, I always felt self-conscious and awkward at dance auditions. And auditions were a piece of cake compared to demonstrating choreography to a group of high school students.

My heart pounded and I began to sweat before Devlyn turned on the music. But if there was anything I'd learned in my short tenure as coach it was that, as with dangerous animals, you can never show fear to teenagers. Not unless you want to lose all control.

Thank God Devlyn was a fabulous dancer and an even better partner. After he hit play, Devlyn grabbed my hand and pulled me close to his chest so we could demonstrate the first lift. He spun me away from his body and then twirled me back to face him. I placed both hands on his shoulders and jumped. He put his hands on my hips and lifted me up and around before putting me down on the other side. The lift was fun, flirty, and flashy but easy to execute.

After ten minutes, the team had the gist and we moved onto the second, more difficult lift. This one involved being hoisted onto Devlyn's shoulder and staying there for four beats before dropping into a basket catch. From that position I'd be flipped up and over onto my feet. It had taken Devlyn a lot of convincing to persuade me to try this lift and several attempts before I landed on my feet instead of on my now very bruised backside. Mentally crossing my fingers that I'd avoid landing on my ass, I jumped and found myself up on Devlyn's shoulder. Four counts later, I dropped into his arms and watched the world spin before it righted again. Hurray.

While Devlyn worked with the boys on partnering the lift, I talked the girls through their part. Then we performed it twice more so the kids could see the technique before they attempted it. By the time the first bell rang, four couples could perform the lift flawlessly and the other three were close. Not bad for a morning's work.

"Good work, everyone. I'll see you after school for another rehearsal." Before Chessie could ask, I added, "Be ready to audition for the solos. Mr. DeWeese says he'll be in his office during lunch so you can use the choir room at that time to practice."

The students snagged their backpacks and made a mass exodus toward the door as Devlyn and I put the room back in order for class. As we pushed the grand piano back in place, I spotted Eric loitering in the choir room door.

Doing my best impersonation of a real teacher, I said, "You're going to have to hurry or you'll be late for class."

The kid didn't budge. "I have a couple minutes until the next bell."

My eyes flicked to the clock above the door. School would officially begin in two minutes. Eric didn't just look like the blond, all-American kid; he was that kid. He dressed well, was polite, and always arrived to every rehearsal or voice lesson on time. For Eric to risk being late, he had something important on his mind.

"What's up?" I asked.

"The cops don't always get it right." His eyes were filled with shadows. "You know they don't."

"I'd like to believe they do most of the time."

Eric jammed his hands in his pockets as he considered my words. At the beginning of the year, Larry and Devlyn had said Eric was considering majoring in music. Since his near-arrest, he'd shifted his focus. His college applications now read criminal justice/pre-law. Eric's brush with the legal system had left its mark.

The bell rang, but instead of bolting for class Eric hitched his backpack onto his shoulder and said, "I hope the cops get it right this time. I really do. But if they don't, I wanted you to know that I'd like to help."

Before I could respond to his pronouncement or offer him a hall pass, Eric disappeared through the door.

"Well, that was sweet."

I turned to see Devlyn smiling at me from his perch on the piano bench. "Sweet?" If the kid decided to tackle a murder investigation, he could end up in the clink for obstruction. Colleges tended to frown on extracurricular activities that came with rap sheets.

"When a teenage boy is willing to risk after-school detention to offer a teacher his help—" Devlyn stood up and walked over to me. "Yeah, I'd call that sweet."

Maybe. But now instead of worrying about Eric's interest in the murder, I was panicked that his tardy would merit a detention. "Should I track down his teacher and let him know Eric was late because of me?"

"I'll handle it." Devlyn's hand brushed my arm. "How are you doing?"

If the door to the room hadn't been open, I would have taken advantage of the warmth of his arms and the comfort they offered. But we weren't alone. Not really. Kids and faculty were roaming the halls. Larry and the band director were in a meeting next door—a meeting I needed to get to. This wasn't the time.

"I'm fine," I assured him. "Or I will be, if I don't walk into my meeting and hear Larry tell me I'm already fired."

"Larry isn't stupid. He knows how much better this program is because of the work you've done. Once the concert is over, the school board will know it, too."

I was thankful Devlyn was right about Larry. I still had my job, which was good. But the phone call I got as the meeting ended had my stomach tied in knots. Detective Frewen hated disturbing my day, but could I stop by the police station when I had a moment to chat? Yikes. I'd seen enough television dramas to translate the polite tone and humble-sounding request. Detective Frewen wanted to see me, and he wanted to see me now.

Chapter 5

The Evanston Police Station was a large, two-story brick building located a few blocks to the south and west of Cahn Auditorium. Detective Frewen had left word at the information desk that I was coming. Minutes after my arrival, I found myself seated in a small lounge with a cup of coffee that no amount of sugar and cream could make drinkable.

"Ms. Marshall, thanks for coming so quickly. I'm sorry to keep you waiting." Detective Frewen walked into the room and made a beeline for the coffeepot in the corner.

As he took the seat across from me, I scanned his jeans and brown sport coat for handcuffs. None that I could see. Considering that a good sign, I sat back and gave him my best "I'm innocent" smile as he said, "I just need to ask you a few more questions and have you sign a witness statement. It shouldn't take long."

True to his word, the questions were quick and mostly a

replay of the night before. When he ran out of questions, he asked me to wait for the statement to be typed so I could sign it. No problem. I would also need to be fingerprinted before I left.

Problem.

"Fingerprinted?" I swallowed hard. Fingerprints were for suspects and bad guys. This wasn't a good sign.

"For elimination purposes. We need to know which prints on the water bottle are yours. I hope you're okay with that."

As if I had a choice.

Of course, I might have put up more of a fight about the prints had the detective pointed out to me that the ink wasn't going to come off my hands. After three rounds of scrubbing with hot water and antiseptic-smelling soap, my hands were red, tingly, and still tipped with black. Crap. I had show choir rehearsal in a matter of hours. The last thing I needed was Chessie reporting my blackened, guilty-looking fingertips to her influential parents. I'd lose my job for sure.

I was still feeling put out when Detective Frewen escorted me to the front door and thanked me for my time. My annoyance over the ink on my fingers was probably why, when he asked if I had any questions, I was brave enough to say, "Why didn't David taste the poison in his water?" When the detective didn't answer right away, I explained, "I was watching his face when he drank. He never tasted it. Why?"

Detective Frewen's steel gray eyes met mine. "You're Mike's friend, right?"

The whole "friends" thing was debatable, though that probably wasn't of interest to Detective Frewen. "We met a couple months ago."

"Right." His expression said he was aware of how Mike and I had met.

"I'm not looking to stick my nose into police business," I assured him, just in case Mike told him otherwise. "I just . . . I watched David die. It would help if I could understand why it happened."

The detective's eyes softened. "The lab reports haven't come back yet, but if you ask your fellow singers they'll tell you that David Richard was known for adding two things to his water: zinc and a dash of vodka. That was probably the reason he was worried you had the right water bottle after your confrontation."

Zinc was a favorite tool of performers to keep healthy and in good voice. I kept a stock of zinc lozenges in my bag. In fact, I'd been taking them since I started sneezing on Saturday. This meant I was familiar with the strong metallic, bitter flavor of zinc. One that would have no problem masking the taste of the poison. And if I were to place a bet, I'd say the killer was familiar with the taste of zinc, too.

I'd intended to avoid my well-meaning but overly protective aunt today. Instead, I found myself smiling as I spotted her signature pink Cadillac in the garage. If anyone could remove fingerprint ink before show choir rehearsal, it was Millie.

"Do you know how to get this stuff off my hands?" I asked as I spotted Millie stirring something on the stove.

"The police fingerprinted you?" The spoon Millie had been using dropped into the pot, spattering red liquid across the counter and onto her hot pink apron. "There's no way you killed David Richard. This is police harassment. I'm going to make some calls. By the time I'm done, those cops will never eat donuts again."

Before my aunt could dial the National Guard, I said, "I'm not a suspect. They needed my prints for elimination purposes. But now I can't get the ink off my hands. Do you have anything that will help?"

Aunt Millie put her cell phone on the counter and walked over to look at my hands. When faced with a choice between righteous indignation and a skin-care emergency, my aunt picked skin care every single time.

It took almost two hours and a half-dozen phone consults with fellow Mary Kay associates before the ink was removed along with what had to be half of my skin. The air smelled of smoke from the pan my aunt forgot to move off the stove, and my fingers stung from the combination of lemon juice, nail polish remover, passion-fruit sugar scrub, and whatever other products my aunt employed. Ouch.

Aunt Millie handed me a bottle of moisturizing lotion. "I'm going to set up a meeting with research and development. We could make a killing with a skin-care line aimed at law enforcement."

Leave it to my aunt to turn my personal crisis into a business opportunity. "Your company is lucky to have you."

"The high school is lucky to have you." Her eyes narrowed behind her pink-framed glasses. "I was going to make some phone calls this morning, but Aldo told me I should wait and talk to you first."

When I next saw Aldo, I was going to kiss him atop his semi-bald head. "I appreciate the support, but phone calls aren't going to help. The show choir will turn in a great

performance on Thursday and the problem will be solved."
I hoped.

I tried not to squirm as Millie studied my face for hints
of deception. Whatever she saw must have satisfied her
because she picked up her cell phone and shoved it into her
pocket. "Aldo and I have invited lots of friends to the concert
on Thursday. If that school board steps out of line, they
won't know what hit them."

Yikes. Time to change the subject. "Where is Aldo?"

"He's playing piano for a charity luncheon at the country
club."

"Why didn't you go with him?" The ladies who lunch
bought makeup by the gross. It wasn't like my aunt to miss
an opportunity to rake in the orders.

Now it was Millie's turn to look uncomfortable. "I don't
want to give Aldo the wrong idea about our relationship."

"He's living in your house."

"That's just geography. But I think he's starting to believe
we're a couple. I can't imagine what would have given him
that idea."

Holding hands. Making dinner together. Sharing a bed.

"I thought you liked Aldo." I did. Who wouldn't like a
guy who played Mozart and whipped up a killer manicotti?

Millie blushed. "I do."

"Then, what's the problem?" From what I could see, having Aldo around not only made Millie happy, it saved her
from buying new pots and pans every month. It was a
win-win.

"You wouldn't understand. Let's just say that I'm a career
woman. Aldo's a traditional man. We're both set in our ways
and have standards for our lives that aren't negotiable."

The fact that Aldo was willing to live in a house inhabited by four lifeless dogs told me Aldo's standards were totally negotiable. But what did I know.

Before I could say something in Aldo's defense, Aunt Millie adjusted her glasses and grabbed her purse off the counter. "I have to do a consult before I pick Aldo up from the club. Remember, use that lotion at least once every hour and feed Killer before you go."

Since nothing was too good for Millie's baby, Killer's dog food was made by a personal chef who also happened to be a Mary Kay client. The food was healthy, well-balanced, and smelled like musty fish. I dumped a bunch of it in Killer's bowl and decided to get a snack of my own before I headed for rehearsal.

I froze as Killer sauntered into the kitchen, nails clicking. His eyes zeroed in on me, and his pompon tail stopped wagging. Then he walked straight to the refrigerator, stopped, and planted his butt on the floor with a short menacing woof.

My stomach growled. I had two choices. Show the dog who was boss or go hungry. I took a step toward the fridge and Killer's lips curled back into a snarl, making me back up several steps. Killer knew how to be scary. When Millie was around, Killer tolerated me. When she wasn't, his mission in life was to see me starve.

Well, two could play at that game.

Careful not to turn my back to Killer, I put the dog food bag back in the pantry and walked over to his doggie dish. "Do you want to eat?" I picked up the rhinestone-studded bowl.

Killer growled again, this time giving me a nice view of his professionally whitened teeth. Giving Killer a wide smile,

I walked toward the garbage can in the corner of the room and put my foot on the pedal. The lid popped open.

"Do you want your food?" I dangled the bowl of food over the open trash can. Killer got to his feet. A high-pitched whine mixed with the throaty dog growl. "Millie won't be back for hours. If I don't eat, you don't eat."

Killer took a step forward and whined again. This time without the snarl. His big brown eyes stared at the bowl, and the whine dissolved into a whimper. Slowly he edged toward me, making pathetic doggie sounds. When he was about three feet away, his pompon tail drooped as he lowered himself to the floor. With another pitiful whine, he lowered his fluffy white head to the ground in between his paws and looked up at me.

"Okay, fine. You can have your food." I stomped over to the mat embroidered with the fancy French version of his name and put the bowl down on the ground. "Are you happy now?"

Killer got to his feet, barked, and lunged toward my ankle. Yikes. I bolted for the door, trying not to feel embarrassed that a poodle had gotten the best of me.

By the time I pulled into the parking lot at the high school, I was feeling better, which no doubt had something to do with the extra-large order of fries I'd consumed. My phone rang as I cut the engine. It was probably Devlyn wondering where I was. Normally, I was at least ten minutes early. Today, I was going to be exactly on time.

Wiping salty, grease-coated fingers on my pants, I slid my phone out of my purse. I hit the on button as I climbed out of the car into the cold.

"Paige, it's Bill Walters. I'm calling about tomorrow night's rehearsal."

"Did Maestro Tebar move the rehearsal time up?" I asked, hoping the answer was no. I'd thought I'd have time to work on the Mozart *Requiem* piece today. My unexpected trip to the police department meant that I needed all the time tomorrow I could get to practice.

"Maestro Tebar has asked that I send her apologies but she will be unable to attend tomorrow's rehearsal. The associate conductor will be running rehearsal in her stead."

"Why?" I stopped in my tracks, causing a couple of girls to scowl as they dodged around me. "Did something happen to Magdalena?" The idea that someone was bumping off *Messiah* staff made my mouth go dry.

I braced myself for the news that Magdalena was dead and instead heard, "Magdalena has been detained by the police. The producers are hoping this is just a minor setback that will be cleared up by Saturday. Otherwise . . ."

"Otherwise what?"

"They will have no choice but to cancel the show."

The choir room was a madhouse. Music was blaring from the CD player, and a couple of kids practiced dance steps on one side of the room while others flirted, shared makeup techniques, or texted. A red-faced Larry stood in the middle of it all, waving his hands and yelling to get the kids' attention. Unfortunately, whatever he was saying was lost in the wave of teenage chatter. While Larry was an excellent choral conductor, he had a lot to learn about vocal projection.

"Hey!" All eyes swung toward me. A moment later, the CD player was turned off and everyone was quiet. If nothing else, my opera training had taught me how to be loud. "Since you're all so busy doing stuff other than practicing, I'm going to assume it means you've perfected the new number—lifts and all. So, let's see it."

The kids scrambled to get into position. I marched over to the CD player and queued up the music, trying not to think about Bill Walters's news. If Magdalena had killed David Richard, she deserved to be arrested. Still, the prospect of losing both my day job and my potential career-breaking gig in the same week was enough to make me curl up into a ball and cry. But there was no way I was going to lose it in front of Chessie Bock.

The opening steps went off without a hitch. The harmonies were dead on. Suddenly, I felt as though everything might be okay. The kids would rock this out. The school board would love it. My job would be safe.

Then the kids reached the lifts and everything fell apart.

Crap.

"Okay." I stopped the music before anyone got injured or worse. "Let's run both lifts, couple by couple so I can make sure you have the technique down."

Thank goodness Devlyn arrived before Larry could insist on helping to demonstrate the moves. While Larry's current girlfriend had him going to the gym and doing marathon sessions of Yoga, neither had given him the upper-body strength needed to get me off the ground. At five feet seven, I wasn't the light-as-a-feather type.

After two hours, the group could execute the lifts without bodily harm and sing the song, which was good. Unfortunately, they were still having problems doing both at the same time. That was bad. I could only hope that after a night of practicing on their own they'd be able to remember both the words and the steps.

A quick glance at the clock made me sigh. I couldn't put it off any longer. I needed to audition the solos and make a decision—give Chessic another feature with the hope it would save my paycheck or cast the singer I thought would do the best job.

"Everyone line up. It's audition time."

My stomach was in knots as I listened to the boys sing first, then the girls. When the auditions were over, I looked at the row of nervous faces in front of me and knew exactly which ones should be cast. Plastering a smile on my face, I said, "I'm going to think it over tonight and let you know tomorrow who the soloists are going to be."

Was I stalling? Absolutely. Sue me.

"Chessie's parents won't be angry if you don't give her one of the solos," Devlyn said after the last student had vanished out the door.

"Are you sure?" I wanted to believe him, but I had Christmas gifts to pay for.

Devlyn shut the door and then walked over to put his arm around me. Larry had left with the students. He hadn't wanted to be late for Yoga, which meant Devlyn and I had to lock up. "The group looks better than they ever have."

"They still can't sing and execute the final lift."

"They will."

"If they don't—"

My thought was cut off by the brush of Devlyn's lips. For a second, my mind went a little fuzzy. After his mouth left mine I said, "Can we simplify the ending to make—"

Okay, maybe I started protesting again because I knew

it would get me another kiss. Can you blame me? And Devlyn didn't disappoint. His mouth met mine again and all choir concerns disappeared. My fingers dug into Devlyn's shoulders as my knees went weak. His lips brushed mine twice before settling for a longer taste. And wow, did he taste good. Like lemon. I was going to have to start drinking Devlyn's lemon-flavored water. Yum.

I went back for more, but Devlyn glanced at the door and eased away. "We should probably take this conversation somewhere else. Just in case."

Devlyn was right. A school was no place to be caught kissing. Twenty minutes later, we were wedged into a booth at an Evanston Irish pub. Devlyn had chosen the place based on its tasty food and the slim-to-none chance that Prospect Glen students would make an appearance. If they did, the lighting in our corner was dim enough the students wouldn't notice either of us. While I appreciated the ambiance, the idea that we needed to hide our relationship put a dent in the romantic mood.

Still, it was hard to complain when Devlyn's deep blue eyes were focused on me. "I wanted to come by last night after your aunt called, but I wasn't sure if you'd want company. Are you really okay?"

I intended to say yes, but as my lips started to form the word my throat tightened and tears pricked the back of my eyes. When Devlyn took my hands in his and gave them a squeeze, I was a goner. A tear escaped down my cheek. Then another. I sniffled and tried to hold back the tears, but now that they'd started, there was no stopping them. Putting my head down on our joined hands, I gave up fighting and cried.

I hated crying. It made my eyes puffy, made my nose

run, and made me feel like a wimp. Even worse, I was crying on a date and I didn't have a tissue to mop my face or blow my nose. I was a mess.

Suddenly grateful for the out-of-the-way dining location, I took a deep breath and sat up. Devlyn didn't tell me it was all going to be okay or say that things weren't as bad as they seemed. He just handed me a napkin and pushed his glass of wine across the table to me.

It's hard to blow your nose in a discreet manner. Feeling stupid and embarrassed, I shoved the used napkin into my pocket and took a sip of Devlyn's wine before saying, "Sorry about that."

Devlyn gave me one of his killer smiles and brushed a strand of hair away from my mouth. "Don't apologize. Watching a man die and the threat of losing your job is enough to upset anyone."

"Don't forget having my *Messiah* gig canceled." If we were going to list my problems, we might as well be thorough.

"What do you mean, canceled? My mother told me she called the theater this morning. The box office said the performance was going on as scheduled."

Knowing Devlyn had planned to bring his mother to see me sing was enough to make me want to cry again. "The stage manager called a couple hours ago. Our conductor, Magdalena Tebar, is currently under investigation for David Richard's death. If she's arrested, the show will be canceled. The worst part is that it's all my fault."

"That the conductor killed David Richard?"

"No. That the cops are going to arrest Magdalena." The waitress arrived with our food. Over fish-and-chips, I gave Devlyn the rundown on Magdalena's right hook.

"But you don't think she killed him?"

"I don't know," I said, spinning a French fry between my fingers. "She could have, but I've been thinking about the look on Magdalena's face after she hit David. She looked happy. Satisfied. Like she'd done the job she set out to do. Not like she was getting ready to take him down. And when she realized he was dead, she fainted."

"She could have faked it."

I pictured the way she'd toppled into the arms of the violist with quick reflexes. The billowy purple skirt she'd worn had hiked up to the top of her thighs as the violist laid her on the pit's concrete floor and checked her pulse. She didn't seem like the type to allow the entire string section a bird's-eye view of her lacy red underwear. "Maybe."

"But you don't think so."

I shrugged and stabbed a piece of fried fish. Did I really believe Magdalena was innocent or did I just want her to be so I could sing in the show this weekend? It was hard to tell.

"Eric wasn't wrong this morning." Devlyn put down his fork. "The cops aren't always right. Eric would be in jail if you hadn't trusted your instincts. Maybe you should trust them now."

Devlyn and Eric both had a point. My eyewitness account was the reason the police suspected Magdalena. That meant it was my responsibility to make sure the conductor wasn't getting a bum rap. Right?

By the time Devlyn walked me to my car and gave me a toe-curling good-night kiss, I'd convinced myself that asking a couple of questions wasn't just self-serving. It was my moral obligation. While the performers involved would cooperate with the police, they'd be hyperaware of the press generated by David's murder. My fellow performers wouldn't share anything that didn't make them look good. Which meant the police would be lacking information. Unless someone else got it for them. I could only hope the other singers felt more comfortable sharing juicy industry gossip with one of their own.

And when it came to the gossip sources, I knew exactly where to start.

Chapter 6

●

While the cops might be focused on the people who performed in front of the curtain, I knew where the real power
in the performance world lay—with the stage manager.
Stage managers know all. They are in charge of everything
in front of and behind the stage, and have the ear of the
producers, directors, and performers. They are also in
charge of making sure the performers are given the support
they need to perform to the best of their abilities. Which is
why Bill Walters had agreed to meet for coffee and a chat.
The last thing he needed was a performer wigging out.

Since the coffee shop was located near the Northwestern
University campus, the place was teeming with college kids
hunched over laptops while sucking down copious amounts
of caffeine. Even had Bill not been waving, I would have
spotted him on a couch in the back of the café. The receding
hairline and button-down pink shirt were dead giveaways.

He was armed with two cups of coffee and a reassuring smile that didn't quite reach his hazel eyes.

"Thanks for coming out to talk with me," I said, taking a seat on the couch.

"I'm happy to do it. The lighting designer was supposed to finish focusing lights tonight, but the police won't let us back in the building until tomorrow." Bill sat down and handed me a coffee cup. After being out in the cold, my hands soaked in the warmth. "I know you're worried about the show."

I took a deep breath and plunged into the script I'd created for myself during the drive over. "The show's important to me, but what happened last night . . ." I looked down at my hands. "David Richard didn't seem like a nice guy, but I can't imagine anyone wanting to kill him."

"Honey, everyone who worked with David wanted to kill him. The man was a menace." Bill took a sip of his coffee. "Most big opera houses refused to work with him. It's one of the reasons he agreed to be an artist in residence at Northwestern this year and do this show. David and his manager were working hard to reinvent David's public image."

"I didn't know that. Was it working?"

Bill chugged some more coffee and shrugged. "Probably. David knew how to turn on the charm when he wanted to."

I took a sip of coffee and smiled. "How did you know I liked gingerbread lattes?"

Bill shot me a gapped-tooth grin. "Your manager gave us a list of your likes and dislikes. Yours was the shortest of the five preference lists, which makes it easy to remember."

The idea that anyone in show business thought I was important enough to worry about my coffee preference made me flush with pleasure. It also gave me a new line of questioning. "If you know everyone's preferences, did you also know that David Richard added zinc to his water?"

Bill's smile disappeared. "Why do you want to know?"

Busted.

Hoping to look worried and vulnerable, I gnawed on my bottom lip and said, "I almost took his water bottle. The idea that I might have drank from it has given me some bad moments."

"I heard about that from Jonathan." Bill gave my arm a sympathetic squeeze. "Just about everyone who worked with David knew about his *special* water. The whole zinc thing isn't all that unusual. I've stage-managed a lot of shows where singers have listed zinc lozenges or drops on their preference riders. I had to make sure that Jenny and the rest of the production staff took special precautions on this production considering Magdalena's allergies."

Allergies? "What allergies?"

Bill blinked. His reddish-tinged cheeks told me he'd spoken out of turn. "I shouldn't have mentioned Magdalena's personal business."

Probably not, but now that he had, I wasn't about to let him off the hook. Taking a sip of coffee, I employed a technique my mother used to use when she wanted to know something—silence. Bill put his coffee on the table, wiped his hands on his pants, and picked the cup back up. Looking into the dregs of his drink, he said, "Look, Magdalena is a very private person. The staff knows they need to take special precautions, but they don't know why. Magdalena's allergies weren't even listed on the rider because she was afraid someone could invade her privacy. But I had to take notes and do some research on the Internet to make sure I didn't screw up and buy the wrong kind of hand cream or serve her too much red meat, otherwise she'd end up in the hospital."

Since Bill didn't seem inclined to dish further on Magdalena, I asked, "What about Vanessa and Jonathan? Did they have any unusual requests? I'd like to get them both something for opening night and I don't want to get the wrong thing."

Bill smiled. "Well, don't take offense if Vanessa hates anything you get her. She's only going to like you and your gifts if you can do something for her career."

"Which means she's never going to like me."

"I think you're sensational, and I overheard Magdalena telling David Richard that you have the spark. That's something Vanessa would be jealous of, too. She's a strong singer and a decent actress, but she doesn't have that extra something. David Richard had it. So does Jonathan, only Jonathan would rather teach than travel. You have to be willing to travel to be an opera star."

Which is why I kept my passport current. Too bad I hadn't had reason to use it recently.

"Were David and Jonathan friends, then? I know they were both teaching at Northwestern this year."

Bill laughed. "Jonathan knew how to play the game. He acted friendly with David in public, but I've worked a couple shows with the two of them. They weren't friends. Jonathan's one of the nicest singers in the business, but David had a history of pushing Jonathan's buttons. I hated the idea of putting them in the same dressing room for this, but I didn't have a choice." He looked back into his coffee cup. "Now I guess I don't have to worry about it."

History? What history? Before I could ask, Bill's phone rang. Apologizing, he got up in search of a quieter spot, leaving me wondering if the police knew about Jonathan and David's past. That the kind and debonair Jonathan could have had anything to do with David Richard's death was hard to believe. Still, I'd learned firsthand that while psychopaths in movies looked the part, real-life killers could appear completely normal.

I drained the rest of my coffee and waited for Bill to return. When he did, his face was pale and his eyes a little wild.

"Is everything okay?" I asked.

Bill might work with actors, but the look in his eyes said none of the performers' training had rubbed off. "Everything's fine. Just a few details that need ironing out," he stammered, shrugging into his coat. "Let me know if you need anything before tomorrow night's rehearsal. Okay?"

Without giving me a chance to answer, Bill hurried to the door and disappeared into the cold. Grabbing a latte for the road, I headed back to Millie's with the radio tuned into the local news channel in case the police had made an arrest in the case. By the time I arrived home, I'd learned someone had stolen Baby Jesus from the Old St. Patrick's nativity and replaced it with Yoda. No arrests in either that bit of strangeness or my *Messiah* case.

My fingers were raw and tingly from the cold when I peeled off my gloves and walked into the kitchen. Since Killer was nowhere in sight, I made a beeline for the refrigerator, grabbed a diet soda, and contemplated a snack.

"You forgot your moisturizer." Millie's voice made me jump, sending my can of soda crashing to the ground.

I picked up the dented can and looked over at my aunt. She was standing in the kitchen doorway in a sexy pink satin robe and fuzzy pink slippers. From the careful application of her makeup and the wafting scent of floral perfume, I guessed sleep wasn't my aunt's next activity of choice.

She grabbed the soda and put it on the counter. Taking my hands in hers, Millie examined my fingers and gave a sigh of dismay. "Regular moisturizer isn't going to do the trick. You're going to need something stronger. Come with me. I have extra-emollient cream in my office. That should do it."

I followed Millie down the hall into the cosmetics command center. The room was painted a pale pink. Aside from that splash of color and the taxidermied border collie standing guard at the door, the room could have belonged to any Fortune 500 CEO. Framed college degrees hung on the wall along with photographic evidence of the sports figures and television journalists who made up Millie's clientele. In the center of the room was a massive mahogany desk equipped with a high-powered laptop, an array of computer accessories, and a phone system that NASA employees would have a hard time using.

Millie went to the back of the office and plucked a small pink tube off one of the meticulously organized shelves. "Here. Try this."

My aunt's tone said it would be best not to argue. I unscrewed the top, slathered a bunch of cream on my fingers, and felt immediate relief. When it came to skin creams and cosmetics, my aunt was always right. Which made me wonder. "Do you know of an allergy that makes a person sensitive to hand lotions and red meat?" Since the question sounded strange even to me, I added, "One of the suspects in David Richard's murder is allergic to both those things."

The minute I mentioned the murder, Aunt Millie's eyes narrowed. "Hand-cream ingredients can trigger all sorts of allergies. Do you know if the lotion had a fragrance or doubled as a sunscreen?"

"I haven't a clue."

My aunt fired up the computer, rolled up her sleeves, and started to search through her database of cosmetics. As the minutes ticked by, I began to fidget. Finally, I said, "You don't have to spend time on this now. I don't want to interrupt your plans."

"Plans?" My aunt gave me a quizzical look. "What plans?" The tiny red flush blooming under the perfectly applied base makeup belied her innocent tone.

Now I had a decision to make. I had to feign ignorance of my aunt's sex life or meet it head on. When I was growing up, my parents taught me to steer clear of uncomfortable conversations. They believed in avoiding unpleasantness at all costs, which is probably why they didn't call or visit. My parents loved me, they just didn't understand my life choices. While they wanted me to be happy, they would rather that happiness occur on the farm down the road doing something they understood. Growing corn and milking cows made sense. Singing and dancing on stage? Not so much. Even if the *Messiah* went on as planned, the tickets I'd set aside for my folks would most likely never be used. Millie, on the other hand, would be front and center. She believed in facing life head-on.

Which is why I asked, "Isn't Aldo waiting for you upstairs?"

Millie looked back at the computer screen and began typing away. "He's finishing up a facial treatment. The face mask he tested last night gave his skin a slightly cerulean undertone. I'm hoping the new treatment will help bolster his mood."

"If not, the lacy number you have on under the robe should do it."

My aunt blushed, but flashed a wide grin. "That was kind of the idea. Wait. I think I have a couple possible answers for you. According to the cosmetics forum, the most common hand-cream allergies related to food are triggered by milk and soy products. But your suspect could also be allergic to zinc oxide and certain oils." My aunt kept talking, but the mention of zinc oxide had my Spidey senses tingling.

I was so distracted, I barely noticed Aldo when he bopped through the door wearing a black silk robe and what might have been a come hither smile. His blue-tinged face made it hard to tell.

Excusing myself, I raced upstairs, fired up my laptop, and looked up zinc oxide. Zinc oxide was an ingredient in a number of sunblock skin creams. All of which said they shouldn't be used by people with allergies to zinc. A person highly allergic to zinc could break out in a rash or hives if her skin came in direct contact. A few more keystrokes told me people with zinc allergies often avoid red meats.

Bull's-eye.

If Magdalena was allergic to zinc, and my nonexistent investigator instincts were telling me she was, why would she risk handling a water bottle that was full of the stuff? Risking a rash didn't seem like the best plan for getting away with a crime. Magdalena had been wearing short sleeves the night David died. Gloves would have protected her hands, but not the rest of her arms. An allergic reaction would not have gone unnoticed.

My gut told me this was important. While the cops might not say an allergy to the murder weapon was definitive proof of innocence, I was pretty sure it would at least cast some doubt on her guilt. Doubt would keep her out of jail, and behind the podium for the concert.

Of course, this all hinged on Magdalena actually being allergic to zinc. There was only one way to find out. I glanced at the clock. It was just after ten. Betting Bill was still awake, I dialed his number. When he answered, I asked, "Is Magdalena Tebar allergic to zinc?"

The stunned silence spoke volumes. Score one for me.

"Has she mentioned her allergy to the police?"

"No." The word was barely a whisper. "And the nondisclosure agreement I signed won't let me tell them."

"Well, I could—"

"You can't say anything." Bill sounded panicked. "Magdalena will sue me, and I promise she'll find a way to end your career before it begins."

Yikes. My stomach went squishy at the idea of Magdalena Tebar using her influence to blackball me. Still. "Doesn't she know her zinc allergy makes it less likely the police will look at her as a suspect?"

"She says she has her reasons for keeping her medical condition quiet." A voice murmured in the background. Bill whispered something I couldn't quite make out back before saying to me, "Look, Paige, I have to get going. Magdalena wants to handle this her way. I'd strongly suggest that you let her." And with that, Bill was gone.

———

Between the worry that Magdalena would be falsely arrested and the knowledge that Millie and Aldo were doing "skin care treatments" down the hall, I had trouble sleeping. So it wasn't a surprise it took several growls and a loud bark from Killer to rouse me out of bed. I was thankful that by the time I got to school for rehearsal, the two cups of coffee I'd chugged had kicked in and I was ready to sing and dance.

The minute I spotted Chessie waiting at the choir room door, I felt my caffeinated energy sag. With my attention focused on David Richard's murder, I'd forgotten about casting the solos. The gleam in Chessie's eyes and the fact she was fifteen minutes early for our 6:15 A.M. rehearsal told me she had not.

My stomach knotted as I unlocked the door and flipped the light switch. While I hadn't given this decision much thought since yesterday, I knew what I was going to do. If a choice had to be made between doing what was best for me or best for the choir, it was my job to choose the choir. Pulling off my jacket, I turned to Chessie and said, "I'm sorry, but you're not going to be assigned one of the new solos. I'm giving the female feature to Megan."

Chessie dumped her bag on the floor and planted her hands on her hips. "If there is something I should have done differently—"

"There isn't." I took a deep breath. "You're a strong singer even when you dance. Right now, the group is struggling to project sound while doing the choreography. If I take you out of the ensemble, the whole thing will fall apart." Was that the whole truth? No, but it was part of it. Besides, complimenting Chessie was always the best way to get her to cooperate.

Chessie's eyes narrowed. "You know my father is on the school board, right?"

So much for cooperation.

The implied threat of her father's position hung in the air. I could see Chessie waiting for me to back down. Yeah, right. "If your father wants to talk to me about why you have only one solo in the concert, I'll be happy to explain my reasoning to him. Feel free to tell him that."

Ignoring the angry stare, I began setting up for rehearsal. By the time the room was rearranged, the rest of the choir had arrived. They were bleary-eyed but ready to work.

Instead of practicing on the new song, I ran them through the older numbers, hoping familiar songs would build their confidence. In doing so, it also built mine. While watching the kids twist and twirl and sound fabulous through the numbers, I felt a kick of pleasure. While I was often proud of my own performances, this was different. These kids were good when we started. They were better now. Whether I'd wanted this job or not, I'd made a difference. That meant something.

"Okay. Time for the new number. We're going to run through it first, then make adjustments for the soloists as needed. Remember—your singing matters just as much as the dancing. I want to be impressed by your volume and your feet."

The dancing was better than yesterday. The opening was solid. The first lift went off without a hitch. Then things started to fall apart. Two of the girls zigged when they should have zagged, and one of the guys tripped trying to avoid bumping into them and took two other singers down in the process.

Crap. Crap. Crap.

"Okay, let's try it again."

I made them dance through the number again. And again. By the time I worked with my two soloists, Megan and Trevor, and added them into the mix, Devlyn and Larry had arrived. Devlyn and I worked through the glitches while Larry did his best not to get in the way. The choir ran the entire song again, and the number looked good. Maybe better than good. Despite Chessie's angry scowl, by the time the first bell rang

I was optimistic at my group's chances of impressing tomorrow night's crowd.

"Don't worry," Devlyn said as the last teen walked out the door. "They'll be ready. We'll have the dress rehearsal after school today, and you'll be able to go off and sing tonight without a care in the world."

"I'm glad to hear the *Messiah* hasn't been canceled. I was worried it was going to be." Larry dumped a load of papers on the piano and gave me a red-faced smile. "Then again, knowing the cops are close to making an arrest will probably make the audience feel like it's safe to attend the show."

"Close to an arrest?" My legs went limp. If I hadn't grabbed onto the piano, my backside would have hit the floor. "Where did you hear that?"

"I heard it on the news report this morning."

I swallowed hard. "Did they say who?"

"I don't think so, but . . ." Several folders of music slid off the piano. Larry tried to catch them, but while Yoga had improved his breathing, it had done nothing for his reflexes. Within seconds, the folders hit the ground and burst open, sending music skittering across the floor and under chairs. With his ears turning the same vibrant shade of red as his sweater, Larry crawled around the floor, collecting papers. Devlyn and I leaned down to help, but Larry waved us off. "Y . . . y . . . you guys have other w . . . work to do. I can take c . . . c . . . care of this. Please."

Normally, I would have insisted on helping, but the stuttering told me Larry's embarrassment was at an all-time high. Sticking around would just make it worse.

Since I didn't have voice lessons until after lunch, I grabbed my stuff and headed for the door. Devlyn looked up and down the empty hall before giving me a kiss on the cheek as we parted ways—him for his office, me on a mission to discover whether Magdalena had been locked up and the show was on its way to being canceled.

First, I checked to see whether Bill had left a message. Nothing. Stepping into the cold air, I debated calling him. Theater people weren't known for being early risers. Then again, if Magdalena had been arrested, Bill was probably long awake and dealing with the fallout.

With my conscience cleared, I pushed send and waited for an answer. Voice mail. Drat. I'd try again later. Shoving my phone in my pocket, I walked to my car and smiled as I spotted a brightly wrapped gift resting on the hood of my car. The show choir kids had been doing the Secret Santa thing for the last week or so. I'd even helped a couple of kids slip cards or silly little gifts into one another's bags to keep identities hidden. I couldn't help feeling a warm glow at being included in the fun.

Getting in the car, I put the package on the seat and revved the engine. While waiting for the heater to kick in, I picked up the box and turned it over in my hands, looking for clues to my Secret Santa's identity. No card. Just snowman paper and a bright green bow.

I smiled as I ripped the shiny wrapping, flipped open the lid, and dug through the tissue paper. My smile disappeared. Sitting in the box was a Santa ornament with a noose around its neck. Underneath Santa was a note.

If you're not careful, you'll be next.

———

Okay, I knew I should be freaked. I mean, someone hung Santa. But I was pretty certain who had to be behind this.

When I first took the job, Chessie had used threatening notes in her campaign to get me to quit. Obviously, she hadn't learned her lesson.

Neither had I. The warm glow of acceptance I'd felt finding the gift was replaced by icy rejection. No matter how much I tried to succeed at this job, the kids were always going to consider me an outsider. Watching them improve and grow, writing them recommendation letters, and talking about their college dreams hadn't changed a thing. Chessie might be behind this, but she wasn't the type to wage battles against popular opinion. Maybe the stress of everything was unhinging me, but, to me, hangman Santa sent a message loud and clear—my team wanted to win and they still thought I wasn't good enough to help them reach their goal.

My chest tightened. Unexpected tears made my throat ache as I fought to keep them from falling. I wasn't going to cry over a couple of spoiled teenage kids. Hell, I didn't even want this job. If things worked out and the *Messiah* went on as planned, I wouldn't need it. I could quit and make everyone happy.

Brushing aside an idiotic tear, I pulled out my phone and dialed Bill again. Voice mail. Damn. Time for plan B. I fished an Evanston Police Department card out of my purse and punched in Detective Frewen's phone number.

If he didn't sound happy to be answering a call at eight o'clock in the morning, he sounded less thrilled when I asked, "Did you make an arrest in David Richard's murder?"

"No arrests have been made." Phew. "But we currently have a person of interest in custody."

Crap. I asked for a name, but the detective wasn't in the mood to share. Before I could consider telling him what I knew about Magdalena's medical condition, Detective Frewen thanked me for my cooperation and disconnected.

Double crap. Now what?

Digging through my bag, I came up with the *Messiah* contact sheet, which listed Bill's phone number and home address. If Bill was sleeping in, he might not know Magdalena had been taken into custody. He could call her manager and have him give the police the information about her zinc allergy. Bill wouldn't get sued, and the cops would have to think twice about their suspect. Problem solved.

Bill lived in a redbrick bungalow a couple blocks from the Northwestern University campus. I parallel parked my car and tried his phone one more time. Still no answer. Rehearsing my arguments for Bill to get involved in clearing Magdalena's name, I locked the car, marched up the sidewalk, and rang the bell.

No answer, but I could see a light on inside. Time to knock. I banged on the heavy wooden door and was surprised to feel the door shift and open a crack.

"Bill?" I yelled.

Okay, this was getting spooky. Pushing the door open the rest of the way, I peered into what had to be a living room. Worn brown couch. Scarred wooden coffee table. On the table was an open binder, two empty coffee cups, and a dish with a crumb-filled muffin wrapper. Bill's winter jacket hung on a coat tree just inside the door. Bill wouldn't go outside in this weather without that coat. Not unless he wanted a spectacular case of frostbite. That meant he had to be somewhere inside.

"Bill?" Still no answer. If the guy was in bed, he slept like the dead. I headed for the hallway at the back of the living room, calling Bill's name, and stopped cold in the doorway. My stomach rolled, and my knees went weak. I sucked in air and felt a scream build inside me.

Swinging on a rope from the kitchen's ceiling fan was Bill. I had been wrong. He wasn't sleeping like the dead. He was dead.

Chapter 7

My brain screamed at me to jump into action. To cut Bill down and get him help. But my feet wouldn't move—and even if they would, I could see Bill was beyond assistance. His face was pale. His head hung to one side. His body was still.

Hands shaking, I found Detective Frewen's number in my call log and hit send. I had to swallow twice before I could speak and even then I barely recognized the thin, terrified sound. The minute I identified myself, Detective Frewen sighed. "I appreciate your interest in this investigation, Ms. Marshall, but I'm not at liberty to discuss any details."

"Bill Walters is dead." Once the words started, they flew out of my mouth. I gave the detective the address, assured him I hadn't and wouldn't touch anything, and promised to go outside and wait for his arrival—all while feeling like I was being watched by Bill's lifeless eyes. I needed to get

out of here. After the sadistic Secret Santa gift and seeing
Bill hung from the ceiling, I was about to completely lose it.

Wait . . .

A part of my brain that had shut down after seeing Bill's
lifeless body turned back on. Could the similarity between
that gift and Bill's death be a coincidence? If so, it was a
pretty big coincidence, and while coincidences were possible, this didn't feel like one. That meant a pissed-off
Chessie hadn't given me the gift—the killer had. A killer
who warned me I might be next.

Shit.

The room swam in front of my eyes, and I hung onto the
doorjamb for support. Finding a dead body was bad. Learning the person who killed that person might want to kill you,
too, was even worse.

Out of the corner of my eye, I noticed a piece of paper
with black writing scrawled on it on the kitchen table. A
suicide note? I took two steps toward the scarred wooden
table and squinted to read: *I never meant for anyone else to
take the blame. David Richard deserved to die, and so do I.*

Next to the paper was a mostly empty bottle of wine and
a bottle opener. But no wineglass. Huh.

Trying my best to ignore Bill's corpse, I peered over the
counter into the sink. No dirty dishes. No dishwasher, either.
Did I think that Bill wrote his confession, downed most of
a bottle of wine, and washed and put away his glass before
taking his own life? No way in hell.

Taking several deep breaths, I scanned the kitchen one
more time before heading back to the front stoop to wait for
the cavalry. My nose was frozen by the time Detective
Frewen pulled up in a black SUV. He instructed me to stay
where I was and went inside. A few minutes later he was

back and barking into his phone for assistance. When he hung up he glanced at me. "You look cold."

You think? Red, runny nose. Arms wrapped around myself, shivering. No wonder he was a detective.

He crooked a finger toward the street. "We can sit in my car while I get your statement."

The SUV had heated seats, which had my butt thawing long before the rest of me. But even warm and toasty, my hands continued to shake. Detective Frewen shifted to look at me. "Tell me again why you came to see Bill Walters this morning?"

I took a deep breath and weighed what I should say. Telling everything meant risking my career—a career I'd worked hard to get off the ground. But a man had died. As far as I was concerned, my would-be career paled in comparison. So I spilled. I told Detective Frewen about Bill's mention of Magdalena's secret medical condition. My concern that the information would impact the investigation. My hope that talking face-to-face with Bill would convince him to share the information with Detective Frewen himself or beg Magdalena's manager to do it.

I could see the vein in the detective's neck begin to pulse under his scarf. To his credit, his voice was calm as he walked me through the events of the morning, including the hangman Santa I'd unwrapped. I could tell he wasn't sure whether the two events were connected, but he retrieved the items from my car anyway. More emergency vehicles arrived, filling the street with blinking lights. As police officers and paramedics climbed out of their cars, Detective Frewen told me to call him if I remembered anything else. Then he headed into the house, leaving me out in the cold.

Back in my car, I looked at the empty seat beside me.

The more I thought about it, the more I was convinced Bill's death and the mysterious gift were connected. And while I hadn't had the opportunity to compare the writing on both notes, my gut was telling me the same person wrote them. But why? Why threaten me? I barely knew the victim.

The question plagued me as I steered my car back to the Prospect Glen High School parking lot. As I walked the halls to the performing arts wing, I thought I might have an answer. Bill must have told someone about the questions I was asking. Someone who didn't want me poking into areas they'd rather have left alone.

Great. Being stalked wasn't on my Christmas wish list. Neither was tracking down another killer. I'd been there, done that, and almost died in the process. Detective Frewen and his team seemed competent, but they hadn't fingered the killer in time to save Bill. Which really sucked. As a stage manager, Bill had been organized and professional. As a person, he had been considerate and kind, which was too often a rarity in this dog-eat-dog business. Bill deserved to have his killer brought to justice and at the moment, I wasn't sure he was going to get that. If I wanted Bill to rest in peace, and if I didn't want to end up swinging from the ceiling myself, I was going to have to take matters into my own hands.

Since I had forty-five minutes before my first private lesson began, I slipped into Larry's office and fired up the computer. It was time to learn more about my fellow *Messiah* cast members, starting with murder victim number one, David Richard.

On the other side of the door, the freshman choir belted out its rendition of "Sleigh Ride," complete with slapstick claps and jingle bells. I clicked on David Richard's website.

His deep blue eyes stared back at me from his headshot in a way that felt like he was looking into my soul. Creepy. Ignoring the photo, I started reading.

The man was forty-five years old, single, and childless, and, according to his biography, had sung every popular, and some not so popular, tenor roles in the operatic repertoire. From the list of past performances, it looked as though David rarely spent more than a month or two in any city before jetting off to his next performance—until this year, when he landed the guest artist gig at Northwestern University. From what I read, the man had arrived here to give a Fourth of July concert and never left.

Weird. Stranger still was the lack of performance engagements on his calendar for the rest of the year. The website cited his dedication to the yearlong teaching commitment, but the person I'd bumped into in the greenroom didn't seem dedicated to anyone but himself.

David's discography boasted twenty-five albums with a new one to debut early next year. Trying not to be jealous that David Richard had recorded his first solo album at twenty-eight, I clicked back to his performance résumé and hit print. The best way to discover who wanted David Richard dead was to figure out who in the *Messiah* cast knew him well enough to harbor a major grudge. I'd just have to cross-check his résumé with the rest of the cast and see how many of them connected.

Next search: Vanessa Moulton. Her website was brightly colored and filled with review quotes from past roles. The quotes were comprised of words like "rising star" and "amazing potential." I couldn't help noticing the quotes were from shows Vanessa had performed over a decade ago. Her résumé since then was made up of minor roles in small companies or ensemble roles with a few of the bigger houses. She was far from the rising star her reviews once predicted her to be.

Feeling a tug of sympathy, I hit print and scanned her list of credits as I headed to the practice rooms. Time to teach my voice lesson.

The student was late.

Normally, I'd be annoyed, but the extra minutes gave me time to compare David Richard's extensive performance list to Vanessa's respectable but much smaller one. As Christy Masonic bopped through the door muttering her apologies, I spotted the overlap between David and Vanessa: Glimmerglass Festival in New York almost fifteen years ago. Vanessa spent the summer in the ensemble. David performed Don Ottavio in *Don Giovanni*.

While I played Christy's warm-up vocal exercises, I thought back to what Jonathan had said in the dressing room about David not remembering Vanessa. While that might tick a girl off, it wasn't exactly a rousing motive for murder. Not even for a woman with Vanessa's inflated sense of self-importance.

I tortured Christy with an intense breathing exercise and moved on to her college audition pieces. Christy was planning on going into music education. That meant she needed to sing two classical songs for her auditions for the college programs to which she'd applied. The English song went beautifully. Christy had a pure tone and good command of dynamics. Unfortunately, her memorization of the Italian piece left a lot to be desired. After three tries, I asked her to get out her music and use the words so we could work on the rest.

Ten minutes later, Christy walked out of the practice

room with a stern warning from me to get the Italian song memorized. Then my next lesson walked in. This one was a freshman who had trouble not only with memorization but with nerves. Anytime I looked at her, she turned three shades of red and lost all ability to sing. But in the odd moments she wasn't in a total panic, she showed huge potential.

My last lesson of the day was out sick. Left with time on my hands, I closeted myself in Larry's office and ran a search on Jonathan McMann. The length of the man's résumé wasn't a surprise considering he was at least a decade older than the other soloists. According to the website, Jonathan traveled extensively for the first fifteen years of his career before settling down here in Chicago. Since then he'd taken the occasional out-of-town gig, but mainly performed at the Lyric. For the past seven years, he had moonlighted as a Northwestern professor.

On a whim, I brought up the university website and clicked until I found the vocal music faculty page. Wow. I wondered how Jonathan felt about David Richard's picture being front and center. The page was also strewn with quotes regarding David's outstanding work with young singers.

After a few more clicks, I found an article the *Daily Herald* had run trumpeting David Richard's arrival on the Northwestern faculty. The chair of the music department was quoted as saying, "We hope this partnership will extend past this current academic year. With luck, David Richard will decide to make Chicago his permanent home."

Setting aside the info on Jonathan, I pulled up whatever I could find on Magdalena. She and David had crossed paths at least a dozen times in the past decade. Magdalena and Jonathan had also worked on a handful of shows together.

Not surprising, but I had to wonder if either of those past relationships factored into the current murders.

The end-of-day bell rang as I hit print on an article about Magdalena's foray into composition. I added the pages to my enormous pile of investigative materials and then grabbed my stuff and headed to the theater for rehearsal. Time to put the murders out of my head and get the kids ready for tomorrow night's concert.

"Ms. Marshall."

I turned and spotted Eric racing down the hallway toward me. His all-American face was filled with concern.

"Are you okay?" he panted. "I was listening to the news during study hall. The reporter said that a member of the *Messiah* production team died and that one of the singers from the show found him and called the police."

While I really wanted to play the responsible teacher card and chastise Eric for listening to the radio during study hall, the concerned look on his face had me saying, "I'm fine, Eric. Honest. The cops are handling it."

"What if a serial killer is targeting members of the cast? You could be next."

Cheery thought. Sadly, there was a chance he wasn't far off the truth. "Look, I'm okay. I'll be even better when you and the rest of the choir show that the new number is ready for tomorrow night's performance. Otherwise, I have a feeling Chessie and her parents will get to me before any serial killer does."

Eric's face reddened at the mention of his girlfriend, but his eyes didn't lose their determined focus. Thank goodness the girlfriend in question had great timing. Chessie bounded down the hall, snaked her arm through Eric's, and gave a toss of her long brown hair. "You forgot to wait for me after ninth period." Her pink-glossed lips pouted.

"Sorry." Eric gave her a wide smile. "I needed to talk to Ms. Marshall about the second lift in the new number. The last time we ran it, I felt a little shaky. I don't want to risk dropping you."

I had to give the kid props. He lied like a champ. Chessie beamed at her boyfriend's concern and dragged him into the theater while chattering about plans for some party or another. I waited a few seconds and then followed them inside.

Today was the dress rehearsal with the band. When I'd started this job, I hadn't realized that competitive show choirs have their own band. According to the band director, Jim Williams, being chosen for the show choir band was a huge honor. That kind of made me think the band kids needed a life, but I wasn't about to complain. Getting the most talented instrumentalists in the school to accompany the choir made my job a whole lot easier. At least it would if Larry and Jim didn't let their perpetual power struggle get in the way. Jim was chairman of the music department. Larry ran the more high-profile program and had the financial backing of the choir boosters. Each wanted things done his way, or else. I just hoped the "or else" part didn't happen today. My nerves couldn't take it.

The band was setting up their instruments on stage right. Jim was directing traffic while Larry stood next to him, whispering in his ear. From the way Jim's eyes bulged, I'd guess Larry wasn't asking him to catch a drink after rehearsal. Time to step in.

I dumped my stuff on a chair, climbed onto the stage, and sauntered over to the band as Jim pointed a finger at Larry and yelled, "I don't care if your choir needs extra space to dance. The band can't move any farther stage right or we'll be in the wings."

Larry actually seemed to be considering that option, so I hurried to say, "I think a couple of the freshman guys are having trouble with their bow ties. Why don't you help them, Larry? I'll work with Jim to get things set up here."

Once Larry disappeared into the wings, I gave Jim my widest smile and asked, "How can I help?"

Jim was a sweet guy with two college-age kids and a wife who baked cookies at least once a week for the teacher's lounge. He was also a sucker for flattering words and a couple of well-placed giggles. Was I flirting with him? Maybe a little, but it got things reorganized in a way that gave the dancers more space and still allowed the band to be seen by the audience. Sometimes a person has to resort to a little eye-batting to get things done.

Walking away from Jim, I had to wonder if Vanessa had flirted with David when they ran into each other all those years ago. Maybe things went further than flirting? Not an unusual thing to happen among performers—especially ones who were looking to make a name for themselves. Hooking up with a rising star to bolster a career wasn't my style, but it might have appealed to someone as ambitious as Vanessa. And his lack of memory of that relationship years later would certainly be a slap to her ego.

Of course, even if my speculation was close to the truth, it was a pretty far jump from a woman scorned to murderess. Still, it might be worth asking a few questions. Just in case.

"Ms. Marshall."

Oy. I plastered a smile on my face and turned. "Yes, Chessie?"

The teen looked stunning in the red satin dress trimmed with faux white fur. "My throat feels scratchy. Would it be okay if I didn't sing today? I'd hate to lose my voice before tomorrow night's performance, especially after you said how much you depend on me."

Yeah, right. The girl's eyes flashed with malicious mischief. The energy rolling off her was of pure glee. One thing was certain, if Chessie wanted Broadway in her future, she'd have to invest in acting classes. Lots of them.

Chessie was waiting for me to question whether she was really sick or push her to sing through the phantom illness. If I questioned her vocal distress, she'd run to her parents and report my lack of sensitivity. Since I wasn't about to give her more ammunition to use against me, I said, "If you don't want to sing today, you don't have to. I'm sure Megan will be more than willing to step in and sing your solo."

Ha! Chessie didn't see that one coming. Her eyes narrowed as she contemplated the implications of Megan singing not one, but two features. After a moment, she smiled. "Maybe I could try to sing the first number and see how I feel. I'd hate to put Megan on the spot. She's already nervous enough about the solo you just assigned to her."

Right, and hell was paved with ice-cream sandwiches.

"Let's see how you feel." My voice oozed sympathy. "I'll tell Megan to be prepared just in case." Before Chessie retreated, I decided to put one other issue to rest. "Hey, Chessie, how is the Secret Santa thing going? Have you figured out who your Santa is?"

I looked for glimmers of guilt or excitement in the kid's expression. Coincidence was hard to swallow, but I'd rather believe the hanging Santa was an evil prank pulled by a willful teen as opposed to a warning from a cold-blooded killer.

Instead of guilt, annoyance flickered across Chessie's face. "The whole Secret Santa thing is lame. I'll be glad when it's over."

With a toss of her hair, she tromped off, not knowing her parting words caused more damage than anything else she'd said or done. Chessie's lack of acting skills made one thing certain—she wasn't behind Suicide Santa. The killer was.

My stomach dropped. The killer knew where I worked. If the killer came after me here, I wouldn't be the only one in danger. My students would end up in the line of fire, too.

Chapter 8

Chessie's singing voice was strong and clear throughout rehearsal. Not a surprise. The rest of the choir looked and sounded fabulous as they finished the seasonal portion of their repertoire. Then they darted off to change costumes for their competition set.

Ignoring the knot lodged in my chest, I asked Jim to have the band lower the volume in a few specific spots. I then settled back in my seat in the center of the theater to watch the next part of the show. Devlyn joined me as the choir members took their places for the second half of the program.

"Relax," he whispered. His hand closed over mine and gave it a quick squeeze. "I saw the first set from the light booth. They're looking good."

I bit my lip and nodded as the lighting changed. The band started playing, and the choir began its next number. Sequins sparkled under the stage lights. The kids twisted, twirled, and sang their hearts out. There were a few spacing issues that needed fixing, and a harmony or two that I wanted to tweak. I jotted notes and held my breath as the band played the intro to the new number. The soloists were strong. That was good. The background vocals were better than they had been earlier. But the kids' lack of confidence with the dance steps was obvious. Though not bad, the dancing wasn't as polished as the other numbers and didn't have the spark. Eventually, it would. The potential was there. Would the school board agree?

I had the choir practice its costume changes, smoothed some of the trouble spots, and gave a few additional notes to the band. Finally, I said, "No rehearsal in the morning. I want you to be rested and ready for the concert tomorrow night. Mr. O'Shea, Mr. DeWeese, and I have asked a lot of you this week. We're all incredibly proud of the work you've done."

I meant every word. My chest tightened. My throat ached as I sniffled back the tears.

Pushing aside the swell of emotions, I choked out, "Get changed. Go home and get some rest. I'll see you tomorrow." And the kids raced off stage.

"No rehearsal tomorrow?" Larry scrambled up the escape stairs. "But they need rehearsal. What about the school board?"

"The team will perform better if we ease off and give them a break." Not to mention that a killer couldn't target them if they weren't within fifty feet of me. I wouldn't step foot on school property tomorrow until our call time for the concert. And only then if I could guarantee the students would be safe.

A text from our assistant stage manager, Jenny, told me tonight's *Messiah* rehearsal was still on. There was also a text from Aunt Millie. She'd heard about the newest death and wanted to make sure I was okay.

I considered going back to Aunt Millie's house to grab dinner and reassure her of my safety but decided against it. Millie's message implied she wasn't home. Without my aunt in residence, Killer would be guarding the refrigerator, which meant another showdown. I wasn't up to that battle, so I opted to stop at McDonald's instead. Supersize fries always made me feel like I could take on the world. On top of that, the closest restaurant happened to be a hop, skip, and a jump from a person I really needed to talk to.

I had just sat down with my salad and monster-size fries as Mike Kaiser appeared in the doorway, looking cold and annoyed. He scanned the room, spotted me in the back, and nodded. A couple minutes later he slid across from me with his own tray.

"Glad you decided to take me up on the date." He winked as he unwrapped a double-stacked hamburger. "We could have gone somewhere a little nicer. Cops don't make a fortune, but I know how to treat a girl right."

I rolled my eyes. "I told you this wasn't a date. I need help with something." Mike's cocky grin said he didn't believe a word I was saying. "Have you talked to Detective Frewen today?"

The smile disappeared. The eyes narrowed. Mike went into cop mode. "I called him after you called me. You've had another busy day."

"Not intentionally."

"Which is scary considering how many dead bodies you've found. Most people don't ever stumble across one, let alone three."

Technically, I'd only stumbled across two—Greg, the murder victim Mike had investigated, and Bill. David Richard died in front of a lot of us. I doubted Mike would be impressed by the distinction. Instead of quibbling over details, I admitted, "I need help. There's a possibility that whoever killed David and Bill might come after me."

Mike crossed his arms across his chest and leaned back in his seat. "What did you do?"

"Someone is threatening my life and you're asking what I did?" Call me crazy, but I was pretty sure I wasn't to blame for someone else's homicidal tendencies. If Mike was going to say I was, he was going to get a French fry upside the head.

His expression didn't change. "The killer wouldn't come after you without a reason. Now, what did you do?"

I put down the French fry. The man had a valid point. Taking a sip of my soda, I gave him the rundown on my meeting with Bill and the hints he'd dropped about Magdalena's mysterious allergy. As I talked, a sick, oily sensation spread through my gut. "You don't think Bill died because I asked him to meet with me last night?"

I waited for Mike to offer immediate reassurance. When he didn't, the salad I'd eaten threatened to reappear. "I'm the reason Bill died?"

"No." Mike leaned forward, looking me square in the eyes. "The killer is the reason Bill's dead. Bill either knew something the killer didn't want getting out or the killer thought the cops would buy the suicide/confession routine."

"Which they don't."

"Not for a minute." He took a sip of his soda. "Contrary to popular belief, most suicide victims don't leave notes. The killer got creative. He also got too clever cleaning up after himself. Detective Frewen is waiting for the medical examiner to rule officially, but he's betting the same person who murdered the singer offed the stage manager, too."

The same guy who was now after me. Gulp.

I pushed my food to the side. "The killer knows where I work. I'm worried he'll come after me and end up hurting one of my students."

"I'd like to say he won't, but at this point anything is possible."

That was not the answer I wanted to hear. "We have a concert tomorrow night. It's been advertised in the newspaper, and it's listed on the school's website. Do you think there's a chance the killer will show up?"

"Maybe."

Note to self: Never go to Mike when you want to feel better about anything. The guy had a gun, however, and knew how to use it. At this point, that meant more than words of comfort.

Sneezing, I tried to ignore the panic bubbling inside my chest. "What are you doing tomorrow night?"

Mike grinned. "Already setting up a second date?"

"I want you to come to the concert and keep an eye out for anything suspicious."

"You want me to watch a high school choir concert?"

The horror in his voice made me laugh. "I promise it won't be as bad as you think." If it was, it would be the last high school choir concert either one of us would see. "I'll feel better if I know you're there to protect my kids in case of emergency."

"I've had to sit through my niece's choir concerts. They're brutal."

"This one won't be." At least, I hoped not. Mike didn't look convinced, so I added, "You'd never forgive yourself if the killer showed up and you weren't there." Mike still didn't cave. "How about I buy you a drink after the concert to say thank you?"

"It's going to need to be a really big drink."

"It will be. I promise."

"The chances of the killer showing up at the school are slim. You know that, right?"

I nodded.

"Good." Mike grinned. "Then I can pretend this was an elaborate ruse to ask me out on a date." He stood up and brushed a wayward sesame seed off his lap. "I'll see you tomorrow night. Wear a sexy dress and don't do anything to antagonize the killer before then. Keep your head down, your mouth shut, and let the cops do their jobs. Okay?"

Without waiting for an answer, Mike winked and strolled out the restaurant door, leaving me to clean up his trash. Who said chivalry was dead?

Bolstered—albeit slightly queasy—from my dinner of salt, greenery, and grease, I steered my car through traffic to the theater. During the drive, Mike's warning to keep my head down rang in my head. The idea of further antagonizing a killer had zero appeal. Maybe if I followed Mike's advice and avoided asking questions, the killer would see I was keeping out of things and leave me alone. While it went against my nature to sit back and do nothing, I was more than happy to go against type if it kept me alive. Alive was good. Dead . . . not so much.

Vowing to make myself look as disinterested in the murderer's identity as possible, I walked through the stage door and scanned the sign-in sheet. According to the cast list, I wasn't the only one who had arrived before call time. Both Jonathan and Vanessa were somewhere in the building, as were a large number of chorus and orchestra members. While being surrounded by other people hadn't helped David Richard, knowing I wasn't alone with an unmasked murderer did loosen the knot in my shoulders.

Taking a deep breath, I double-checked to make sure the water bottle I brought was sealed and then headed downstairs. With any luck, Vanessa wouldn't be in our dressing room. Call me crazy, but the idea of being alone with Vanessa's sunny disposition was low on my bucket list.

A number of choristers and orchestra members were milling around the greenroom. Their voices were subdued. From the tension and tears, I could tell they'd heard about Bill's death. Like me, they were wondering if this rehearsal was only to inform us that the show had been canceled.

The tears continued in my dressing room. I opened the door and found Vanessa sobbing in Jonathan's arms. "I can't believe Bill's gone. If only he'd told someone how unhappy he was . . ." Vanessa's bottom lip trembled, and her eyes swam with tears. Either the woman was miserably unhappy or she had better acting abilities than Chessie.

Vanessa spotted me in the doorway. She pulled out of Jonathan's arms, wiped at her face, and went from devastated to diva in two seconds flat. "This is a private conversation."

My new "don't antagonize homicide suspects" mandate had me stepping backward. I'd almost made it to safety when Jonathan insisted, "Paige, don't leave. Vanessa, it isn't fair to yell at Paige." Jonathan's voice was low. The tone sounded as though he was comforting a wounded and potentially dangerous animal. "Just because she didn't know Bill and David as well as we did doesn't mean she isn't upset." Jonathan looked at me with tired eyes. "I hope you'll forgive us for being on edge. Bill was a good friend. Getting a call from Jenny telling us that Bill committed suicide knocked us for a loop."

Clearly, our assistant stage manager hadn't heard that the police didn't buy the suicide routine. Since I'd vowed to be seen and not heard, I opted to keep that information to myself.

Not that Vanessa would have cared what I had to say anyway. From the way she threw herself back into Jonathan's arms and pressed against him, I'd say she was interested in more than comfort. Jonathan didn't look like he minded. Feeling like three was most definitely a crowd, I ran through a list of excuses to get me out of this dressing room before lifelong therapy became a necessity.

Thank goodness the feminine but firm voice of Jenny Grothe rang out from the monitor. Places. It was time to sing.

Magdalena took the podium, looking poised. Behind her, an anxious-looking Jenny hovered with a clipboard. Magdalena's lightly accented voice was controlled as she thanked everyone for coming to rehearsal under such difficult circumstances. "This week has been a tragedy for the opera community. The producers and I discussed canceling the show, but ultimately it was decided the best way to celebrate the lives of David Richard and Bill Walters was to share the music they loved with the world. To help with that mission, several radio stations have agreed to broadcast a recording of this concert as a part of a musical tribute to my friend David Richard."

My heart skipped into my throat. My voice broadcast beyond this theater into people's cars and homes was a dream come true. The publicity surrounding the broadcast could potentially launch my career into the stratosphere. This was everything I ever wanted. Too bad I was finding it hard to be happy. Knowing two people had died in order for my dream to come true made it impossible to celebrate. I wanted to earn my success, not walk across the memories of the dead to achieve it. A glance to my left told me Vanessa wasn't having the same moral dilemma. She looked thrilled.

"Andre Napoletano has agreed not only to sing the tenor role but also to perform a number I composed in David's, and now Bill's honor. Together, we will make sure that those we have lost are remembered around the world."

Magdalena's final words drew applause and sniffles. The minute she raised her baton, both ended and rehearsal began. Another member of Northwestern University's voice faculty stepped in to sing the tenor role for the night. His voice was strong and beautiful, but it didn't hold a candle to the memory of David Richard's final performance.

My muscles tightened as I waited for my first aria. The French fries from earlier rolled in my stomach, and I made a mental note not to eat before Saturday's performance. Finally, my turn came. My legs trembled as I stood. My heart thundered in my chest as I reminded myself to take deep, controlled breaths. The orchestra hit a chord, and I started to sing.

The opening line was just my voice over the held note in the orchestra. I could hear a slight quaver. Nerves. The quaver disappeared as I finished the opening line and the strings played a series of moving notes. By the time I sang the next line the nerves were gone, and I lost myself in the joy of making music. Magdalena cued the chorus as I finished the last note of my opening salvo and smiled. For the first time in days, I felt a spurt of joy. With so much recent unhappiness and stress, it was easy to forget why I was here. Why I struggled day after day to make it as a performer. It was this feeling—the giddy happiness at being able to create something magical out of notes on a page. These moments made all the auditions and the inevitable slew of rejections worthwhile.

The chorus sat down. The orchestra played the opening to my aria, and I concentrated on the music. The long passes of running notes in this aria tripped up a lot of singers. I'd practiced this aria for weeks so I could execute it with precision, passion, and flair. My goal was to make the vocal gymnastics of the aria sound and look easy. In Millie's living room, I'd accomplished all of the above. Now it was time to see whether my practice had paid off.

The music was fast. I reminded myself to breathe slow and low. While I wanted to hit every note just right, the only way to do that was to trust the prep work I'd done and relax. The opening notes sounded strong and clear. The first passage of fast, running notes was dead on. So was the next. I stopped thinking and let the music flow out of me until Magdalena directed the orchestra into the tempo change.

While the opening section of the song was light and happy, this part of the music required a tone infused with warmth and compassion. The audience needed to feel the peace and kindness I was singing about.

The music returned to the bright, effervescent tempo and

I worked to sound buoyant and effortless. When I finished the final notes and the orchestra played the last section of the piece, Magdalena smiled up at me. Sitting down, I basked in the unspoken praise. And when I caught Jonathan's nodding approval, I knew beyond a shadow of a doubt that I had nailed it. For the first time since my manager had called to tell me I'd landed this part, I felt as though I belonged.

The rest of rehearsal flew by. I lost myself in the joy of the production until the end of my last solo. As I finished singing the final measure, I looked away from Magdalena and spotted Detective Frewen. He was seated on the aisle near the back of the theater. His arms rested on the seat in front of him as he studied the players on stage. Not just players; suspects. For the last two hours, I'd forgotten that I was more than likely sharing the stage with a murderer. Now reality came crashing back, and I struggled to eke out the notes of the last ensemble number.

When the last chord was sung, Magdalena put down her baton and smiled. "Very good. Friday night's rehearsal will be even better with a couple of changes." She gave notes to the orchestra and asked the chorus master to work with the ensemble on a few sections. Out of the corner of my eye, I watched Detective Frewen rise, walk down the aisle, and fold his arms across his chest as he watched us.

No. Not us.

Detective Frewen's attention was focused squarely on one person. Not one of the soloists or Maestro Tebar, but a person seated in the orchestra pit immediately to the left of the conductor. A person I had never formally met and only knew by her stunning red hair and intimidating reputation—principal violinist and concert master Ruth Jordan.

Chapter 9

Ruth shifted and fingered the bow resting across her lap, making it clear she was aware of Detective Frewen's scrutiny. Since the violinist was known equally for her playing and her spectacular beauty, there was a chance the detective was just being a guy and admiring the view. But I didn't think so. His eyes were too steely. His jaw was clenched. No, this wasn't a man hoping to bag a date. This was a guy looking to catch a killer.

Which had me baffled. Why would Ruth Jordan be a suspect in David's and Bill's deaths? Despite his illustrious career and ability to turn on the charm, David Richard was a vocalist. For most people that wouldn't be a negative, but Ruth Jordan had a reputation in the musical community for avoiding personal encounters with singers. Several of my friends warned me to steer clear of Ruth when they learned she'd be playing this show. While it wasn't unusual for instrumentalists to crack jokes about their superior talent, Ruth Jordan wasn't laughing when she claimed singers impersonated real musicians. Still, while her attitude might not rate the Woman of the Year trophy, I doubted it rated high on the motive for murder scale. And Bill? Well, Bill had been a stage manager. In performer terms, that was like being Switzerland: neutral and interested in everyone getting along.

I was so busy watching the bi-play between Ruth and Detective Frewen, I almost missed Jenny announcing the end of rehearsal. Grabbing my water and my book, I stood up and almost walked smack into Jonathan.

"You sounded great tonight."

My cheeks warmed with pleasure. "Thanks. That means a lot coming from you."

"A few of us are going out to raise a glass to David and Bill. I'd love if you could come along."

For a second, I felt like I was back in high school, only this time the cool kids weren't ignoring me. They were asking me to sit at their lunch table. Too bad one of them might be a stone-cold killer.

When I didn't answer right away, Jonathan lowered his voice and asked, "Are you worried about Vanessa? I know she can be a little abrupt around people she doesn't know well. You'll like her once you get to know her better."

Something told me Vanessa and I were never going to exchange beauty tips and swap clothes. And to be honest, I wasn't certain I wanted to go out drinking with a couple of murder suspects. "I'm not sure if I should go. Tonight is a school night."

"I didn't realize you had kids."

"I have fourteen of them." I laughed at his confused expression. "I coach the show choir at Prospect Glen High School."

Jonathan smiled. "I didn't know you were a fellow teacher. I'd love to compare notes, and I promise I'll make sure you get home in plenty of time to get your beauty sleep. Although you certainly don't need it."

My heart skipped several beats at the compliment. Not only was the guy handsome, he knew how to flirt. If several people hadn't died, I would have jumped at his offer. As it stood, I was still tempted. Having drinks with a group of accomplished professional performers was appealing. And Jonathan had looked genuinely shocked to hear I taught at a high school. That made me feel marginally better, since my sadistic Secret Santa knew exactly where I worked. Desire to network and be accepted by the Chicago music community warred with my sense of self-preservation. Turning down a chance to schmooze with people who could help my career seemed like a really bad idea. Going into a potentially dangerous situation without someone watching my back seemed even worse.

While Jonathan gave directions to the after-party location to a couple of chorus members, I pulled out my phone, waved it around to find a signal, and dialed. Twenty minutes later, I'd followed Jonathan's directions to a local sports bar and found Devlyn waiting for me out front.

I hurried as fast as I dared across the icy parking lot to meet him. "Thanks for coming."

"I should thank you," Devlyn said as I made it safely to the sidewalk. "Playing Watson to your Sherlock is more entertaining than reading my sophomores' thoughts on

Hamlet. And getting to do this makes it even better." Before I could ask what *this* was, Devlyn kissed me.

Devlyn's lips were warm despite the cold temperature. When his arms pulled me up against him, I forgot about the biting wind as the rest of me heated up. Too bad we were here to mingle.

Classic rock blared as Devlyn and I walked into the bar. The place was dimly lit by florescent signs hawking a variety of beers and other spirits. A dozen televisions broadcasted whatever sporting events were happening around the world. Chandeliers hung low over high-top tables filled with patrons. A couple of jean-clad guys were playing pool to my right. Clustered around the tables to the left were at least a dozen people I recognized from rehearsal, including Jonathan and Vanessa.

We walked over to the bar and placed our orders. While we waited for our drinks, Devlyn asked, "Do you want me to stick to your side or mingle and pump people for information?"

I was about to tell him to stay nearby when the front door opened and Ruth Jordan strolled in, accompanied by a sandy-haired man. She wore an emerald green coat and an angry expression. The man took her jacket and went off to a table, leaving her hovering near the entrance on her own. "Why don't you make nice with the woman who just walked through the door?" I suggested. "I think the lead detective has her on his suspect list, and I haven't a clue why."

"Why don't you ask her?"

"She doesn't like singers." Besides, I was supposed to be convincing the murderer that I had backed off and was letting the cops do the investigating. "I'll be over there if you need me." I pointed in the direction of an empty high-top table in the corner and grabbed my diet soda with lime. Weaving through the crowd, I said hello to a couple of castmates then perched on a stool and watched Devlyn work his charm on the principle violinist.

After a couple of words from Devlyn, Ruth's scowl disappeared. He bought her a drink, and her mouth spread into a sultry smile. A few minutes later, they were seated at the end of the bar talking as though they were old friends.

"Your friend seems to have deserted you." Jonathan's voice reached over my shoulder.

I turned and smiled. "Devlyn will come back at some point. We have some school stuff to discuss."

Jonathan slid onto the stool next to mine. "He teaches with you?"

"He's the drama teacher and helps with the show choir choreography."

Jonathan's eyes swept over the lilac shirt and turquoise blue scarf that Devlyn had worn to work today. "Is your friend a good dancer?"

Translation: Is your friend gay?

I assured Jonathan that Devlyn was an exceptional dancer, and Jonathan slid his stool closer, saying, "I meant what I said about your singing tonight. It's an honor to share the stage with you."

Huh. From the way he was acting, I'd guess Jonathan would be honored to share more than a stage. According to the articles I'd read, Jonathan had settled permanently in Chicago just after a divorce that left his ex-wife living in the suburbs with custody of their two sons. Since then, he'd been photographed escorting a number of beautiful women to charity events and opera openings. So far he hadn't been interested enough in any of them to take a second plunge into the matrimonial pool. I had no illusions that he was interested in taking more than a dip with me. That being said, I couldn't help being flattered.

I spotted Vanessa over Jonathan's shoulder. "From the way Vanessa is glaring at us, I'm guessing she doesn't share your sentiments."

"Vanessa only gets along with male singers or female ones whose talent doesn't match or exceed her own. When you factor in your age and your appearance . . ." He picked up his beer and lifted it in my direction. "Consider her dislike as what it is: a compliment."

"Well, when you put it that way . . ." I laughed. "Although, the other day you said she was upset with David Richard. Wasn't he Vanessa's type?"

Oops. The words popped out before I could reel them back. I was supposed to be demonstrating my lack of interest in the murder investigation. Actively talking about the victim wasn't going to help my cause.

Thank goodness Jonathan appeared more amused than concerned. Leaning his elbows on the dark wooden table, he said, "David Richard was exactly Vanessa's type. And according to the grapevine, she was his. Or one of his types. David went for variety. He wasn't interested in hitching his star to any one woman. Vanessa was disappointed when she couldn't change his views on commitment when their paths crossed years ago. She thinks her career would have been different had David gone along with her plans. I have a feeling she was hoping when he saw her again he might undergo a change of heart."

So my guess had been right.

My thoughts must have showed on my face, because

Jonathan said, "You don't approve of Vanessa's methods for advancement?"

"Networking is important in this business. It's one of the reasons I came out tonight instead of going home."

"But . . ."

I took a sip of my soda, contemplated the value of honesty, and decided to give it a whirl. "I want to make it in this business, but more important, I want to know I've earned whatever success I have. I don't want to land a role simply because I'm dating the right guy."

"But you don't mind being cast because you're related to the right person?"

I blinked twice. "What are you talking about?"

"I'm talking about how you got this role." Jonathan drained his beer and signaled to the waitress for another. "I'm friends with the producer."

"And?"

Jonathan's smile faded. "You honestly don't know what I'm talking about." I shook my head, and he sighed. "Maybe I got it wrong. How did you get cast in this production?"

"My manager submitted my CD. I was invited to audition. A couple days after the audition, my manager told me I got the part." I'd earned this role. Or had I? The look on Jonathan's face made my heart sink into my toes. "What did the producer tell you?"

Jonathan developed a sudden interest in the wood grain of the table. "Vince said a friend asked him to pull some strings and get her niece an audition."

Millie.

I closed my eyes. Embarrassment wedged in my throat. The happiness I'd felt at landing this job, and with my performance tonight, vanished like smoke. Instead of feeling pride, I was lost and more than a little sad. I looked down at my drink and wished the glass were filled with something stronger than caffeine.

Jonathan's hand rested over one of mine. "The producer told me he expected to turn you down. He already had a soprano in mind for the part. The audition was a technicality—until he heard you sing. Your aunt might have gotten you in the door, but your talent landed the role."

I wanted to believe Jonathan. Was he telling me the truth or did he add that last part out of guilt?

Shaking off my insecurities, I assured Jonathan I wasn't upset by his unexpected news and let him introduce me to a group of his students who were part of the *Messiah* chorus. As Jonathan talked to the students and complimented their work, I could see how much he loved teaching. And the way he fielded questions about a number they were struggling with told me he was good at it. I taught because I needed the cash. Jonathan worked with students because he loved it.

As the students began talking about other things, Jonathan noticed our assistant stage manager hovering in the background and asked, "How are you doing, Jenny? I know this has to be hard—losing Bill and having to take over his job."

Jenny's lower lip trembled. "Bill had everything so organized. There isn't much for me to do right now, which is good. I haven't slept very well since David's death." She pulled out a tissue and dabbed her eyes. "I think the producers might bring in someone else to make sure the performances run smoothly, which is probably for the best. My boyfriend keeps telling me I can handle the job, but he's in retail. He's never worked in the theater. He doesn't understand. Bill worked so hard on this show. I don't want to screw anything up."

After reading her bio, I knew that the slight, dark-haired Jenny was majoring in theater management at Northwestern. She was also a music minor, probably in order to feel more comfortable working on these kinds of shows. Jenny was technically the assistant stage manager, but the position was more internship than real authority. Up until today, Jenny's biggest responsibility had been to make sure everyone signed in for rehearsal. It was no surprise that the death of her mentor and her promotion to stage manager, no matter how short-lived the promotion might be, had her looking overwhelmed.

In many ways Jenny and I were a lot alike. Both outsiders trying hard to fit in. Smiling, I said, "You're doing a great job. Whether they bring someone else in or not, the show is going to run like clockwork."

"Thanks, Paige." Her eyes filled with gratitude. "I should probably get going. There's an early production meeting tomorrow. See you at the dress rehearsal." She gave one last sad smile, struggled into a puffy green coat, and walked away. At the door, Jenny was stopped by Ruth Jordan. Ruth barked something, to which Jenny shook her head and said something back that made Ruth's eyes narrow. I inched closer, pretending to check messages on my phone while straining to catch what the two were talking about.

No dice. Billy Joel was wailing over the loudspeakers, and Ruth and Jenny were speaking in hushed tones. The combination made it impossible to hear anything. The man Ruth had walked in with appeared. Whatever he said had Jenny in tears as she opened the front door and hurried out into the icy wind. Ruth's lovely faced looked more than a little annoyed when the guy hurried outside after Jenny.

"I always thought classical music types were more refined than the rest of us." Devlyn appeared at my side. "After talking to both Ruth and Vanessa tonight, I'm humbled to admit I was wrong." He slipped an arm around my waist and my pulse danced at his touch. "Do you want to hang around or are you ready to get out of here?"

I looked to where Jonathan was holding court with his students. Vanessa was sitting on the stool next to him, one perfectly manicured hand resting on his arm. Neither looked as though they were leaving anytime soon. I could stay and network or go home and sleep.

Sleep won.

"Let's get out of here." I waved good-bye, shrugged into my coat, and headed out into the arctic air. When we got to my car, I asked, "What did Ruth have to say?"

Devlyn adjusted his scarf to cover the bottom of his chin. "She thinks my fingers are the perfect shape and length to play the violin. A strong but sensitive personality is required to play violin, you know."

"Right." I rolled my eyes and jammed my hands into my coat pockets to keep them warm. "Did she say anything that didn't pertain to your anatomy?"

Devlyn flashed a cocky grin. "I'll have you know, Ruth's fixation with my anatomy was the only reason she'd answer any of my questions. The woman has a one-track mind, not to mention grabby hands. She also has a serious dislike for your dead tenor. Ruth claimed he was a mediocre talent who skated by on his looks and what she considered questionable charm."

"She knew him personally?" I found that strange considering her reputation for avoiding singers.

"It sounded like it to me." Devlyn blew on his hands and rubbed them together. "Ruth tried to convince the producer to replace David Richard weeks ago. She was more than a little upset that her request was dismissed. Had she not already signed a contract to play this show, she would have walked. From our little chat, I've learned Ruth considers singers a necessary evil, but her desire to oust David Richard seems to go beyond typical prejudice."

Why? Devlyn didn't know. And the wind was cold enough to discourage speculation. I was thankful it didn't discourage Devlyn from pulling me close, though. When the kiss deepened, I shivered in a way that had nothing to do with the temperature and everything to do with the man next to me. His tongue brushed against my bottom lip for one taste. Then another. My fingers dug into his shoulders as my knees went weak. My nose was cold, but the rest of me was very, very warm. When the kiss ended and we stepped apart, we were both breathing hard.

Devlyn's hand brushed my cheek. "Once this week is over, we're going to spend lots of time getting to know each other. Right?"

"I have my calendar marked."

His smile was slow and sexy. "Good. Get some rest. Tomorrow's a big day."

After one more heart-stopping kiss, Devlyn held open my car door and I climbed in. He didn't walk to his car until I pulled out of the lot and started to drive away. A real gentleman. Was I lucky or what? I hoped that when this week was over and Devlyn and I had quality time to spend together, we'd both get a whole lot luckier.

I was so wrapped up in thoughts of Devlyn that it took me a while to realize the silver car behind me had made every turn I had. Or maybe I was just being paranoid. After two murders and a threatening package, who could blame me? To prove I was jumping at shadows, I turned right at the intersection and then waited for the headlights of the other car to appear in my rearview mirror.

Nothing.

I let out a half laugh, half sigh, and then almost stopped breathing as a pair of headlights eased onto the street behind me.

Was it the same car? It was silver; beyond that, it was hard to tell. The streetlight caught the license plate, most which was covered by snow. All I could make out was the letter C.

At the next intersection, I made another right turn and then held my breath. I was halfway down the block when headlights appeared. Same car. Same mostly snow-covered license plate.

Oh, crap!

I pressed on the gas and my car sprang forward, leaving the other car behind. Three more turns and a dozen more glances in the mirror told me I'd ditched my tail. I was also lost in a maze of residential one-way streets. Ten minutes later, my heart rate was back to normal as I turned onto Millie's street. The beacon of pink lights made me smile with relief until I spotted the pair of headlights on a silver car coming from the other direction. The car was barreling down the road—right at me.

Chapter 10

The silver car's lights reflected off the snow and ice as it swerved across the road into the path of my car. Out of reflex, I started to jam on the brakes, but then realized the silver car wasn't slowing. Stopping wouldn't do me any good. Not unless I wanted to end up flat as a pancake. Wrenching the steering wheel to the right, I prayed for a miracle. My car jolted and then climbed up, on, and over the snowpacked curb.

Oh my god! A brightly lit evergreen tree appeared in my path. I pulled the wheel to the left and jammed my foot onto the brake. My car skidded. I hit a patch of ice, fishtailed for a minute, and then came to a complete stop in one of Millie's neighbors' driveways. Taking fast, shallow breaths, I turned and looked out the rear window for the next attack. But there wasn't one. The silver car and whoever was driving it were gone.

My heart slammed against my rib cage, and I looked up

and down the residential street for signs of the silver car's return. Nothing. No cars. No lights other than the ones decorating the front lawns and houses. Whoever had followed me from the sports bar was gone.

My hands shook as I slowly backed the car down the driveway and drove down the street to Millie's. When I parked safely in the garage, I sat in the car and waited until my breathing returned to normal before going inside. If Millie was still awake, I didn't want to freak her out. Hell, I was freaked enough for both of us.

The downstairs lights were off. I flipped the switch, dumped my bag on the kitchen table, and shed my winter coat. The house was warm, but I was chilled to the bone. Even after a shower with the water cranked to boiling, I was still shivering. I guess a near-death experience will do that to a person.

Wrapped in my ratty but comfortable blue flannel pajamas and green terry-cloth robe, I closed my bedroom door, wondering what had happened. The car following me had to belong to the killer, but why had he come after me tonight? If I'd been asking lots of questions at the bar I would almost understand the motivation to scare the hell out of me. But I'd backed off, just like the killer asked, and it hadn't made a difference. The fact that it didn't both pissed me off and scared me silly.

Sitting on the bed with my legs crossed, I considered my options. I could call Detective Frewen and report the car incident. While on the surface that seemed like the logical choice, I was pretty sure all it would get me was a condescending pat on the head and a lecture on police department jurisdiction. I could call Mike. He at least would believe my story. Other than looking at the tread marks my car made while sliding across the neighbor's lawn, however, there wasn't much he could do. The only real solution to the threatening note and the silver stalker car was to catch the killer and have him locked away. Of course, for that to happen someone would have to figure out the murderer's identity.

Sliding off the bed, I went downstairs, grabbed a snack of holiday cookies, and then headed back upstairs to my room to fire up my laptop. Munching on one of my great-aunt Gertrude's famous sugar cookies, I sat at my desk and waited for the computer to boot. The odds of me putting my finger on the killer before the cops were pretty low, but I had to try. I couldn't just wait around for someone to run me off the road again. I had gotten lucky and no one was hurt. Next time . . .

I clicked open a browser and ran a search on our concert master, Ruth Jordan. Unlike Jonathan and Vanessa, Ruth didn't have her own website—but that didn't mean there was a shortage of information. Ruth wasn't shy and appeared in the local papers a lot. There were articles, reviews, a snide mention of her divorce from a French journalist, and society shots of her and whatever man she was currently dating. The newspaper photographs suggested Ruth liked older men. Much older. Which was interesting, considering her play for Devlyn tonight.

The critics praised Ruth's playing from coast to coast. Like Jonathan, Ruth had settled here in Chicago when she took a position with the Chicago Symphony Orchestra eight years ago. She wasn't the principle violinist with the CSO, at least not yet. That probably stung the well-developed ego Devlyn referred to. Ruth was a woman who wanted to be recognized as the best. Which begged the question—why would she take an orchestra position on this production of the *Messiah*? For someone like me, saying yes to this gig was a no-brainer. Singing with a name like David Richard could launch my career. Ruth was the concert master, which had to make her feel good, but this still was a step down for a violinist used to playing at Orchestra Hall. Sure, the production would get press due to David Richard's performance. That was enough to encourage almost any performer to take the job. But Devlyn said Ruth had threatened to quit when David was hired, which nixed that motivation. She took this gig for a reason. Too bad I had no idea what that reason was.

Since I wasn't going to have any epiphanies while sitting here in my pajamas, I put my questions about Ruth Jordan to the side and moved on to a more pressing issue: How had the murderer gotten his or her hands on the potassium cyanide used to kill David Richard?

While there were several sources that sold potassium cyanide through the Internet, I was happy to see potential buyers had to provide documentation that authorized them to purchase the poison. Potassium cyanide was most commonly used in gold mining, as a jewelry buffer, and occasionally in photography. The deadly compound was also used in something called electroplating, which had to do with metal ions and electrodes. My mind glazed over after reading the first paragraph about the process. I hoped staying alive wasn't going to hinge on my comprehension of anodes and anions and a bunch of other words that had never come up in high school chemistry. Otherwise, I was screwed.

Making the executive decision to leave electroplating to Detective Frewen and people way smarter than me and leaping to the assumption that none of my fellow cast members moonlighted as gold miners, I turned to the two things on the list I understood: jewelry and photography. First up: jewelry.

Oy. There was electroplating again. At least this time the article used small, non-technical words. I now understood that electroplating had something to do with transferring metal from one source to another.

I skimmed past more electroplating stuff and learned that potassium cyanide was used by jewelers as a cleaning agent. As far as I was concerned, a person had to love sparkly jewelry a whole lot to risk death in order to make her rings and necklaces shine. Then again, who was I to judge?

Pulling out my file on my four suspects, I looked to see whether any of the newspaper articles mentioned one of them having a jeweler in the family. No dice.

Mulling over ways to learn about my fellow performers' interest in gold, I began my research on the use of potassium cyanide in photography. As a rule, modern-day photographers didn't tinker with the poison, which in my mind made them smart. But there was a photography technique from the mid-1800s called wet collodion process. It used a potassium cyanide–based solution to create a glass negative, which in turn led to a very detailed print. The style had become obsolete before the 1900s. For some reason, however, modern-day fine-art photographers had revived the historic technique.

Interesting.

I typed in another search and leaned back in my wheeled chair as I read the results. Northwestern University offered several photography classes. They also offered options for independent study in all art disciplines. With Jonathan's and David's connection to the university, it might be smart to ask the photography instructor whether she demonstrated the uses for potassium cyanide in her classes. If nothing else, it was a place to start. Comforted by the illusion of being proactive, I shut down the computer and went to bed hoping tomorrow would be a better day.

I woke to the beeping of the alarm clock. Drat. I'd forgotten to turn off the damn thing last night. No early morning rehearsal meant there was no need to get up at the crack of dawn. Eyes closed, I reached over to smack the off button and felt something cold and wet touch my arm. Then the growling began. I shifted, opened my eyes, and came nose to nose with Killer. The festive red and green bow Millie had affixed to his collar did nothing to detract from the scariness of the dog's currently bared teeth.

The alarm clock continued to beep. Killer continued to growl. Yeah—this day was getting off to a rollicking start.

Determined not to show Killer any fear, I reached for the clock and jumped when Killer's growl transformed into a pissed-off bark.

"Look," I said, "I don't like the alarm any better than you. If you'd let me shut the thing off we could both go back to sleep." Sleeping in the same bed with a dog that was doing his best to starve me to death didn't seem like a great option. But I'd learned the hard way that chasing Killer out of the room was fraught with more peril than letting him stay.

The barking stopped. Reaching over Killer's fluffy white head, I smacked the button on top of the clock. The beeping mercifully stopped, too. Killer let out a whimper, put his head down on his paws, and promptly closed his eyes. I tried to do the same, but thoughts of last night's threatening car chase and Killer's whistle-like snores made me give up on my wish for extra shut-eye.

I pulled on a fitted, deep blue sweater, a pair of jeans, and my fuzziest socks and headed downstairs. At least with Killer asleep on my bed I was guaranteed a clear shot at the refrigerator.

"Good morning!" A robe-clad Aldo beamed as I bopped into the kitchen. The white of his teeth gleamed, making the azure tint of his skin more obvious. Whatever skin magic Millie had tried clearly hadn't worked. The man looked like the Smurfs' very cheerful Italian uncle. Only I doubted the Smurfs knew how to brew coffee like Aldo.

He handed me a mug doctored perfectly with sugar and cream and pointed to a kitchen counter stool. "Sit. You need a good breakfast to keep up your strength. Millie has been worried about you. I worry, too."

Guilt gnawed at my heart. "I left messages to let Aunt Millie know I was safe and I was going to be later than expected."

"Yes. Yes. We get the messages." Aldo opened the fridge and pulled out a grocery cart's worth of ingredients. "You're a good girl, but we love you so we cannot help but worry. First you see David Richard murdered. Then you find your stage manager dead. And tonight you have to convince the school to keep you working for them. Your aunt wants to talk to the school people, but I tell her you no want us to interfere."

"I really don't." My job. My problem. I wanted to handle it my way. The mention of Millie's possible interference made me think of my conversation with Jonathan last night. I took a large hit of coffee, stared into the half-empty mug, and asked, "Did Millie talk the producer into letting me audition for the *Messiah*?"

Aldo blushed. The addition of the red in his cheeks

turned his face a pale shade of purple. The blush also answered my question. Damn. There went my appetite. "Why?"

Aldo gave an exaggerated shrug and cracked an egg into a glass bowl. "Your aunt only wanted to help you. She always say you are too talented to not be discovered. If only the right person would hear you sing . . ." His voice trailed off as he cracked egg after egg. By my count, nine eggs went into the bowl. Either Aldo was distracted or he was expecting a barbershop quartet to turn up for breakfast.

"Millie offered to help me in the past," I said. "I turned her down."

"I know." Aldo kept his eyes on the cutting board as the knife he wielded skillfully slashed across an onion. "She was worried you'd get too busy teaching and forget to pay attention to your career."

"I'm only teaching to pay the bills." And after today, that might not even be the case.

"She has money, and you won't take it." Aldo put down his knife and met my eyes with his deep brown ones. "I understand why you won't. I would no take it, either. But my Millie thinks of you as a daughter. She wants the best for you. It frustrates her when you won't allow her to help. She talked to her friend just this once and asked for you to have an audition. The friend told her you wouldn't get the job, but she told him that was okay. She just wanted you to have a chance to shine."

I understood Millie loved and believed in me. In fact, I counted on Millie's unshakable faith in my talent when I had to face the hope of another audition only to find rejection. But getting this job had boosted my confidence because I'd believed I had gotten it. Me. On my own. That I hadn't cut deep. Knowing my aunt had a hand in my casting took away the faith I had gained in myself. I wasn't sure what to do about that.

"Are you going to tell your aunt that you know?" Aldo poured the egg mixture into a pan and then looked over his shoulder at me.

"No." I wanted to, but telling my aunt wouldn't change a thing. It would just upset her. There was no reason for us both to be unhappy.

"Good." Aldo beamed as he slid the pan into the oven. "Millie is planning on doing some Christmas shopping today. Shopping always makes her happy. The happier she is, the better chance I have when I give her my Christmas gift."

"What gift?" The glint in his eye had me guessing the gift wasn't a pair of hand-knitted socks.

He sat down his spatula, hurried over to the kitchen door, and peered into the hallway. After verifying the coast was clear, he turned and announced, "I bought your aunt a ring. I am going to ask her to marry me."

Uh-oh. "Aunt Millie said she never wants to get married."

"She does not mean it." Aldo laughed. "Every woman wants to get married."

Not Millie. The last guy who had asked for her hand in marriage found his ankle clenched between Killer's jaws moments before being escorted to the door. Killer didn't draw blood, but Millie's "Let's be friends" kiss-off before slamming the door did. I was fond of Aldo. I didn't want to see him meet the same fate.

"Maybe you should give Aunt Millie a little more time before popping the question. You two haven't been dating all that long."

Aldo shook his head, and he grabbed three plates from Millie's polished oak cabinets. "Years ago, when I first met your aunt, I told myself to be patient. Not to rush her. Back then, your aunt slipped through my fingers. This will not happen again. This time will be different."

This time was going to be a train wreck.

The telltale sound of Millie's heels against the hallway floor cut off the conversation before I could take another crack at convincing Aldo to hold off on his proposal. I'd have to find another time to have a heart-to-heart with him. As Millie stepped into the kitchen and said good morning, Aldo slid a plate filled with fresh fruit, potatoes, and a perfectly browned omelet onto the kitchen table. He added a mug of coffee. Then, with a flourish, he pulled out her chair, kissed her on the cheek, and pushed the chair in after she was seated. A second heaping plate of food followed right behind and was placed in front of me. Yeah—if Millie didn't say yes to Aldo, I probably would.

"This looks lovely, Aldo," Millie said, but instead of picking up her fork, she laid her hand over mine. "I'm glad you're here so I can see for myself that you're all right."

There was fatigue and worry shimmering in Millie's eyes. Both meant she hadn't slept until I'd gotten home, and maybe not even then. My heart sighed. There was no way I'd tell Millie she'd been outed for getting me the gig. While my mother loved me, it was Millie who understood me.

"I'm okay. Honest." As though to prove the point, I picked up my fork and dug into the eggs. Ham, peppers, onions, and pepper Jack cheese. Yep—Aldo was a keeper.

Millie continued to stare at me instead of her food, so I added, "I admit that having another member of the cast murdered worries me a bit." More than a bit, but who was counting? "I promise I'm being careful. I even asked Mike to come to tonight's concert on the off chance something bad may happen."

"You arranged for Mike and Devlyn to be in the same room?"

Yikes. I hadn't thought about that. Mike and Devlyn weren't known for getting along. Not only did Mike know and disapprove of Devlyn's sexual secret, both men felt the need to be contrary to any male I might feel an attraction to.

"My students' safety is more important than macho male posturing. They both know that." And if they didn't, I'd make them well aware of it by night's end.

Aldo slid into the seat next to Aunt Millie and gave her a wide smile as she finally began to eat. While we scarfed Aldo's gourmet breakfast, I gave Millie a brief rundown of last night's successful rehearsal and then redirected the conversation to what Millie had planned for the day. As we finished our meals, my aunt happily discussed her desire to buy out the North Shore stores.

Once our plates were stashed in the stainless steel dishwasher, Aldo headed upstairs to try the new skin treatment Millie had devised to de-Smurf him. When he was gone, my aunt turned to me. Her eyes were steely as she asked, "Okay, tell me. What's your plan?"

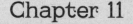

Chapter 11

Plan? "What plan?"

She gave me the Look. When I was a teenager, it made me feel as though she could see not only my open pores but deep into the recesses of my soul. "Paige Ellen Marshall, do you for one minute believe I think you plan on doing nothing while a madman or -woman is eliminating members of the *Messiah*?"

"The police are working on catching the killer."

"Without much success." She cast a furtive glance at the hallway and lowered her voice. "I didn't want to talk about this in front of Aldo; he's the artistic, sensitive type. The idea of you going toe-to-toe with a lunatic would have his blood pressure skyrocketing, but I don't see how you have any other choice. The killer could come after you next."

So much for not worrying my aunt.

I poured myself another cup of coffee and took a hit

before admitting, "You're right. The cops are doing everything they can, but I don't want to wait for the murderer to knock on my door. I've been researching people I think are on Detective Frewen's suspect list, and the poison used to murder David Richard."

"How can I help?"

An instinctive refusal sprang to my lips. Discreet wasn't in my aunt's vocabulary. If she started nosing around this case, the murderer would know. Then Millie would end up in the line of fire. My stomach went squishy at the thought of Millie being hurt or worse.

Unfortunately, the look on my aunt's face spoke volumes. She was not going to take no for an answer. If I didn't accept her offer of assistance, she'd "help" in her own way. If she worked with me, I could do my best to limit her visibility. And, I had to face it: Millie had contacts all over the city. I was betting she had a source inside the Northwestern music department who could dish up the dirt on Jonathan and David's working relationship.

Resigning myself to Millie's assistance, I asked about her Northwestern contacts. Without missing a beat, Millie pulled out her phone and dialed. I glanced at the clock on the microwave and cringed. If someone called me before eight in the morning, I'd cheerfully tell her where to shove her phone before I hung up and crawled back into bed.

Whoever Millie contacted must not have shared my aversion to early morning wake-up calls. After a discussion of the weather—yes, it was cold—and a small chat about the perfect concealer for tired eyes—because tracking down a killer couldn't get in the way of a sale—Millie asked the person on the other end of the line if he would be willing to meet and talk about Jonathan and David. After several "uh-huh"'s, Millie hung up the phone with a smile. "Jack will meet us for breakfast in a half hour."

"We just ate breakfast." If I shoveled any more food into my stomach, it would explode. As it was, my pants were feeling uncomfortably snug.

Millie laughed. "We'll order something and push it around our plates. Jack won't mind. He equates dainty eating with ladylike behavior. It was one of the reasons I stopped dating him. If I order a steak, I want to eat every juicy bite. Dainty be damned. Still, Jack loves to gossip. That makes him perfect for this little project. Now, excuse me. I need to make myself presentable. Meet you at the car in ten minutes."

Making myself look presentable included fluffing out my hair and dabbing on pink lip gloss. Millie's version involved pink rhinestone-studded stilettos, a tulip-style pink skirt, and a formfitting white sweater with a neckline that left little to the imagination. She'd also bejeweled herself with dangly diamond-and-gold earrings and a teardrop diamond necklace that sat in the crease of her very ample and exposed cleavage. On anyone else, this breakfast meeting ensemble would look a little silly. On Millie, the sparkles and tight-fitting top looked absolutely right.

From the way Jack's eyes bugged out, it was obvious he thought so, too. The man was tall with wavy black hair streaked with silver that perfectly matched his tailored suit. Out of our trio, I was definitely the underdressed one.

Once introductions were made and breakfast (ugh) ordered, Millie got down to business. "Jack is a Northwestern alum. He spends a lot of his time fund-raising for the music department. Something he excels at. He's even talked me into writing a check."

"And I plan on getting you to write another one." Jack winked at my aunt and then turned his brown hound dog eyes on me. "I was a business major, but I have a great appreciation for the School of Music. My daughter is currently attending Northwestern, majoring in piano performance. Her senior recital is scheduled for March. You should come hear her play."

"That sounds lovely, Jack. You'll have to remind me when the date gets closer." Millie leaned forward, giving Jack a great view of her chest. "My niece is one of the soloists in the sing-along *Messiah*. I bet you were just as shocked as we were to learn David Richard was murdered."

Jack's expression turned serious. "David Richard's death was a tragedy. I'm assisting in arrangements for the memorial service. We're waiting until January, when the university is back in session."

"What kind of teacher was David?" I asked, as the waitress set a plate of silver-dollar pancakes in front of me. Just looking at the food made my stomach groan. Still, I picked up my fork, poked a pancake, and said, "I only met David once, but I didn't get the impression he was easy to get along with."

"The man was a royal pain in the ass." Jack cheerfully sawed at his breakfast steak and popped a piece into his mouth. He spoke while he chewed. "And from what I've heard, David wasn't much of a teacher."

I ignored the view of partially masticated meat in Jack's mouth and asked, "Then why did he accept a guest artist position when it was offered to him?"

Jack shook his head and shoveled more food. "He wasn't offered the job. He asked for it."

My fork clanged against the side of my plate. "Why?"

"The dean said it was because David loved the city and was compelled to give back to the next generation of singers."

"You don't believe that?" I asked.

Jack slathered an English muffin with butter and grape jelly before taking a big bite. "The man canceled half the lessons he was scheduled to teach and was late to every one of his master classes. Teaching was the last thing David Richard wanted to do."

"So why was David Richard really here at Northwestern?" Millie touched Jack's fork-free hand. He promptly turned three shades of red and started to choke. Millie didn't blink. She just leaned over and smacked him on the back—hard. The momentum pitched him toward his plate of food. Before I could react, Millie stopped his forward movement and pushed him back in his chair a split second before his nose made contact with his steak. Looking serene, Millie picked up her coffee cup and took a small sip. Clearly, the agility classes she was taking Killer to had rubbed off.

Jack cleared his throat and looked down at the table as though wishing it would swallow him whole. When the table didn't comply, he picked up his fork, straightened his shoulders, and did the next best thing to disappearing—he pretended the embarrassing event had never happened. "What did you ask again, Millie?"

My aunt gave him a sweet smile. "If David Richard didn't like teaching, why was he at Northwestern? He must have had hundreds of other opportunities to choose from."

"He did." Jack resumed eating. "At the two fund-raisers I got him to attend, David told anyone who would listen about the opportunities he gave up in order to take the one-year guest artist position. London, Rome, Tokyo, New York.

He put them all on hold so he could help discover the next great opera singer. At least, that was the way his public relations team was spinning it to smooth out the rough edges of his reputation. Too bad the only thing he discovered was how to rub his colleagues the wrong way."

"He wasn't well-liked by the faculty?"

Jack laughed. I winced. The combination of red jelly and meat in his mouth looked like blood. It was disturbing to say the least. Jack didn't notice my discomfort as he explained, "The other faculty members were counting the days until David's contract expired. Especially Cynthia Goodrich, Mark Krauss, and Jonathan McMann. The three of them went wild when they heard David asked the dean for a permanent, full-time teaching position."

I knew Cynthia Goodrich by reputation. Strong soprano voice. Even stronger teaching skills. Cynthia's former students were gracing opera stages across the world. The opportunity to work with her was one of the reasons vocal performance students wanted to attend Northwestern. Jonathan I knew, but while the name Mark Krauss rang a bell, I couldn't remember why.

Thank goodness Millie jumped to my rescue. She asked about the other teachers, which gave Jack a chance to flex his fund-raising muscles while extolling the virtues of Northwestern's teachers. As he talked about Mark's wonderful work with the university's choral program, it hit me. "Mark Krauss is the tenor section leader for the *Messiah* ensemble."

Jack nodded. "He also sings in a number of award-winning chamber groups. The man is a good singer, but his real passion is teaching. He takes pride in Northwestern's dedication to the students. That's why he organized the petition to keep David Richard from being offered a permanent faculty position. The petition drew criticism from some of the higher-ups, but Mark didn't care. He's the kind of guy who puts students first."

He was also a guy with possible motive and opportunity. That put him smack at the top of my suspect list. Hoping to learn more about the motive part, I asked, "Do you know why Mark wanted to keep David from being offered a spot on the faculty?"

"The petition said it was to maintain the high standards of teaching at the school." Jack shoveled the last of the home fries into his mouth. "While I'm sure that was part of it, teaching standards aren't the typical reason men get into fistfights. You know?"

Nope. I didn't know. But I was dying to find out. "When did Mark and David get into a fight?"

"It was during the faculty meeting just before the end of semester. From what I've heard, one minute Mark and David were talking in the corner of the room, the next the two were brawling."

"Why?" I asked.

"Probably over a woman," Millie guessed as she adjusted her glasses. "Men think women are impressed by out-of-control testosterone. Personally, I've never been all that excited when men fight over me. They always expect me to tend their wounds and clean their clothes. Do you know how hard it is to get bloodstains out of linen shirts? After the sixth or seventh time you start to get the hang of it, but still . . ."

Jack gaped at Millie. I just shook my head and asked, "Did anyone tell you what the fight was about?"

"A few people speculated that David insulted Mark's wife, but no one really knows. When I ran into Mark, I asked him about it. He said he overreacted and clammed up about the rest." Jack shoved the last third of his English muffin into his mouth and chased it with coffee. He swallowed, then changed subjects and told Aunt Millie how fabulous she looked.

I tuned out Jack's attempts at flattery and considered my newest suspect. If the university had been in session, I could have sauntered into the School of Music and arranged to bump into Mark Krauss. Unfortunately, school was out until January. That put a crimp in my nonexistent investigation style. It's not like I could march up to Mark's door and ask him questions. If he was the killer, that tact would most likely land me in the same state as David and Bill—dead.

Since I wanted to keep breathing, I decided to let the whole investigating Mark problem simmer in the back of my brain while I shifted my focus to tracking down the poison. Finding where the poison was acquired meant finding the killer. I needed to start focusing on jewelry stores and photographers. The sheer volume of jewelry stores in the North Shore alone made investigating that avenue daunting at best. Photography seemed more manageable. How many artsy photographers could possibly be using potassium cyanide for their work? The number had to be low, right?

By the time Jack had finished putting the moves on Millie and Millie had sufficiently deflated his hopes, I had my next investigative move planned.

I settled into the passenger seat of the hot pink Caddy and asked, "Do you know any artistic photographers?"

Yikes. I smacked against the seat belt as the car that had just started moving jolted to a stop. I looked around for the cause of Millie's sudden braking and saw nothing. No other moving cars in sight.

I turned to my aunt and was floored by the anger shimmeiling in her eyes. Pointing a finger at me, she said, "Paige Marshall, if you need money, you only need to ask me for a loan."

I blinked. "I don't need a loan." What I needed was a translator, because I didn't understand my aunt's train of thought.

"Look." Millie put the car in park. "I know you don't want to take money from me. I admire that. You know I support a woman's right to make whatever choices are correct for her and her career. But I want you to think twice before making a decision that will impact both your performing and teaching."

Okay, now I was really confused. What did seeing an artistic photographer have to do with my career? I was going to ask when it hit me. Oh my God!

"You think I want to be in *Playboy*?"

Millie sighed. "I know those kinds of magazines pay well . . ."

I couldn't decide if I was insulted that Millie thought I'd pose naked for cash or flattered since I was past the age of a typical Playmate. I opted for the flattered route. It required less emotional angst. Carefully, I explained about the role potassium cyanide played in the wet collodion photography technique.

Understanding dawned in my aunt's eyes, along with a healthy dose of embarrassment. Putting the car back in gear, she said, "Kitty Upson is always going to art galleries. She took some art classes a while back. Her work was horrendous, but it wasn't a complete loss since the art teacher became husband number four. So far the marriage and the gallery attending have stuck. If anyone would know who the artistic photographers are, it would be them."

Millie found the number and hit send on her cell with one hand while steering the car out into traffic with the other. She cut off three cars, blew one stop sign, and almost plowed into a garbage truck while she chatted with Kitty. By the time she hung up the phone, I'd promised my first-born child to the automotive gods and Millie had the names of two Chicagoland photographers known for their wet-plate technique. Aunt Millie also had a thousand-dollar order for Mary Kay products, which she promised would arrive in time for Christmas. No grass growing under Millie's feet.

First stop: LaVon Brady. Kitty's husband said LaVon was a black-and-white photographic specialist whose most recent gallery show featured the wet-plate technique. A quick Google search on Millie's phone landed the number for the gallery in question. We also ended up in an intimate relationship with a Dumpster, which I was working hard to pretend never happened. Taking Millie's phone from her hand, I instructed her to concentrate on driving. I called the gallery and got a recorded message: Due to the holiday shopping season, the gallery was now open two hours earlier. Score.

The Brady Gallery was located in a warehouse loft on the north side of the city. While the redbrick warehouse appeared several decades old, the condos and shops on the street looked brand-new.

After a ten-minute search for parking, Millie and I hurried through the biting wind down the sidewalk to the Brady Gallery. A large sign on the front door advertised the show of a new up-and-coming artist. Inside, the warehouse space had hardwood floors, brick walls, and wooden rafters. The paintings on the wall looked like something Killer could create if Millie provided him with Crayola watercolors and some paper. The nearest canvas was streaked with an indecipherable pattern of blue, purple, and a strange brown-green color that couldn't possibly be found in nature. A quick glance at the price tag made me yelp. Murder wasn't the only crime being committed this holiday season.

"Can I help you ladies?" An impossibly tall, dark-skinned woman, made that much taller by spiky pink heels and a pink and turquoise turban, sauntered toward us.

I smiled. "My aunt was hoping to see some of LaVon Brady's work. We're told Ms. Brady is one of the few artists in the city who experiment with wet-plate technique."

Turban Woman straightened her shoulders, which made her look even taller. "I'm LaVon Brady, and yes, I am one of two artists in the city who use the wet-plate technique. It's a historic and time-intensive practice that requires a great deal of skill and patience. I believe that no time is wasted when it is dedicated to great art."

If what was on the walls was LaVon's idea of great art, I would have argued that the time used would have been better spent on a nap.

Nodding, I asked, "Are any of your wet-plate photographs still available for sale? We've heard so much about them. It would be an honor to look at your work."

LaVon beamed. "A great number of pieces sold during my last show, but I do have one or two here in the gallery. There are also a few back in my personal studio."

"Can we see the ones that are here?" my aunt asked. "I'm looking for a holiday present for a very special friend." Before LaVon could say yea or nay, Millie added, "Cost is no object."

I could see dollar signs dancing through LaVon's head as she asked us to follow her. By the time we reached the back of the gallery, my head was spinning from the wild array of colors and vegetable-like shapes we'd passed. LaVon claimed the paintings were getting rave reviews in the art world. Clearly, the art critics were blind or insane.

We stepped into a small side room and the colorful veggies were replaced by stunning black-and-white photographs. Chicago buildings. Shots of the lake. And one of a little girl and her grandmother feeding the pigeons in a park. While the two people were smiling, something about the shadows gave the scene an ominous feel. LaVon had talent.

LaVon led us to a corner of the room and pointed. "Those two photographs are part of my recent show." Both photographs were portraits. One was of a little girl with enormous eyes and lots of freckles. The other was of a woman who looked as though she'd spent the last several hours mailing her holiday packages at the post office. Both photographs drew attention to the subjects' eyes. The price tags were as exorbitant as the ones on the vegetable paintings, but in my opinion the photographs were worth the money.

Too bad complimenting LaVon wasn't going to get me the answers I was looking for. I needed to know if my suspects were her friends or clients.

Frowning, I said, "These are fantastic, but I don't think they're exactly what my aunt is looking for."

"My friend prefers photographs of objects or landscapes." Millie adjusted her glasses. "It's a shame you don't have anything like that here. You do such beautiful work. You mentioned having others back in your studio . . ."

LaVon preened under my aunt's praise. "I have an album of all the work that appeared in my most recent show. Several of the ones I still have at my studio might fit what you're looking for. I'd be happy to bring out the book and let you flip through it. If a piece is to your liking, I can arrange for you to see it in person. Wait here."

LaVon moved like lightning on those ice-pick heels. Within moments, she'd returned with a huge black binder and placed it in my aunt's hands. Each page had a 5 x 7 photograph of one of LaVon's pieces. Beneath each photograph was the title of the work, a typewritten description, and the price. If the work had already been sold, the name of the buyer was listed.

I read each buyer's name as Millie slowly turned the pages. My heart tripped when I saw one that was familiar. Listed as the purchaser of one of the less expensive but still pricy wet-plate photographs was a man I'd last seen hanging from his kitchen rafters: our former stage manager, Bill Walters.

Chapter 12

Millie cooed over the photos and asked questions. LaVon smiled as she talked about the techniques involved in using nineteenth-century equipment to capture the images. I couldn't get my mind to focus on anything but Bill's name written in neat block handwriting under that photograph.

Out of all the names I might have recognized, his was the last I'd expected to see. Bill's complete access to the theater made him an obvious suspect. Or would have, had he not been dead. Maybe Bill had killed David and someone learned he was the murderer. That person could have been angry enough to avenge David's death. But I found that scenario hard to swallow. Why take that kind of risk? If someone wanted Bill punished, all he or she would have to do is pick up the phone and dial 911. Besides, while lots of people admired David's talent, I doubted anyone cared enough to kill for him.

Could Bill owning a wet-plate photograph be a coincidence? Anything was possible. Too bad I was having a hard time convincing myself of that.

When LaVon started giving Millie the hard sell, I interrupted and asked, "Isn't it dangerous to use the wet-plate technique?"

Annoyance flickered over LaVon's features before they settled back into a smile. "Great art always involves risk."

She turned back to Millie, and I asked, "Death is a pretty big risk for your art, don't you think?"

The woman's head swung toward me so fast her turban slid precariously to the left. "The chemicals involved in wet-plate technique are dangerous if used improperly. That's one of the reasons schools don't often teach the process and what makes photographs using the technique so valuable. Now, if you like one of these—"

"If the chemicals are dangerous, are the photographs safe to own?" I bit my lip and put on my best concerned face. "My aunt's friend has children. They might not want to hang something on their wall that has potassium cyanide on it."

LaVon's eyes bulged and her turban hit the floor with a thud, exposing hair that clearly hadn't recently seen a brush. Taking deep breaths, the artist stooped down, picked up her head covering, and gave me a scary-looking smile. If Millie weren't around, LaVon would be using me for turban target practice. Good thing I wasn't here to make friends.

Through clenched teeth she said, "I can see how you might be concerned, but I assure you that none of my photographs have been created with potassium cyanide." Her nostrils flared, but I gave her huge credit for the calm tone. "I have chosen to use hypo thiosulfate. While this is not historically accurate and I don't make it widely known, I am of the belief that all art must evolve. I have chosen to take place in that evolution."

Translation: LaVon Brady didn't want to die.

Since I was equally opposed to death, I decided I should probably get out of there before LaVon could inflict damage with her long, pink nails. Still, there was something I had to know. "I saw that Bill Walters purchased one of your wet-plate photographs."

"Many people purchase my photographs." The tone told me my worry about LaVon using her nails wasn't all that far off. It was time to ask my final questions and clear out.

"Bill and I are friends." Or were. Sort of. "Do you know him personally? A referral from him would go a long way to convince us that the photographs are safe."

LaVon looked to my aunt, who nodded on cue.

With an exaggerated sigh, LaVon said, "Give me that," and pawed through the pages of her book until she reached the photograph purchased by Bill. "I vaguely remember this sale. It took place a couple weeks ago, just before my show closed. The gallery was busy, so one of my staff handled the transaction. However, when I'm in the gallery I insist on meeting any customer who buys one of my pieces. I regret to say this record of sale is wrong."

"Why?"

LaVon closed the book with a snap. "Because the purchaser I met was a woman."

Too bad the only other details LaVon was almost positive she recalled was that the woman was shorter than LaVon herself (which only eliminated players in the WNBA) and wearing a black dress. When asked about hair or skin tone, LaVon shrugged and said the person was white.

Back in the car, I considered what I'd learned. Bill's purchase of the photograph, or lack of one, was important. Whoever killed Bill must have purchased the photographs and signed his name to the sales certificate weeks ago in order to frame him for David's murder. If the cops had bought into the suicide, they would have most likely found the purchase logs at LaVon's gallery and assumed Bill had managed to get the potassium cyanide for David's murder from her studio. Two cases closed. Problem solved.

Only, the killer didn't do enough research. LaVon was too squeamish to use potassium cyanide in her work. So, even if the cops believed Bill's suicide note, they would have traced the poison source to the gallery and realized that the whole thing was a setup. The murderer, whoever he or she was, had made a mistake. I could only hope that as I continued digging I'd find a few more.

While Millie drove back to the North Shore, I placed a call to the other wet-plate photographer on Kitty's list. Yes, the artist used potassium cyanide in his work. To do otherwise would be less than true to his art form. I rolled my eyes and said, "I'm looking for a holiday gift for a friend who loves historical art, but I'm concerned one of my other friends might have beaten me to it. Would you mind looking through your records to make sure they haven't yet purchased something? I would hate to look unoriginal. How tacky would that be?"

Millie snickered as she recognized my impersonation of one of her best clients. The woman gravitated toward anything that was one of a kind, no matter the expense or the tackiness quotient. I'd last seen Millie's client at the country club's incredibly dull Give Thanks dinner-dance. Her gown was puce silk embellished with gold beads and turkey feathers. Throughout the night, Aunt Millie and I waited for Elmer Fudd to come through the door with his gun to liven things up. Sadly, the only lively event was Aldo tripping over a seeing-eye-dog's leash and ending up headfirst in the bowl of champagne punch. I laughed. Millie was mortified. Aldo was thrilled. He said it was the best bubble bath he'd had in twenty years.

The artist on the phone was either impressed by my impersonation or bored silly, because he agreed to fire up his computer and do a search of his buyer list. I went through each suspect, adding in Bill Walters's and David Richard's names for good measure. None of them appeared on the list. Huh.

After thanking the artist for his time, I hung up and tried to decide what my next move should be. It wasn't until the car had come to a stop that I realized Millie had already chosen our next adventure: shopping at the mall. As though having a killer stalking me wasn't enough—now I had to face down desperate shoppers and crazed clerks. Talk about joy to the world.

Before I could protest, Millie jumped out of the car and trekked through the slush to the stores far in the distance. Despite my aunt's choice of high-heeled footwear, she streaked across the icy asphalt like she was wearing snowshoes. My boots slipped and slid as I hurried to catch up. Maybe it was a good thing we were going to the mall. I needed better footwear.

It wasn't until we walked through the doors of the first store that I asked, "Why are we at the mall?"

"I need help picking out Aldo's gift."

"Why?" My aunt had a black belt in object acquisition. She never needed help selecting gifts.

"I want Aldo's gift to convey the correct message."

"It's a Christmas gift, not a fortune cookie."

Aunt Millie frowned while the soundtrack playing over the speakers sang about Grandma getting plowed over by reindeer. "Aldo is very dear to me. I want this gift to demonstrate how I feel about him."

Maybe Aldo was right. Maybe Aunt Millie had changed her outlook. Maybe this time *was* going to be different. Picturing my aunt in a hot pink bridal gown, I followed her to the men's department and watched as she made a beeline toward a deep burgundy satin robe cut in the style of an old-fashioned smoking jacket. The color was sexy, the fabric expensive. And bedroom-wear always screamed romance.

I started to say the robe was perfect when Millie brushed by it on her quest to pick up . . . a pair of cashmere socks. "What do you think of these?"

Oh God! "You want to give Aldo socks? That seems kind of . . ." Like a kiss-off? "Impersonal."

"Aldo has cold feet."

I had a feeling Aldo's feet weren't the issue. The only cold feet that really mattered belonged to my aunt. And the only way Aldo was going to get my aunt to say yes to his proposal was through divine intervention.

Since God had a lot on his plate, I decided to take a crack at it. "Those socks look more like something you'd buy Great-Uncle Ed. Don't you think?" Great-Uncle Ed was known for making sock puppets to entertain me and my brother. When we were little, we thought it was delightful. Now that we were adults, we found the continuing behavior a little creepy. Not to mention the fact that Great-Uncle Ed wasn't known for his faithfulness to showering.

Seeing my aunt falter, I took the opportunity to steer her back to the satin robe. "I think this would be a much better choice for Aldo."

My aunt ran a finger down the fabric and frowned. "It's the perfect color for him, but don't you think this is too . . . intimate? I wouldn't want to give him the wrong idea."

The man was sleeping in my aunt's bed. The robe wouldn't misdirect him any further. "Why don't you buy it now—just in case. You can always take it back if you find something you like better."

"You're right." Millie grinned and plucked the robe off the rack. "I don't know what I was so worried about."

Bolstered by the purchase, Millie tore through the store like a champ. By the time she was done, she had purchased several sweaters, two pairs of pants, a set of embroidered handkerchiefs, and a pair of silk pajamas for Aldo—all of which she would probably return. The socks she bought for Great-Uncle Ed. Score one for me.

Loaded down with bags, we walked out of the store into the brisk December air. "Now what?" I asked.

"I thought Aldo might like a pair of cufflinks."

The crowd roaming the sidewalks of the outdoor mall had multiplied since we first arrived. And while it was sunny, the wind was cold. Walking around the mall didn't have much appeal.

"They had cufflinks in there," I said, pointing to the warmth of the store we had just exited.

Millie's eyes twinkled. "I was thinking we need to visit a high-end jewelry store. You said those are the ones that use potassium cyanide, right? I just so happen to have a friend who owns a jewelry store in Evanston. Why don't we pay her a visit?"

I smiled and linked my arm through hers. "That sounds like a great idea."

The jewelry store in question was housed in a beige building with black awnings in the heart of downtown Evanston. I closed my eyes as Millie wedged her Caddy between two SUVs, and then followed my aunt inside. After a mall teeming with crazed shoppers and blaring holiday music, the jewelry store with its softly played Tchaikovsky and half-dozen sedate customers was soothing.

A gray-haired woman in a smart black suit nodded at us as she pulled a tray of rings out of a gleaming glass case. Aunt Millie nodded back and whispered, "That's Gayle. She owns the store and designs most of the pieces she sells."

Gayle's customer tried on a dozen rings, hemmed and hawed, and eventually left empty-handed. Calmly, Gayle placed the rings back in the case and waved us over.

"Couldn't get the customer to make a decision?" my aunt asked.

"Oh, Barbara made a decision." Gayle laughed. "Now she'll go home and drop the card to the store on the kitchen table so her husband will know she was here. He'll come by tomorrow and purchase the ring she liked, along with a couple of other things I pick out for her. Then the rest of the year they'll tell everyone how he always guesses exactly what gift she wants. It's been our little tradition for the past fourteen years."

Gayle gave Millie a sly smile. "Are you here to start your own holiday tradition? We're having a fantastic sale on tourmaline jewelry. There's a terrific hot pink necklace with your name on it."

Millie's eyes brightened, and Gayle led her over to a case along the back wall. The white gold, tourmaline, and diamond necklace was pink and sparkly and perfect for my aunt.

"We used to have a matching diamond and pink tourmaline ring, but I sold it earlier this week. Tourmalines are popular this year. If you like this piece, you might want to snap it up."

While my aunt contemplated the bright and shiny object in front of her, I said, "Gayle, I've read a story that some jewelry stores use potassium cyanide to clean jewelry. Is that true?"

Gayle raised an eyebrow and looked at my aunt. Millie said, "My niece is investigating David Richard's murder," and promptly went back to admiring the sparkly jewels.

The eyebrow raised higher. "You're a police detective?"

I sighed and shot my aunt a dirty look, which she didn't have the decency to notice. "I'm a classical singer. I was at rehearsal the night David was murdered. Whoever killed him used potassium cyanide."

Gayle sighed. "I heard about the murder, and I apologize if you think my questioning your motives for asking was rude." A small frown crossed her face. "At least once or twice a year someone asks me if they can buy potassium cyanide. It's a popular choice for suicides."

There was a cheery thought. "What do you tell people when they ask?"

"That we don't have potassium cyanide in the store and that, while it does a wonderful job cleaning gold, the poison is too difficult to obtain for us to bother with it."

"Is that the truth?" Millie asked. Her attention had shifted from jewelry to murder.

"No." Gayle lowered her voice. "I have potassium cyanide

tablets under lock and key in my studio upstairs. None of the staff know they're there."

I noticed several of the staff members in question watching our little powwow with interest. Perhaps they weren't as unobservant as Gayle might like to believe. "How can you be sure?"

"I suppose I can't be 100 percent certain," Gayle admitted. "But I only use potassium cyanide under very specific circumstances and only when I'm certain I'm alone in the studio. I wouldn't want to be responsible for a member of my staff inhaling the fumes too deeply or ingesting it by mistake. As you've seen firsthand, potassium cyanide can be incredibly dangerous."

Millie frowned. "Then why use it?"

"Because jewelers are crazy." Gayle smiled. "The cyanide solution strips the gold, which might sound like a bad thing since it means a small fraction of the gold is removed. But it leaves the metal looking much brighter. I use the cyanide solution after I complete a new piece to get it ready for display in the showroom."

"Have you used it recently?" I asked. "I guess what I'm asking is would you know if any of the potassium cyanide in your studio is missing?"

"I have. I would, and no, nothing is missing." Gayle leaned across the jewelry case. "If you think there's a chance someone took cyanide from a jewelry store, I'd be happy to ask around to make sure none has gone missing. Most stores don't use it, but a few, like me, still do."

"That would be great," I said. Detective Frewen was no doubt questioning jewelers about their stashes of potassium cyanide, but I was betting Gayle could get that information faster. Which left one last question. "Where do you buy the potassium cyanide? Do you need a special permit or something?"

Gayle gave me a small smile. "With a business license and photo ID, a person can obtain potassium cyanide at any jewelry supply store."

While it was nice to know jewelry supply stores had a record of everyone who purchased potentially lethal products, I wasn't all that hopeful about tracking the killer that way. He or she would have had to be pretty stupid to purchase a murder weapon under a real name. If I was wrong, Detective Frewen would have the culprit behind bars in no time. And boy would I like to be wrong.

On the off chance Detective Frewen wasn't at this moment making an arrest, I decided to forge ahead with my own investigation. Tracking the poison was proving more difficult than I'd originally thought it would be. For now, I'd leave that avenue to the pros and focus on an area I might be able to make some progress. While Millie succumbed to bejeweled temptation and forked over her credit card, I considered options for getting information about David's relationships with my primary suspects without drawing attention to myself. I had a cast list at home with Jonathan's and Vanessa's addresses on it. Maybe I could "happen" to bump into them . . .

The ring of my cell phone cut off my train of thought. I fished through my purse and looked at the display.

Larry.

He was probably calling to say we didn't have enough tinsel on the front of the stage. The man was obsessed with making the theater look as shiny as possible. I wasn't sure if that was a commentary on his decorating aesthetic or his worries that the audience would need something to distract them during my choir's performance.

I flipped open the phone prepared to talk Larry off the ledge. Yep—I was right. Larry was upset. Only this wasn't about decorations. Between the high pitch of his voice, bad reception in the store, and Larry's stuttering I could only understand a few words. The ones I caught made my knees buckle.

"Come now . . . trouble . . . Megan . . . dead."

Chapter 13

I took several deep breaths and asked, "Did you say Megan was dead?" No response. I looked down at my phone. Crap. No bars.

I walked toward the front doors, hoping to regain my phone signal. "Hello? Larry?" My phone display told me I now had a signal. Larry, however, was long gone.

Punching in Larry's number, I waved my thanks to Gayle, told my aunt we had to go, and hurried out the door knowing Millie would be right behind. The phone rang five times and went to voice mail. Larry must be in a reception dead zone or he was too busy to answer. I left a quick message telling him I was on my way, hung up, and dialed Devlyn. Maybe he'd know what was going on. Straight to voice mail. Damn.

I considered calling the school's office and decided against it. If something terrible *had* happened, the office staff would be swamped with calls from panicked parents. While I was freaked, parents would be even more upset.

Their needs came first. And on the off chance Larry was overreacting, clueing the office staff in on the problem wasn't going to help anyone.

Saying a quick prayer that Megan was okay, I hopped into Millie's car and gave her the rundown on Larry's phone call. I asked my aunt to drive to Prospect Glen High School—fast—and turned on the radio. Something bad happening at a high school would be a lead story. At least it would be after the station was done hawking HoneyBaked ham.

It took an array of colorful language and a couple of bumper collisions before Millie extricated the car from its parallel parking spot. She pulled into traffic and hit the gas. My stomach lurched into my throat, and I reached for the safety bar. Horns honked. Aunt Millie gave the middle-finger salute, and I reminded myself to breathe as the guy on the radio began reciting the news. Fire in the city . . . blah, blah, blah. Armed robbery   yadda, yadda, yadda. Kids throwing snowballs from an overpass onto the road, causing several accidents.

Nothing about Megan Posey or Prospect Glen High School. I took that and the lack of emergency vehicles in front of the school as a good sign. Millie let me off at the front entrance and I raced inside. The hallways were quiet as I strode across the scarred linoleum toward the performing arts wing. The clock told me the quiet wouldn't last long. The bell signaling the end of fourth period was about to ring.

My hand was reaching for the choir room doorknob as the bell jangled. I jumped out of the way as the door flew open and a herd of kids stormed out. When the coast was clear, I peeked into the room, braced for the worst. Larry was seated at the grand piano, gazing off into the distance, his cell phone clutched in his hands. For some reason, the quiet pose disturbed me more than if he'd been yelling at the top of his lungs. Larry wasn't exactly a sit-still kind of guy.

"What's going on?" I asked.

Larry yelped and spun around. The fast motion combined with Larry's lack of coordination caused him to slip off the edge of the piano bench, smack onto the tile floor.

I raced over, grabbed Larry's hand, and hauled him upright. "Are you okay? Is Megan? I only caught a couple of words before the phone connection cut us off." Just enough to scare the hell out of me.

Larry's eyebrows knitted together. His mouth trembled. Oh my God. Megan really was dead. Did the killer come looking for me and find one of my students? My throat closed up and a flood of tears churned behind my eyes as I waited for the news that would make them fall.

"Me . . . Me . . . Megan caught her hand in the shower door and pulled off one of her nails. Her hand st . . . st . . . started to bleed and she fainted and hi . . . hi . . . hit her hea . . . hea . . . head. Her sister came by last hour to tell me Megan's doctor won't allow her to perform in the concert t . . . t . . . tonight."

I grabbed the piano as a wave of relief hit. Megan being injured was bad, but dead would be worse. Way worse.

"Okay," I said, trying to pull my thoughts together. "We have to get a message to the Music in Motion kids. We need an extra rehearsal before tonight." The bell rang again, signaling the beginning of lunch. Since the school was so large, the lunch period was divided into three separate sections. Kids attended class during two of those sections and lunch during the other. Since most of the choir kids didn't have a study hall, Larry allowed them to come to the choir room instead of the cafeteria during their lunch breaks. I'd been around during enough lunch periods to know that my choir kids rarely opted for the lunchroom. They also rarely used the extra study time to study. Which gave me an idea.

"Can we get a message to the choir to come here during lunch?" I wouldn't be able to practice with everyone at once, but I'd at least be able to start figuring out how to work around Megan's absence. Between lunch rehearsals and a quick run-through with the entire group during seventh-hour choir, we might be able to save the show.

Larry agreed. Lunch rehearsal was a good idea. He hurried to the office to make an announcement over the PA system, and I called my aunt to tell her the students were safe and she could go home. I would be here for a while longer and didn't want her to wait. If Larry or Devlyn couldn't give me a lift home, I'd call a cab.

As Larry's voice echoed over the loud speaker, I closed my eyes and envisioned the dance numbers that were supposed to be performed tonight. Because Megan was a strong singer but not a strong dancer, I'd positioned her and her partner in the back for most of the numbers. There was only one number where she and her partner were front and center. I would have to move another couple forward to fill the gap. I'd also have to recast the solo that she'd just been assigned. Chessie would think she was the obvious choice, and if rehearsal didn't go well today, giving her the feature might be the only way to save my job. Oy.

I'd deal with that later. The real question I needed to focus on was whether or not to ask another student to fill in for Megan tonight. The Music in Motion choir had two female and two male understudies. Those understudies were both part of Larry's Singsations group, but attended the

Music in Motion rehearsals to practice with the squad in case of emergencies. Well, this was an emergency. I just hoped one of the female understudies had been practicing her moves.

Since it would be at least another twenty minutes before the first students would arrive, I used the time to call for backup. Devlyn's phone went to voice mail—again. I gave him the update on Megan, told him about my emergency lunch rehearsals, and asked if he could come by the theater early tonight to help boost the kids' morale before they went on with the show. Devlyn had a way of building students up so they thought they could leap tall buildings in a single bound. If I was going to save tonight's performance, I'd need all the superpowers I could get.

I hung up and dialed a second number. The recorded music we typically used for rehearsal was okay, but what I really needed was an accompanist who could start and stop and pound out the understudy's part if necessary. As luck would have it, my aunt was shacking up with a guy who fit the bill.

Aldo agreed be at the school in time for seventh period, so I walked down to the office, gave the rent-a-security guy Aldo's name, and asked if someone could show Aldo to the choir room. The last thing I needed was a still slightly turquoise Italian man wandering aimlessly up and down the halls. He'd get pegged upside his head by a spitball for sure.

Out of the fourteen members of Music in Motion, eight had "B" lunch, which gave me something to work with. One of the female understudies also arrived wide-eyed and pale as a ghost. Not a good sign.

Nope. Not a good sign at all. The girl knew the notes and the steps, but the minute she had to dance with Megan's dark-haired, blue-eyed partner, Jacob, everything fell apart. Her pale skin turned beet red when Jacob put his hand on her waist. She stepped on his feet, forgot the words, and looked like she was going to hurl through it all.

I couldn't decide if the hurling was due to stage fright or the proximity to the handsome boy next to her. Probably a combination of both. Had I not been desperate to keep my job, I might have found the girl endearing. Instead, I was telling her "thanks, but no thanks" and sending up a prayer to the show choir gods that the next understudy was immune to Jacob's charms.

The girl in question arrived with the "C" lunch crowd. As luck would have it, the understudy was Megan's younger sister, Claire. The two girls weren't exactly the best of friends. Both were blonde and average height. That's where the similarities stopped. Where Megan was shy and sweet and struggled academically, sophomore Claire was outspoken, abrasive, and highly intellectual. More than once, Claire had thought about dropping show choir because it interfered with her study time. Luckily, I'd managed to talk her out of it because, while Claire didn't have the sensational voice of her older sister, Claire could dance. I just hoped the idea of taking her sister's place, albeit temporarily, didn't make Claire wig out.

Jacob was gone, so I asked Eric to act as Claire's partner. The concerned, almost embarrassed look on his face as he took Claire's hand made me wonder whether he and Chessie had had a fight. The last thing we needed in this choir was romantic teenage drama. Oy! Cueing up the music, I shelved my worry about Eric's love life and waited for Claire to show her stuff.

Claire looked nervous, but her feet flawlessly executed

every step of the first number. I cued up the second one. Once again, Claire's dancing was perfection. Too bad her face looked as though someone was stabbing her with a red-hot poker. Something to work on.

By the time lunch was over, I'd dodged Chessie's pointed questions about the now-vacant solo position and was confident Claire could perform all but the newest musical number. The lifts were too complicated to risk it. I'd just have to figure something else out by the time seventh period rolled around.

The next group of kids filed in, and Larry began running through their music for tonight's concert. Since I wasn't needed, I headed down to the cafeteria vending machines to score something that resembled lunch.

My nerves craved deep-fried chips and lots of salt. Unfortunately, the school board had passed a ban on anything tasty in the vending machines. Instead of cheese puffs and salty chips, I was faced with crispy edamame, pomegranate-spiked nut clusters, sunflower seeds, or a dozen other items deemed healthy enough for today's youth. Had these been the snack choices when I was growing up, I would have flunked out of high school for sure. Stress required Snickers. Unless the stress quotient for high school students had reduced drastically since my days of pimples and puberty, these kids were screwed. And at the moment so was I.

After several tries, I convinced the machine to take my dollar, made my selections, and retrieved them from the bin. Pretending the granola bar was slathered in chocolate fudge, I scarfed it down and shoved the wrapper in my jeans pocket. As I headed back toward the choir room, I struggled to open a bag of baked potato chips that advertised being just as good as deep-fried chips. Whoever said there was truth in advertising was just plain wrong.

I spotted Aldo shuffling down the hall in a bright orange coat. He was squinting at room numbers while clutching a hall pass in his purple-gloved hand. A smile lit his face when he spotted me hurrying toward him. "I hope you don't mind. I get here early to look over the music before rehearsal."

"Early is good," I said. Early was way better than being late, although I doubted Aldo needed to look at the music. Not only was he a gifted cook, the man sight-read almost any piece of music without a mistake. I envied his skill. Between grammar school, high school, and college, I'd taken seven years of piano. Those lessons taught me how to play passably well, but I still needed long hours of practice before playing a piece in front of an audience. The taxidermied quintet in Millie's living room didn't count.

Grabbing the music from Larry's office, I led Aldo to one of the practice rooms and listened to him play. I made a couple of minor tempo adjustments and smiled as he played through the songs again without a single flaw. Yep—the man was a genius. Since we had time to kill before seventh period, Aldo began playing his favorite holiday tunes. I didn't wait to be asked. I just started singing.

While music was my job, singing was also therapy. With each note, I felt tension leaching out of my shoulders and my lower back. The dull, throbbing headache that had been building since Larry's phone call began to recede. Aldo played louder. I crescendoed to the end of the song, filling the room with sound. When the last note echoed around the tiny room and faded, I smiled. "Thanks. I needed that."

Aldo flashed a happy grin. "Me, too. I know you are upset

Millie broke her word and helped get you the audition. She might have been wrong to do that, but she is right about your voice. You sing like an angel."

I'd heard a variation on that compliment countless times through the course of my life. In high school, boys complimented my singing in hopes of scoring a date or more. My friends, relatives, and a number of others over the years had been effusive in their praise. But never had I heard the sentiment spoken in such a matter-of-fact tone. The quiet certainty of Aldo's words made my entire body flush with pleasure. Not only was the man a musical genius, he was a really nice guy. Which made it doubly sad that my aunt planned to dance the tarantella all over his heart. Today's shopping adventure with Aunt Millie convinced me her avoidance of a long-term committed relationship with Aldo wasn't due to a lack of emotion for the man in question. Each gift my aunt bought for him made her glow with delight. In fact, now that I thought about it, I'd never seen my aunt happier than she'd been these past months with Aldo. It would be a shame to see their relationship tanked because of a lifestyle decision Millie made three decades ago. Note to self: In between tracking down a killer and saving my job, I needed to find a way to convince Millie that marriage could be a really good thing.

At the sound of the bell, I led Aldo down the hall, introduced him to Larry, and left the two to talk while I rearranged furniture. I noticed a couple kids giving Aldo a sideways glance as they came through the door, but one look from me made them stifle whatever snide comments they might have made about his skin tone.

When everyone was seated, Larry led warm-ups and ran the choir through its concert repertoire. What Larry lacked in coordination, he more than made up for in directorial abilities. The group sounded fabulous.

He made a few adjustments, ran the music again, and turned rehearsal over to me. I glanced at the clock. I had thirty minutes to reassign the solo, reposition, and rework. Chessie looked ready to explode as Jamie stumbled on the words to the coveted solo. Aldo pounded the piano keys as my kids moved their mouths and feet and I shouted out instructions. The new positions of the couples caused four collisions. By the end of rehearsal, I was pretty sure of three things: Megan's sister, Claire, was incapable of smiling, an angry Chessie had zero ability to sing in tune, and tonight's Music in Motion performance was going to be a disaster.

Summoning my acting skills, I plastered a smile on my face and said, "Tonight's show is going to be fantastic. Remember to be at the theater at six. We'll have time to run your songs one last time before the concert."

When the last kid filed out, Aldo patted my shoulder and sighed. "You know what they say—a bad dress rehearsal means a great performance."

"I hope so." Otherwise, sayonara, paycheck.

My dejection must have showed because Aldo added, "You no need to worry about your job. When the school board sees the article in the newspaper, they won't be able to let you go."

"Article?" I looked at Larry, who shrugged. He was just as in the dark as I was. Both of us looked back at a still-grinning Aldo. "What article?"

"A reporter called at Millie's house to talk to you about the *Messiah* murders. Since you weren't home, he asked me a bunch of questions."

Dread knotted my stomach. "What kind of questions?"

"Where you grew up. The shows you've performed. That kind of stuff."

That didn't sound so bad. The knot loosened.

Aldo gave me another pat. "He also wanted to know if you had any theories about who killed David Richard or the stage manager. I said if anyone could help the police solve the case, it was you, and told him about the last murderer you helped catch. Well, one thing led to another and I started talking about your teaching."

The knot tightened. I sincerely doubted a reporter would care whether I had theories as to the killer's identity. Printing that kind of speculation would only land the reporter and the newspaper in hot water. The only person who would be interested in my thoughts on the subject was the killer. And Aldo chatted him up on the phone. Just thinking about that made my granola lunch do backflips.

Then again, I could be overreacting. The fact that I had once before been involved in a murder investigation could be of interest to a reporter. "Did you get the reporter's name or the name of the paper?" A quick phone call would verify that I had nothing to worry about. Problem solved.

"I asked, but the reporter got an important call and had to hang up. But don't worry. You will get a chance to meet him very soon."

"Why do you say that?"

Aldo beamed. "Because he said he would be at the concert—tonight."

I could feel the blood drain from my face and the room began to spin. I grabbed the piano for support as Aldo cheerfully said, "I told him about you and the choir, and he wants to do a story. I am thinking it will help you keep your job. Isn't that great?"

Great? No. Terrifying? Hell, yes. The more Aldo talked, the more convinced I was that the voice on the phone had zero interest in writing an article on my choir. If I was right, Aldo's new best friend had one reason and one reason only to come to the theater tonight—to put an end to me and my personal murder investigation for good.

Chapter 14

The potential coverage of his choir in the paper made Larry vibrate with delight. He gave Aldo a fist bump that almost landed them both in the hospital. With a final thank-you, Larry dashed to his office to spread the good news.

Aldo frowned and looked at me. "You do not think the article is a good thing?"

Well, at least someone had noticed my concern. I gnawed on my bottom lip. "I'm not sure the person who called was a reporter."

"Who else would call your aunt's house and ask questions about you and David Richard's mur—" Aldo's eyes widened as understanding dawned. "*Merda santa*. I invited a killer to a high school choir concert?"

Maybe. "We don't know that for sure. Can you remember what the guy said when he first introduced himself? His first name? His title at the paper? Anything?"

Aldo's forehead crinkled. "No. He never said his name. Just that he was a reporter doing a story. This is no good."

That was a sentiment I totally agreed with. Since dwelling on the negative wasn't going to help, I opted to focus on details that might. "Tell me about the guy's voice. Was it low pitched? Did he have an accent? What did it sound like?"

After my chat with LaVon, I'd moved the men on my suspect list down to the bottom. None of them were the type to sport a black dress. At least, I hadn't thought so. If Aldo's caller was a male, however, it meant not only did one of the men feel comfortable in a skirt and pumps, but, with only two men on my current suspect list, Aldo might be able to finger the killer.

"The voice sounded low."

Mark Krauss was a tenor. I'd never spoken to him, but I was betting money that Jonathan's voice was lower. This was good.

"But the voice got higher as the phone call went along."

Huh. Maybe Mark had tried to disguise his voice?

"And now that I think about it, there were times I thought the voice sounded like my dearly departed wife after she smoked one of her cigarettes."

Well, crap. "So the caller could have been a woman?"

"Maybe. I don't know." Aldo's bony shoulders drooped. "I think I'm confused."

So was I. There was only one thing I wasn't confused about—my students would be in danger tonight. Some of them made me want to tear my hair out, but somehow during the past few months I'd come to care about each and every one of them. Even Chessie. And now they could be hurt. Because of me.

My first instinct was to say the hell with my job and not show up tonight. I was the target. No target, no threat. Right?

Wrong. Bill's death proved the killer was willing to take out anyone necessary to keep his or her identity a secret. The killer could show up, learn I was a no-show, and take out his disappointment on one of my students. Kidnapping or injuring one of my choir members wasn't going to bother someone who had already killed twice. The only way to guarantee my students' safety was to discover the identity of the killer before the concert tonight—and I had under four hours to do so. Too bad I didn't have a clue how to go about it.

While Aldo drove us to Millie's, I racked my brain for a plan. By the time I grabbed a change of clothes for the concert and my *Messiah* contact sheet, I had one. Aldo had heard the killer's voice. Yes, the killer had tried to disguise it, but there was a chance Aldo might recognize the voice if he heard it again. If I could get a recording of each of the suspects, I could make Aldo listen to them. Kind of like an audio lineup. With his ear for tone and timbre, there was a chance Aldo could identify the caller. Not a great chance, but hey—it was better than nothing.

To avoid people identifying me by caller ID, I used Millie's home phone to call my suspects. By the time I'd dialed everyone on the list, I'd learned Magdalena and Ruth were the only two who used their own voices on voice-mail recordings. I played both messages for Aldo. He didn't recognize either voice. Bummer.

Since the others weren't picking up their phones, I was going to have to resort to plan B. Not my favorite option because to get the voices recorded, I had to talk to potential murderers in person. For that, I'd need to bring backup.

Devlyn wasn't available. Mike would just yell at me, with good reason, and I wasn't about to put Aldo or Millic in the line of fire. If I wanted to unmask the killer before my students got hurt, I only had one other option.

The suspect who lived the farthest away was Vanessa Moulton. I opted to visit her first and headed to Lincoln Park. Vanessa lived in a three story condo building down the street from the DePaul University School of Music. I considered finding a parking spot only two blocks away a good omen. Grabbing my purse, I hopped out of my car and walked through the biting wind to the building's front door.

The tiny entrance lobby was warm and empty minus a small topiary tree festooned with silver tinsel and red bows, a bank of mailboxes, and a panel of apartment call buttons. I found Vanessa's name and pressed the button next to it. Then I slid my hand into my coat pocket and wrapped my fingers around my backup—the cold steel of Millie's pink Deretta. A couple months ago, Millie had insisted I carry the gun in case of emergency. When that emergency was over, I'd given it back, but Millie made sure I knew where she stashed it. Carrying a concealed weapon with no permit was a bad idea, but going to a potential homicidal maniac's condo without protection was worse.

I turned on the MP3 recorder app on my phone as Vanessa's voice asked, "Who is it?" The speaker crackled and popped. Drat. So much for hoping I wouldn't have to see Vanessa face-to-face.

"Hi, Vanessa. It's Paige Marshall. Do you have a minute to talk?"

I expected Vanessa to tell me to get lost and was surprised when she said, "Why not. I've got nothing better to do." The door buzzer sounded. I was in.

Vanessa scowled from the doorway of her third-floor condo as I finished my hike up the stairs. "Come on in," she said as she took a step back, tripped over the entryway rug, and lost her balance. Luckily, the wall was there to break her fall. Otherwise, she would have ended up on her denim-clad butt. I kept my right hand curled around Millie's gun and used my left to help Vanessa regain her footing.

When she was upright, she shook off my hand and headed into a stylishly decorated but comfortable living room. The high walls were painted a muted yellow outlined by white crown molding. The sofa and love seat were covered in gray- and wine-colored fabrics. Framed posters from opera performances hung throughout the room. Hanging above the white marble fireplace in the position of honor was an enormous glossy photograph of Vanessa. She was standing on a darkened stage, illuminated by a spotlight, and wearing a spectacular red gown. While the photograph was stunning, I wasn't sure I'd be comfortable kicking back in a room where I was constantly stared at by myself. Then again, I lived in a house with four glass-eyed dogs. I wasn't in a position to pass judgment.

"If you came here to warn me off Jonathan, you can save your breath." Vanessa dropped onto the couch and plucked a glass from the white wicker coffee table. "Jonathan already read me the riot act."

The slight slur in her voice suggested the glass of amber liquid wasn't the first she'd consumed today. Maybe alcohol was the reason I hadn't the faintest clue what she was talking about.

I perched on the arm of the love seat. "Why did Jonathan read you the riot act?"

Vanessa smiled. The smile wasn't friendly; it was one characters use in horror movies before they pull out a knife and start hacking away. "You don't have to pretend with me." Her eyes narrowed. "We both know Jonathan has a thing for you."

Thing? What thing?

"I met Jonathan four days ago." Or maybe it was five. Who was counting?

Vanessa laughed. "What does that have to do with anything?" Before I could answer, she added, "Look, I don't blame you for using Jonathan to climb the ladder. I'd think less of you if you didn't. Talent only gets you so far in this business. Having someone willing to go to bat for you is more important, and Jonathan's a great choice. He's not big-time. At least, not anymore, but he knows the right people. Once he's invested, he'll go the extra mile to help give you a boost. He's different than most of the men I've been involved with."

I was torn between being offended, flattered, and fascinated. Since the booze was making Vanessa friendlier than normal, I opted to focus on fascinated. It would yield the most information.

"Was David Richard one of the less trustworthy types you were involved with?"

"You bet your ass he was." Vanessa drained her glass and looked into it as though waiting for more alcohol to magically appear. "He told me we'd set the opera world on fire. But when I asked him to introduce me to his manager or to some of the directors who came to see the show, he had excuse after excuse as to why it wasn't the right time."

"That must have been upsetting."

"I knew sleeping with David was a risk. Up until then, I'd only dated men a few professional rungs above me. David was on his way to being a world-renowned star and an even bigger horse's backside. I was determined to go along for the ride whether I liked him or not. I never thought I'd fall in love with the jerk. But I did, and when the show was over and he left without a backward glance, I told myself I'd get over him." Vanessa sighed. "I was wrong."

A single tear streaked down Vanessa's cheek. My heart squeezed in sympathy, and I released my grip on Millie's gun. Vanessa might not be my favorite person, but I felt sorry for her. Was there anything worse than pining away after a man you knew wasn't worth it? Suddenly, I felt bad for every negative thing I'd thought about Vanessa. Who knew, maybe after this conversation we'd end up good friends.

"Did you contact David and tell him how you felt?"

"Are you stupid?"

Okay—the good friends thing was totally out.

"If you loved him," I explained, "I would have thought you'd try to contact him. Maybe he was bad at expressing himself." He'd had no trouble expressing his dislike of me when I bumped into him or turning on the charm when he realized who I was, but people can change. Right?

Vanessa snickered. "David wasn't the falling-in-love type. Unfortunately, I am. And I was stupid enough to think being cast in this show was a sign we belonged together. Of course, that was before I actually talked to him." Her lip curled, and her hand turned white as it clenched the empty glass. "I guess I should be glad someone killed him."

"Why?"

Her smile was chilling. "Otherwise I would have had to kill him myself."

———

By the time I was back in my car, I knew three things: Vanessa and I were never going to like each other, she snored when she passed out, and, unless my instincts were totally off, she wasn't the murderer.

Did I think she had the killer instinct? You'd better believe it. The woman was scary. But my gut told me Vanessa was the type who'd want credit for her crime. The cast-aside former lover of David Richard exacting revenge would get tons of media attention. A good lawyer could argue mental distress. Vanessa could score a reduced sentence and a record contract all at the same time. Sure, she might have to wear orange jumpsuits and special bracelets for her appearances, but to someone like Vanessa fame was worth the trade-off.

Cranking the heat in my car, I tried to come up with a good excuse for dropping by Mark Krauss's Andersonville home. Unfortunately, by the time I turned down the bungalow-lined street, only lame excuses had come to mind. I was going to have to improvise.

While I cruised down the street looking for the house number, I spotted a familiar, sandy-haired man skidding on the icy sidewalks in an attempt to keep up with a very large, very energetic Great Dane. Eureka!

I rolled down the window and yelled, "Mark!"

His head snapped around as he looked for the sound. I waved. Oops. The minute Mark's attention focused on me, the dog bolted. The leash flew out of Mark's hand as the dog bounded down the sidewalk. About a hundred feet away, the dog stopped, turned around, and howled.

After pulling over, I killed the engine, climbed out of my car, and gave chase. The dog took one look at my pursuit, let out a loud bark, and bounded into the snow as though daring me to follow. Lovely. I was shown up by Killer on a daily basis. There was no way I was going to let this dog get the best of me as well.

Snow crunched under my feet as I approached the dog. When I got within five feet, the horse-size canine bounded into the next yard, plopped his butt into the snow, and gave me what looked to be a doggie grin. The handle of the red leash sat in front of him as though daring me to take it.

I took several slow steps toward the dog and made a leap for the leash. My fingertips brushed against the handle as the Great Dane dashed to the left. He looked at me and let out a happy bark before dashing into the next yard.

Great. The dog was laughing at me.

I was contemplating a new strategy when a loud whistle pierced the air. The dog stopped, turned, and bounded to the sidewalk, where Mark stood in his camel-colored trench with a Milk Bone in his hand. The Great Dane picked up the handle of the leash with his teeth and dropped it into Mark's waiting hand. Mark then presented the dog with his treat.

"Neat trick," I yelled, brushing snow off my pants.

Mark grinned. "I would have called Penelope sooner, but you looked like you were having fun."

Mark and I had wildly different definitions of the word "fun."

Walking through the snow toward the sidewalk, I scanned the area. Several children were building a snow fort across the street. A woman was watching the kids' progress from a picture window. Knowing there were people around made me feel safe enough to chat without clutching Millie's gun. I feigned receiving a text message and turned the recorder app for my phone on as Mark said, "I didn't know you lived around here."

"I don't. I was visiting a friend a couple blocks away and got turned around heading home." And my music professors said I'd never use my theater improv classes in the real world. Ha!

"Who's your friend? I might know her."

Uh . . . "Sara Smith." Okay—maybe I needed to take another class. Time to change the subject. "I'm sorry I interrupted your walk."

"Penelope likes to play." At the sound of her name, Penelope wormed her head under my hand. Mark grinned. But the smile disappeared as his eyes met mine. "How are you doing? Jonathan was worried you might be overwhelmed due to the show and . . . everything."

If "everything" meant two murders and a killer coming after me—yeah, overwhelmed was the right word. "I didn't know you and Jonathan were friends."

"We're both on the faculty at Northwestern. Jonathan teaches voice lessons. I do conducting and am in charge of the choral program. Our assistant stage manager, Jenny, and a bunch of the Northwestern kids in the chorus are my students."

"Oh." I bit my lip and feigned surprised dismay. "David Richard taught at Northwestern. Were you friends with him, too?"

Penelope got tired of my petting and walked over to sniff at Mark's pocket. Probably looking for more treats. Mark didn't look like he was in the mood to accommodate. In fact, from the way his lip curled, I'd say Mark was pissed.

"David Richard didn't have friends," Mark said. "He had conquests and enemies."

"Which one were you?"

"The man made a pass at my wife. Which do you think?"

Definitely an enemy. "Sorry, I didn't know. I guess you're not all that sorry someone killed him."

"I hate knowing people in the cast will be forever haunted by seeing him die, but, no. I'm not sorry. Whoever poisoned David Richard did the world a favor. David won't have the opportunity to ruin any more lives."

Yikes. The tone of his voice made me cold in a way subzero temperatures couldn't. Swallowing hard, I asked, "And Bill Walters?"

Mark unclenched his hands. "Bill had a weakness for trusting the wrong people. It's too bad. Bill was a nice guy."

Penelope got bored looking for a handout and tugged on the leash. Mark gave her an absentminded pat on the head. "Penelope is ready to go back. Do you need directions to get home?"

I shook my head.

Mark gave me a tense smile. "Then drive safe. I'll see you at rehearsal tomorrow night."

Mark trudged down the sidewalk with Penelope prancing in front of him. I hit stop on my phone's recording app and then hurried to my car and cranked the heat. While I waited for my nose to thaw, I watched Mark and Penelope disappear inside a house at the end of the block. Suddenly it struck me that I knew where I'd seen him in that coat before. He'd been wearing that same camel trench last night when he escorted

Ruth Jordan into the bar. Weird. I guess her attitude toward singers didn't extend toward Mark.

The sky was losing light. The clock said I had less than two hours before I had to be at Prospect Glen High School. Since I was pretty sure Magdalena wasn't the culprit, I only needed a recording of Jonathan's voice for my audio lineup. If I was going to return in time, I had to get moving.

As I cruised down the street, I glanced at Mark's house and jammed on the brakes. Parked next to the redbrick house trimmed with colorful holiday lights was a car. Not just any car—a silver car. And it looked exactly like the one that ran me off the road last night.

Chapter 15

I sucked in air and stared at the silver Malibu in Mark's driveway. My mouth went dry. The light had been too dim for me to see the make of the car yesterday, but the one in front of me was the right color and size. No snow was covering the license plate, making it easy to make out the lettering—CSHRP5. No doubt a musical reference to C-sharp. Knowing tenors, I would guess it was also the highest note Mark could sing.

I found scratch paper in the glove compartment and scribbled down the license plate number—just in case. In case of what? I had no idea, but it gave me something to do besides hyperventilate.

Panicked but feeling more in control, I steered my car north to Jonathan's house. After what I'd just discovered, I thought there was a good chance Aldo would identify Mark's voice as today's mysterious caller. But I wasn't about to leave stones unturned. At least, not while I had the time to flip them.

Jonathan lived in a blue and white two-story Victorian-style house a couple blocks away from Northwestern's campus. The sidewalk leading to the house was shoveled and clear of ice, unlike many of its neighbors. Standing at the etched glass front door, I turned on my phone's recorder before pushing the doorbell. Tchaikovsky's *Nutcracker* chimed as I put my right hand into my pocket and felt for Millie's gun.

The door swung open and a heavy-eyed, rumpled Jonathan gave me a bright smile. Either I'd woken him from a nap or interrupted him in the middle of a romantic encounter. A quick glance south and his invitation inside told me the solo nap was more likely.

Returning his smile, I followed him through a tiny foyer to a rustically decorated living room. A fire crackled in the hearth, giving the room a cheerful glow.

"I hope I'm not interrupting anything," I said, standing near the fire. "I was in the neighborhood and decided to drop by. I wanted to thank you again for your supportive words. They meant a lot."

"It was my pleasure." He folded himself into an over-stuffed leather chair. "But I doubt you just happened to be in the neighborhood."

His green eyes met mine with a knowing gleam. Feigning ignorance, I said, "I don't know what you mean . . ."

"In the last hour, I've talked with Mark and Vanessa. You've been in a lot of neighborhoods today."

Busted.

"I had a lot of errands. Christmas is less than two weeks away."

Jonathan gave me a look that said he didn't believe a word coming out of my mouth. I didn't blame him. My excuse sounded lame even to me. Jonathan stood up and slowly crossed over to where I stood. I swallowed hard and tightened my grip on the gun.

"You don't have to be embarrassed." His voice was deep and soft.

Embarrassed? No. Confused? Yes. I was also starting to sweat standing in front of the fireplace. "Why would I be embarrassed?" I asked.

"Because you came over to do this."

Before I could ask what "this" was his lips met mine in a demonstration. Okay, maybe I should have anticipated this move, but I'd been focused on defending my life, not dodging a pass by a fellow singer. I'd missed the signals. Sue me.

Jonathan's hands framed my face. His lips were warm, strong, and insistent as they slanted over mine. He was probably a good kisser. I mean, he seemed to be doing everything right. But I was finding it hard to pay attention to his technique. Call me crazy, but kissing a murder suspect while clutching a gun in my hand didn't exactly inspire romance.

Jonathan moved closer. I wanted to back up, but going up in flames wasn't on my agenda, which meant I didn't have far to move. Sweat dripped down my back. Yep—this wasn't a romantic moment. But Jonathan didn't seem to notice. His lips brushed my mouth, then my cheek, before he leaned back and gave me a slow, sexy smile.

"I know you're embarrassed that you came here, but I'm really glad you did." His hand trailed down my arm. My right arm. At the bottom of which was a hand currently poised to pull the trigger on Millie's gun. Back in high school, I had a boyfriend who slid his hand into my pocket to link fingers with me. At the time, I thought the gesture was a total turn-on. Today that endearing move would be bad. Very, very bad.

Before tragedy could strike, Jonathan took a step back and leaned against the fireplace mantel. "Unless I'm wrong, you enjoyed that kiss as much as I did."

I blinked. I guess Jonathan deduced that non-participation equaled stunned amazement. Singing he excelled at. His perception skills left a lot to be desired.

Giving me another sultry smile, he asked, "So where do we go from here?"

Mostly, I was interested in going out the door, but I was pretty sure that wasn't what he was talking about. Stepping away from the fireplace, I said, "I have a rule about not getting involved with people I'm in shows with."

"Rules are meant to be broken."

The clichéd line should have been laughable. In Jona than's low, resonant baritone it sounded sexy.

"A few days isn't that long a wait." And heck—by then I might be able to come up with a good way to avoid Jonathan's advances without completely pissing him off. Vanessa was right about one thing: Jonathan wasn't royalty in the opera world, but he knew the people who were. If he wasn't the killer, and currently I was more inclined to cast him as Don Juan than *Carmen*'s evil Don Jose, then I didn't want him holding a grudge. I was having a hard enough time landing gigs without being blackballed. Juggling fear of losing my career and fear of death was tricky.

Taking a step toward the exit, I added, "There's always a chance the thrill of the performance can be mistaken for attraction. I don't want to make that mistake."

The look on his face told me he didn't think another

round of kissing would be a mistake. It was definitely time to get out of here.

I feigned surprise as I checked the clock on my phone. "I didn't realize it had gotten so late. I have to go. There's somewhere I have to be."

"I know. The Prospect Glen High School Winter Wonderland concert."

My heart skidded to a halt.

Jonathan grinned. "I looked you up after you mentioned you were a fellow teacher. The high school has the concert listed on their website."

Yes, they did. But knowing that was true didn't make me feel any better. I wasn't sure if Jonathan's interest was sexual or homicidal, but I was certain of one thing: I wanted out of here—now.

"Look, I really have to get going. A student got injured, and I'm having an understudy rehearsal before the concert." I gave him what I hoped was a non-panicked smile and booked it toward the entrance. "I'll see you at tomorrow's run through."

I was out the door when I heard Jonathan's resonant voice say, "Maybe we'll see each other before then."

Yikes. I found myself glancing in the rearview mirror all the way to Prospect Glen. I took side streets with little to no traffic just to be certain a silver car wasn't following me. My knuckles were white from gripping the steering wheel and my muscles taut when I pulled up to Prospect Glen High School. It was a half hour before the choir's call time. The lot was illuminated but mostly empty. After my run-ins with both Mark and Jonathan and the car chase last night, the shadows beyond the lights freaked me out. Especially since I'd locked Millie's gun in the glove compartment for safekeeping. There was no way I was going to take a gun into the school. I'd just have to count on Mike showing up to protect everyone.

Grabbing my stuff, I booked it from the car to the door in record time. Once inside, I headed for the theater dressing rooms to change clothes and pull myself together. Aldo had promised to meet me at the theater's main entrance ten minutes before rehearsal to listen to my audio lineup. I had to hurry.

A perk of being a professional performer was that I'd had lots of practice at changing clothes—fast. My quickest change to date involved donning a completely different costume, wig, and shoes in thirty seconds. I had to make that change eight shows a week. By comparison, this wardrobe and hair transformation was a cinch.

I went into the dressing room wearing jeans, a sweater, and almost no makeup. I came out sporting a knee-length green satin dress, smoky eyes, and killer silver heels. I also had ten minutes to spare.

My heels clicked as I crossed the stage to check whether everything was ready. Crap. The snowmen had lost its head—again. While a headless snowman might elicit laughs from the crowd, I doubted the school board would find a decapitated Frosty all that funny. Good thing I knew where Devlyn kept the glue guns.

I flicked on the work lights, walked into the scene shop, and headed for the supply closet. Eureka! A glue gun. I grabbed glue sticks and an extension cord and started to back out of the closet when I bumped into something. No. Not something—someone.

Oh crap. My muscles stiffened. Was it a student? A teacher? Or the killer? Whoever it was bumped me, and I stumbled deeper into the closet.

Spinning, I clutched the glue gun in anticipation of defending my life and found myself pulled into a pair of strong arms. I saw Devlyn's smile before his lips touched mine. My body tingled at the sweet, gentle caress. My brain wanted to smack Devlyn upside the head for scaring me.

When the kiss ended, Devlyn grinned. I started yelling. "What is with men freaking me out and kissing me today? You scared the crap out of me."

His eyes narrowed. "Another guy kissed you today?"

Oy. Of course that was the part he focused on. Not the fact that he'd almost made me pee my pants. "While I was looking in to the murders, I ran into Jonathan McMann. Turns out he thinks we'd make a good couple."

"And you told him that you were involved with someone. Right?"

"I thought getting out of the house of a potential killer was more important than a dissertation on my love life."

Devlyn's voice went up about an octave. "You were in his house?"

Oops. I should have kept that part to myself. While Devlyn had tagged along during my last foray into sleuthing, nothing we'd encountered could be considered life-threatening. Going into a potential murderer's home was dangerous. And I had a feeling that telling Devlyn I'd brought a gun with me for protection wasn't going to make him feel any better.

I put my hand on his arm. "Look, I shouldn't have taken the chance, but I was worried the killer might show up here tonight. I was trying to identify the killer before he put any of our kids at risk. You would have done the same." I leaned in to give him a kiss, but Devlyn moved back and placed a hand on his hip. I waited for him to chastise me again and then realized I could hear voices. Student's voices. Devlyn had gone from semi-boyfriend mode to gay-teacher mode in two seconds flat. The actress in me was impressed. The almost-girlfriend was put out.

Assuming the current conversation was tabled, I handed him the glue gun. "One of the snowmen needs a head adjustment. I have something else I have to take care of." Not waiting for Devlyn's reply, I hurried out of the scene shop, kicking up sawdust in my wake.

Since dwelling on the potential pitfalls of my maybe romance with a closet heterosexual wasn't productive, I pulled out my phone and headed to the lobby. Aldo was near the box office, stomping his feet and blowing into his hands. I played each of the recordings several times, although I eliminated the part where Jonathan hit on me. Neither Aldo nor I needed that kind of embarrassment.

At the sound of Vanessa's voice, Aldo nodded. "I have heard that voice. It must be her, yes?"

I played Mark's, and Aldo frowned. Mark sounded familiar, too. By the time we listened to Jonathan's deep baritone, Aldo was completely baffled. My idea to identify the perp was a major bust.

Trying not to look as disappointed as I felt, I assured Aldo the recordings were to blame for his lack of identification and went back into the theater. My investigative skills sucked. I really needed to keep my day job. I just hoped that after this concert ended, doing my day job was still an option.

All the snowmen had their heads attached and my choir was on stage by the time I reached the front row of seats. I did a quick head count. Fourteen members of Music in Motion were here, ready to go.

Since the band wouldn't arrive until showtime, Aldo shed his winter coat and took a seat at the piano. I reminded our understudy, Claire, where she was supposed to stand and counted off the tempo. Halfway through the first number, a panicked Larry ran into the theater waving his arms and stuttering up a storm. The programs were missing. They were here earlier today, and now they were gone.

Reassuring Larry that we would find them, I asked Devlyn to watch the rest of rehearsal and went in search of the missing programs. Part of me was relieved to escape the nasty looks from Chessie and have an excuse to not witness the final run-through. There wasn't time to fix anything. Any major criticism from me would do more damage than good. What the choir needed most was confidence. Devlyn could help with that far better than I. He'd also calm Chessie down and keep her focused. At this point, the best thing I could do to improve the concert's success was to find the programs.

I found the box exactly where I'd watched Larry put it earlier today—on the floor in the corner of his office. Yowzah. The box was heavy. Taking a deep breath, I bent my knees and hefted it up and then teetered down the hallway to the theater.

About two dozen people were wandering around the lobby when I dumped the box onto a chair near the front doors. I scanned the crowd. No one from the *Messiah* cast. There was also no Larry. Thank goodness a teenager in black slacks and a white shirt seemed to know what to do with my delivery. He ripped the box open and began distributing stacks of the glossy white programs to the other ushers. The ushers would open the doors to the theater fifteen minutes before showtime, which was fast approaching.

I watched more audience members trickle into the building. A few parents spotted me and waved. I waved back, took one last look at the growing, suspectless crowd, and headed back into the auditorium.

Kids in choir robes were milling around the auditorium. The band was loading onto the stage. Meanwhile, my choir was finishing up its closing number. The lifts were solid. The singing was good. I only hoped the previous numbers had gone as smoothly.

Devlyn congratulated the kids on their hard work as I climbed onto the stage. He looked happy. That could be a good sign. Then again, he was a trained thespian. He could bluff with the best of them.

Deciding two could play that game, I plastered a wide smile on my face and said, "You guys have done amazing work. You should be proud. Make sure you have fun during the performance and knock 'em dead."

My students gave a cheer and headed off to the dressing rooms. Even Chessie looked excited. Huh. Once they exited the stage, I walked over to Devlyn and whispered, "How were they?"

"Good."

I was torn between hope he was right and worry I was being snowed. "Really?"

He laughed. "There's a few things you'll want them to work on before competition season, but they look good. You can stop panicking."

Yeah. Like that was going to happen.

"Have I told you how amazing you look in that dress?" Devlyn asked. The warm smile combined with the gleam in his eye made my heart skip several beats. "Maybe when the concert is over, we can go out and celeb—"

The sexual gleam in Devlyn's eyes disappeared as he stared at something behind me. Oh God. My muscles clenched. Devlyn must have spotted one of the *Messiah* cast members he'd met last night. Jonathan? Ruth? Mark?

I turned and found myself looking at . . . Mike. He looked every inch the cop in a faded gray sport coat and less-than-pressed blue shirt and jeans. Lurking somewhere under that coat was a gun. Part of me had been certain Mike was going to be a no-show. Seeing him here made me sigh with relief. Devlyn's stormy expression said the feeling wasn't mutual.

"Why is Detective Kaiser here? He doesn't strike me as the high school choir concert kind of guy."

There was violence shimmering under the seemingly calm words. I'd heard the same tone used during a rehearsal for the fall play. I'd poked my head into the room just in time to witness Devlyn's mild speech expressing disappointment in the students for not having their lines memorized. Then he threw them all out of the theater and threatened to cancel the show.

Bracing for an eviction, I admitted, "I invited him." Devlyn's eyes blazed, making me glad I'd never told him about the car that ran me off the road. Hoping to diffuse Devlyn's anger, I hurried to add, "He's got a gun. I thought that might come in handy on the off chance the killer showed up."

Thoughts of the killer made me scan the room again. The choirs that would perform later in the program were filing into the front rows. Millie and Aldo were seated next to Chessie's parents. Gulp. And there was Larry in the back of the theater, talking to Principal Logan and several members of the school board. There was plenty of potential danger lurking even without any sign of a murder suspect.

Mike took the seat next to my aunt. He spotted me looking in his direction, gave me a grimace, and waved. Mike didn't want to be at this concert any more than Devlyn wanted him here. Maybe seeing that would improve Devlyn's mood.

Nope. Still pissed. It was a good thing the show would start soon or I'd probably say something to Devlyn I'd regret. On a normal day, I might find Devlyn's jealousy flattering. Tonight, I really wasn't in the mood.

Devlyn and I walked backstage as the students' families and friends continued to fill the seats. My choir waited offstage for its cue. Music in Motion was kicking off the show with its set of seasonal songs. The competition numbers would come later.

Pretending my stomach wasn't tied in knots, I gave the kids one final pep talk before taking my place in the house moments before the lights blinked on and off. Audience members scrambled for their seats. The band took its place. I stood in the aisle behind the last row of seats. From the back of the theater I could watch the show, keep an eye out for the killer, and bite my nails without being observed. Multitasking at its finest.

The houselights dimmed and then went black. The stage lights glowed to life and the choir members ran onto the stage, decked out in their holiday costumes. My heart swelled with pride as I watched them take their places with confidence. And I realized something. That yes, I wanted to keep my job, but there was something I wanted more. I wanted tonight to be a triumph for my kids.

My kids.

Regardless of the angst they caused—or maybe because of it—they were mine. If the school board decided to fire me tonight, my emotional involvement with them wouldn't end. The paycheck had lured me into teaching them. And despite the monetary motivation, somewhere along the line, I had begun to care.

The music started. My stomach flopped like a dying fish, and I held my breath. I was always nervous before my own performances, but that anxiety paled in comparison to this. For good or for ill, when I was on stage I had control. Here I could only hope for the best.

Even from back here, I could see the sparkle in my students' eyes as they strutted their stuff. Their harmonies were strong. The solos were loud and clear and the dance steps executed with smiles. Even Claire looked like she was having fun—well, sort of.

And then they were done.

I watched my kids race off the stage for their costume change, accompanied by a swell of applause. They were good. Better than good. Mike had to be feeling a bit silly for putting down high school choir concerts. Now I just had to hope the second set of songs would go as well.

Larry took the stage as the freshman choir tromped onto the risers. The pianist played the intro. Larry raised his hands, and the kids began to sing.

Okay—Mike wasn't feeling so silly now.

Doing my best to ignore the creative harmony choices emanating from the stage, I wandered around the back of the auditorium and searched for signs of danger. The faces of those seated in the very back of the theater were mostly unfamiliar. Those I did know belonged to parents of students. While that was reassuring, there were close to one thousand seats in the auditorium—most of them filled. There was no way to see them all.

The all-girls choir took the stage and performed three songs. Then it was the Singsations' turn. Larry's show choir had more than twice as many students as Music in Motion. They danced less, which was good since a couple of the guys were less than coordinated, and sang with half the volume of their counterparts. But the soloists were strong and a couple kids had a spark that drew attention. No doubt they would be part of next year's Music in Motion. Would I?

The concert choir took the stage. Most of the show choir students were in this top choir. Their green and yellow robes currently hid their sequined competition costumes, but I knew they were there. The three songs went fast—perhaps because they sounded really good—and before I knew it, my kids had shed their robes and had once again taken their places center stage.

The lights changed. They were brighter. Rhinestones sparkled. The kids beamed. The band director raised his baton. I sucked in air and held it as the band began to rock out. Then the kids started to sing.

I didn't exhale until the opening lift was successfully complete. The guys twirled the girls into their arms, sending prisms of reflected light dancing across the stage. The girls put their arms around the guys' shoulders and kicked up their legs. The boys held the girls in basket-catch position before swinging the girls around their backs. When the girls came around the other side, the boys caught them in another basket catch before tossing them once in the air and spotting their partners as the girls jumped to the ground.

Perfect.

The execution was sensational. Better than rehearsal. Better than I'd seen them dance—ever. And while the basses could have been louder, the singing was strong, too. The crowd cheered as the music ended with the girls striking a pose while seated on their partners' shoulders.

There were excited whispers in the audience as Claire and her partner raced off the stage. They would sing from the wings while the rest of the choir performed the new number. The remaining twelve members hit their marks, the band started, and away they went.

Devlyn was right. There were things that needed to be fixed: a hand position here, an awkward crossover there. Each lift made my heart stop. Each lift made my heart soar. And while Megan had a slightly better sound for the solo, Jamie's voice was strong and compelling as she belted out the words. I'd watched enough YouTube show choir competition videos to know my group would score well this year. With a few final touches, this group had a chance to win. When I'd started this job, I'd told myself I'd be done with it long before those competitions ever took place. Only, I'd changed my mind. I wanted to be there. I wanted to see this choir compete. I wanted to help them win. Then I could move on.

As the last number started, I couldn't help doing a victory jig as Chessie's voice soared over the ensemble. The kids did it. They learned the new number. They had the crowd cheering for more. I was going to keep my job.

The kid on drums wailed away. The boys flipped the girls in a somersault over their arms, and the girls landed on their feet.

And that's when it happened. One of the guys bumped his partner, who had not completely regained her balance.

She threw out an arm to steady herself and clipped Eric. He turned to look for whatever struck him and lowered his arm a fraction of an inch. That was all it took. Chessie spun toward him, leaned back to where his arms were supposed to catch her, and found his arms weren't where she expected them to be. Her eyes widened. Her smile disappeared. A moment later Chessie's backside and what was left of my career hit the ground with a thud.

Chapter 16

Eric helped Chessie to her feet. The choir kept singing and dancing. Everyone executed the final lift and hit the last pose with huge smiles. The crowd went wild as my students lined up to take a bow. The applause continued even when the other choral students climbed onto the stage to sing the final group song.

Larry waved his arms. The kids sang. Larry turned and indicated the audience should sing along. Most did or at least pretended to. I couldn't. Sound couldn't squeak past the tears in my throat—tears I would never let fall. Not here. Not in front of the school board, who only cared about getting a trophy in the spring. When they fired me, my eyes would be dry. As far as consolation prizes went, it wasn't much, but beggars really couldn't be choosers.

Applause signaled the end of the concert. The houselights flickered to life. The choirs left the stage as parents and friends stood up from their seats. Larry was mobbed at the foot of the stage stairs by audience members wanting to talk about the performance. I spotted Devlyn standing about halfway up a side aisle near an exit door. He was smiling and nodding as he chatted with students and adults. I should be doing the same, but I couldn't get my feet to move.

"You realize I missed the game because I had to come here, right?" Mike leaned against the back wall of the auditorium with his arms crossed over his chest. "But the show was pretty good, if you go for this kind of thing."

I studied Mike's face to see if he was snowing me. Both Devlyn and Mike were hard to read. Devlyn with the whole acting thing and Mike with his cop face. But instead of the flat eyes and expressionless stare, Mike was smiling. My heart lifted. Maybe I was overreacting. I mean, if a guy like Mike enjoyed the show, maybe the school board did, too.

"I'm glad you enjoyed the performance."

Mike's grin grew wider. "The girl falling to the ground was almost as good as watching one of the Bulls' forwards clothesline an opposing point guard."

I sighed. So much for holding out hope.

Mike didn't seem to notice my dejection as he continued, "The girl who fell has moxie. She got up and kept smiling. You gotta admire someone who keeps going after taking a hit."

He was right. Chessie got knocked down, got back up, and finished strong. Could I do any less? Straightening my shoulders, I said, "I have to do the meet-and-greet thing with the parents. Are you going to stick around?"

"Unless dispatch calls, I'm all yours. Consider me your personal bodyguard." He sauntered closer and whispered, "If you feel like taking advantage of my body in the process, so much the better."

I made sure Mike saw my exaggerated eye roll before I plastered a smile on my face and headed into the crowd. Small talk wasn't my forte on a good day. Neither was remembering names, although I was pretty good at faces. Larry excelled at both names and inane conversation. Not only did he remember which parents went with which of his 150 students, he also remembered the names of the students' siblings, the parents' jobs, and a bunch of other useless trivia. While that information would never land him behind the winner's podium on *Jeopardy!*, it made him look brilliant during these after-concert moments. Me—well, at least I only had fourteen sets of parents to remember. How hard could that be?

"Ms. Marshall!" A tall, unfamiliar-looking woman with unnaturally crimson hair that matched her lipstick waved her hands over her head. Either she was attempting to land planes at O'Hare or she wanted my attention. "My husband and I wanted to tell you what a wonderful job you've done with Music in Motion. My daughter is hoping to make your group next year."

I sighed with relief. This wasn't a parent of one of my current students. "Thank you. I look forward to seeing your daughter audition in the spring."

Thinking the conversation was over, I started to turn only to hear, "I'm certain she'd give a stronger audition if she had someone like you working with her on a private basis."

Maybe. Maybe not. Some voice teachers worked well with some kids and failed to connect with others. Finding the right fit wasn't always easy. I avoided the kids with huge egos—like Chessie. She had lots of talent but didn't take instruction well. And while she didn't mind practice, she wanted to practice the stuff she liked instead of the music her teacher assigned. Since I had no idea who this woman's kid was, I had no clue whether the two of us would work well together.

"I only accept a small number of students," I explained. "Currently, all my time slots are filled, but I know Mr. DeWeese has a list of voice teachers from the area he recommends."

The woman's bright red smile disappeared. "My husband and I strongly believe our daughter deserves the very best chance at achieving her goals. If taking lessons with you will help her, we're willing to do what it takes to make that happen."

I glanced at the slightly glassy-eyed husband. He had his hands jammed in his pockets and was staring at the ground in a way that implied a shoe fetish or a strong desire to stay out of this conversation. If only I had that option.

"I'd be happy to add your daughter's name to the waiting list in case a time slot opens up. In the meantime— "

"I don't think you understand. We want her to start as soon as possible." The woman dug into her purse and handed me a business card with her phone number. "Money is no object."

"You know, I see your aunt over there." Mike put his arm around me and smiled at the stage mom from hell. "If you'll excuse us, Paige and I need to say hello."

I tried to shrug off Mike's arm, but he just squeezed tighter and led me away. With the grip he had on me, I found it impossible to move my arms. Which was probably Mike's intent, though I'd never hit the woman. I noticed my hands clenched tight at my sides. Okay, maybe my subconscious wanted to take a swing. Her insinuating that this was an academic version of *The Price Is Right* where the correct bid would get her kid on stage pissed me off.

We reached Millie and Aldo. I was thankful Chessie's parents had abandoned their seats post-concert. It was easier to pretend I wasn't about to be fired if the firing hadn't happened yet.

"So what did you think?" I asked.

Millie beamed. "I think it's wonderful you and Mike have decided to make a go of it."

Drat. I'd forgotten Mike's arm was still wrapped around me. Maybe because in some strange way it felt kind of like it belonged there?

Shaking off both Mike's arm and the disturbing thought, I said, "Mike and I aren't dating."

"Then why is Mike here?"

Good question. One I wasn't about to give an honest answer to. Not while students and parents were within earshot. Mass hysteria wasn't on my agenda.

Before I could come up with a suitable lie, Mike said, "Paige wouldn't go on a date with me. Not unless I proved I could sit through an entire concert without pretending to get a call from the station."

My aunt's eyes twinkled behind her glasses. "He's still here."

Everyone looked at me and waited.

"I said I might go on a date with him. Might." I might also strangle Mike the minute we got out of here.

"Mike did his part. The least you can do is let him take you on the date you promised." My aunt gave me the Look. The look never failed to stymie the client and bring in the sale. It also never failed to make me feel like a schmuck for even thinking of defying Millie's wishes.

While Millie knew Devlyn and I were doing the pre-dating dance, she wanted Mike to take the title of boyfriend. They'd bonded over gun chat a couple months ago. For some reason, Millie translated shooting ability into good boy-friend material. In business, Millie's judgment was dead on. In matchmaking, she was batting zero.

Mike raised an eyebrow as he watched me squirm. He was enjoying the show. Mike was a jerk.

Millie gave another disappointed frown, and I caved. "Okay. I'll go on a date with Mike, but only after the *Messiah* closes."

"That's fantastic." Millie clapped her hands together. "Which reminds me. Mike, do you already have a ticket for the *Messiah*? I hear they've sold out."

Mike's grin disappeared as the Look was directed squarely at him. "I don't." He shifted his feet. "I didn't real-ize tickets would be in such demand. You have no idea how disappointed I am that I'll miss it."

"Of course you'd be disappointed." Millie patted Mike on the shoulder. "That's why you'll be sitting with us Sat-urday night. Aldo bought an extra ticket for a friend of ours. She told us today that she won't be able to make it. That means her ticket for the dinner and concert package are all yours."

"Does the concert happen during dinner?" Mike pulled at the collar of his shirt.

Millie laughed. "Of course not. There's a special dinner before the concert at one of my favorite Italian restaurants. During dinner, there will be a lecture on George Fredrick

Handel and the creation of the *Messiah*. Learning about the music will help us better appreciate it when the concert begins. Aldo and I will pick you up at four thirty. We have to get there early if we want a table close to the lecturer."

For the first time since I'd met him, Mike was speechless. Probably because men with guns weren't used to being steamrolled. As far as I was concerned, going on a date with him was a small price to pay for the joy of this moment.

A parent bumped Mike from behind, which jarred him out of his stunned state. Straightening his shoulders, Mike said, "This all sounds great, but I should probably drive separate. You know—just in case I get a call from the station."

Millie smiled. "I do know, which is why I plan on calling Commander Stringer and asking him to give you the night off. The commander's wife is addicted to Mary Kay products. I slip her a few extra samples every month to help keep the cost down."

"My Millie believes in supporting law enforcement," Aldo announced. "Their salaries aren't good enough for the risks they take."

While that sounded good, Aldo had it wrong. Aunt Millie wasn't looking to help cops keep their hard-earned cash. She cut Commander Stringer a break to keep her driving record clean. Years ago, the two had come to an understanding: If Millie kept Commander Stringer's wife supplied with free products, he would wave his magic policeman wand over her speeding tickets and make them disappear. My single status must really have Millie worried if she was willing to trade in her speeding-for-free card for Mike's presence at my show.

Out of the corner of my eye, I saw Larry trying to flag

me down. He probably had news about my job . . . or lack thereof. Excusing myself, I left Mike in Millie's and Aldo's capable hands, pretended I never saw Larry, and headed in the opposite direction. Yep—I was a coward. Sue me.

I shook hands, made small talk, and smiled so much that the corners of my mouth started to spasm. Parents offered compliments. Students said thanks. The only one who came close to mentioning Chessie's show-stopping moment was a little boy with chocolate smeared across his upper lip. From his height and the Thomas the Train shirt, I was guessing the kid clocked in at around five years old. While his parents complimented the soloists, the kid quipped, "Yeah, the one who fell on her butt was really great," and promptly had a large piece of chocolate shoved into his mouth by mom. The kid's smile as he chewed said he'd made the comment in order to get the treat. The kid was no dummy.

Twenty minutes later, Millie and Aldo had waved good-bye, Mike was nowhere to be seen, and the majority of the audience had gone home. Only students going to an after-concert party at Denny's and a few die-hard choir boosters were left. And, of course, members of the school board. They were huddled in the back left corner of the auditorium. No doubt discussing my fate.

Panic broke through the wall of calm I'd erected. My hands began to shake. My throat went dry. It was only a job, I told myself. Too bad that didn't make me feel any better.

Since waiting for the ax to fall was zero fun, I opted to take action. My plan consisted of two parts. First—get a drink of water. Once I was hydrated, I'd walk up those steps and demand to know whether I still had a job.

Since a bunch of students were hanging around the lobby, I decided to use the drinking fountains outside the band room. My heels clicked against linoleum tile and echoed in the low-lit hall. I took deep, calming breaths and reminded myself that I was a performer. I was used to rejection. I just needed to pretend the school board was one more casting director saying, "Thanks, but no thanks."

The cold water soothed my throat if not my wounded pride. I went back for a second drink and froze.

Footsteps. Somewhere down the hall to my left.

Telling myself not to panic over a student going to his or her locker for a homework assignment, I turned toward the sound and squinted into the dim hall. Nobody there.

"Achoo."

My stomach wedged into my throat. Someone was most definitely there.

A shadow shifted on the wall halfway down the hallway, and my feet started to move. Call me crazy, but I wasn't going to stick around to see to whom the shadow belonged.

Since whoever sneezed was positioned between me and the safety of the theater, I went in the opposite direction, doing my best to walk natural. Maybe if I feigned ignorance, whoever was lurking down the hall would take his time following me and give me an opportunity to hide.

From behind me came another sneeze and then more footsteps. They were getting closer—fast.

I ditched plan A and went for plan B: Run!

On a good day, I wasn't the speediest runner. And when I was in strappy, sexy heels, Aldo could beat me in a foot-race. My heart pumped against my chest as my feet half hobbled, half ran past rows of red lockers. I just needed to get to the end of the hallway. To the left were a boys' and a girls' bathroom, a couple of classrooms, and an exit. If I ducked into the boys' bathroom, there was a chance my pursuer would think I'd raced out the exit or into the girls' lavatory. Either would buy me enough time to take off my shoes and make a quiet getaway.

The footsteps grew louder and even closer as I reached the end of the hall. As I raced around the corner, I looked over my shoulder for a peek at my pursuer. While I squinted behind me, I heard something move to my right. I'd started to turn toward the sound when I felt a burst of pain. That's when everything went black.

Chapter 17

My head throbbed. My eyes felt like they'd been glued shut. The last time I'd felt like this was after the cast party for *Oklahoma!*. A crew member had brought happy-plant brownies. I ate three before someone mentioned the special ingredient. At least when I woke with a headache that time, I vaguely remembered dancing, flirting, and having fun before passing out. This time I remembered nothing.

"Paige?" Devlyn? Wow, did we hook up? It would really suck not to remember that.

"Come on, Paige. It's time to open those sexy eyes and get up."

That wasn't Devlyn. I pried open my lids and squinted into Mike's face. While his voice was all cop, his eyes were filled with concern. That's when I remembered.

"Someone was following me."

"Well, someone must have found you because you have a hell of a lump. Good thing you have a hard head."

I considered smacking Mike as he helped me to a seated position and decided it would just have to wait. I didn't have the energy. "How did you find me?"

Mike hooked a finger at Eric. The kid was hovering in the background next to Chessie, a very worried-looking Devlyn, and a bunch of my other students. "Eric was going to the choir room and heard a scuffle. He found you lying on the ground and called for help."

I tried to stand and the world started to spin. Nope. No standing. Gingerly, I touched the back of my head. No blood. That was a good sign, right? I glanced at Eric, who was looking pale and decidedly upset. "Did you see who hit me?"

Eric shook his head. "No one else was here."

"Whoever it was must have heard Eric coming and ran. Either that or the person hid in one of the bathrooms," Mike explained. "After Eric found you, he ran back down the hall and yelled for help. That would have given your attacker time to get away."

Good to know my escape plan worked for someone. But something felt off; I had been looking behind me when I got attacked. That meant the person doing the chasing and the person performing the hitting were two different people. "What about the person who chased me down the hall?"

"Someone chased you?" Mike's dark eyes narrowed.

"I was getting a drink and heard someone sneeze in the hallway near the theater. When I looked, no one was there. It spooked me. So, I walked in the other direction. That's when I heard footsteps running down the hall toward me. I was looking to see who the footsteps belonged to when I got hit."

Mike turned to Eric. "Did you see anyone in the hallways when you came out?"

202 | JOELLE CHARBONNEAU

Eric bit his lip and shook his head no. For a kid wanting to go into law enforcement, his inability to identify the perp had to be a huge disappointment.

"So now what?" I hoped Mike had a brilliant plan because sitting on the cold tile in my cocktail dress was starting to get old.

"Now we wait for the paramedics to check you out. They should be here any minute."

As if on cue, the door at the end of the hall opened and two emergency workers arrived with a stretcher in tow. A red-faced Larry trailed behind them, rubbing his hands together. He must have been waiting outside for their arrival.

Mike herded the students and random observers back to the auditorium to do his cop thing while the paramedics checked me out. Devlyn and Larry remained for moral support. I waited for Devlyn to go into protective boyfriend mode. Instead, he let Larry hold my hand while he stood several steps back and said nothing. Weird.

The paramedics shined bright lights in my eyes, whacked my knee with a little hammer, had me walk a few steps to see if I'd fall on my ass (I was thankful I didn't), and asked me lots of inane questions. What was my name? What day of the week was it? Who was the current president of the United States? While I was tempted to give silly answers, I played it straight. Making jokes wasn't worth a trip to the hospital and a fashion makeover involving a backless cotton gown.

When the examination was finished, I was declared mildly concussed. The paramedics offered me a ride to the hospital for a CT scan, which I declined, and then handed me an ice pack for the bump on my head, along with some instructions. No strenuous activities for the next couple of days. No driving for the next couple of hours. And most important, have someone wake me every few hours during the night to make sure my brain hadn't started to swell. Oh joy.

We watched the paramedics head out. When they were gone, I turned to Larry and asked, "Did the school board make a decision?" The night had gone so far downhill, I figured there wasn't much farther until I hit bottom. After that there was nowhere to go but up.

Larry swallowed and shot a look toward the auditorium. "I think the school board wants to discuss the choir's performance with you themselves."

I put the ice pack against the back of my head and sighed. "This week, I've seen a guy poisoned, another one hanged, and have just been hit over the head by the person who probably killed them both. Do you really want to make me wait until the school board fits me into their schedule before learning that I'm fired?"

"You're not fired."

Maybe my concussion was worse than I thought. "Say that again."

Larry grinned. "While some school board members question your underutilization of a few of your students, they all believe Music in Motion has a better chance of winning the national competition with you coaching the team."

Translation: Chessie's parents put up a stink but lost the vote. Score.

I started to do a victory dance, felt the world tilt, and was steadied by Devlyn. His smile was wide as he said, "No strenuous activities. Remember?"

"Right."

Grinning like idiots, the three of us headed back to the theater at a slow clip, me barefoot, to make sure I didn't reacquaint myself with the floor. Mike was alone in the theater when we walked through the door. He was lounging against the stage, hands folded in front of him. To those who didn't know him, he'd appear calm and relaxed. I, however, knew what that expression meant. Hell, I'd seen it enough. Mike was pissed.

He pushed away from the stage and walked up the center aisle stairs toward us. "No one saw anything suspicious. I'm going to ask Detective Frewen for photographs of his suspects in David Richard's murder. Maybe someone will recognize one of them, but I'm not holding my breath."

I swallowed hard. "You think the murders and the assault are connected?" As much as I agreed with the assessment, part of me really wished he suspected a disgruntled student or a drunken audience member.

"It would be a hell of a coincidence if they weren't." Mike glanced toward Devlyn. "I've got to go to the station and get a jump on a few things. Can you make sure she gets home safe? She has a knack for finding trouble."

I waved my hand in front of Mike's face. "Excuse me. I can hear you, you know."

Mike smirked. "You have a head injury. There's a chance you won't remember this conversation tomorrow."

"There's also a chance my fist will make contact with your nose."

"Only if you want to go to jail." He flashed his badge and winked. "Cop trumps all. I'll call you later to make sure you got home safe and to set up that date."

Having dropped the date bomb, Mike strolled out the door without a backward glance. Larry hurried after him to shut off the lights and lock up, leaving Devlyn and me alone. Crap.

I waited for Devlyn to ask about the date or do the macho

thing and yell. Instead, he dropped a kiss on the top of my head and said, "Let's get your stuff and get out of here."

We retrieved my things and walked to the faculty parking lot while chatting about the concert. Before climbing into Devlyn's car I remembered something. "Be right back."

I crossed the lot, popped the locks on my Cobalt, and retrieved Millie's gun. While I sincerely hoped I wouldn't have to use it, I knew I'd sleep better with the Beretta tucked under my pillow tonight.

As Devlyn drove, I held a now squishy ice pack to my head and waited for him to mention my date with Mike. Only Devlyn wasn't saying anything. He just had this pleasant, occasionally concerned expression plastered on his face. It was making me tense.

The silence stretched for several blocks. Finally, I couldn't stand it anymore. "I know you're mad about the date with Mike."

Devlyn smiled at me via the rearview mirror. "No, I'm not."

"You threw a fit when I told you I went to Jonathan McMann's house, but you're not upset that I'm going on a date with Mike?" The whole head injury thing was screwing with my perception of reality.

"Going to Jonathan McMann's house was dangerous. Mike is just annoying. Besides, I was watching your aunt in the auditorium. I'm guessing she had something to do with this, which means, technically, the date isn't your fault."

Huh. Either Devlyn felt sorry for me or he was being rational. Whichever it was, I wasn't about to look a gift horse in the mouth.

Now that I wasn't waiting to be yelled at, I began to notice the scenery. "You're going the wrong way."

"Actually, I'm not." Devlyn gave me a smile that made my toes curl. "A girl who would go on a date with a guy who irritates her just to avoid upsetting her aunt isn't going to want to tell that same aunt she was attacked after the concert. The paramedics said someone needs to wake you every couple hours. I've volunteered for the job. This is my place."

As though to emphasize his point, Devlyn pulled into the parking garage of a sleek, five-story building. Part of me wanted to go home. The less cautious half was dying to see Devlyn's living space.

We took the elevator to the top floor and walked down the brightly lit, beige-carpeted hall to his door. His was one of four apartments on this floor. Devlyn hit the lights and led me into an expansive living room. While Devlyn wore pastels to work, at home he was an earth-tones kind of guy. The couch and armchair were deep rust, the furniture was mahogany, and the area rug was gray and cream. Beyond the living room was an equally well-decorated kitchen filled with stainless steel and granite. How he afforded this place on a teacher's salary was beyond me.

Devlyn disappeared into the kitchen. He returned with a glass of water and three aspirin tablets. "The guest bedroom is at the end of the hall on the left. The bathroom is on the right. While you dump your stuff, I'll get us a snack. I could hear your stomach rumbling during the drive."

Moderately embarrassed, I swallowed the pills and walked to the guest room while doing my best to ignore the urge to peek into Devlyn's bedroom. A bedroom said a lot about a person, like whether he watched television in bed or left his underwear on the floor . . . or if he wore underwear at all.

The idea of Devlyn going commando made me flush. Thank God the door I assumed led to his bedroom was closed, preventing my overcurious nature from taking control. The guest bedroom was painted a soft blue. The queen-size bed was covered with a dark blue comforter. A half-dozen blue and white pillows were scattered on top. Never had a bed looked so good to me. My head throbbed. The adrenaline rush from surviving an attack and saving my job had passed, leaving my muscles trembling with exhaustion. There was nothing I wanted more than to fall flat on my face for the next twelve hours. Instead, I ditched my stuff and went to the bathroom to wash up.

Yikes.

My eyeliner was smeared and my hair looked as though I'd plugged my finger into a light socket. Raccoon from hell wasn't my best look. Makeup free and hair problems resolved, I went back to the bedroom and smiled. Sitting on the bed were a pair of gray sweats and a yellow T-shirt.

Dressed in Devlyn's clothes, I padded out to the living room, where the man in question was waiting with scrambled eggs, toast, and tea. How awesome was that? When I was seated, he handed me a plate and a fork. "This was what my mother made for me when I got my first concussion."

"You've had more than one?"

He laughed. "I was a quarterback. Concussions were a way of life."

"You played football?" The only theatrics the football players I went to high school with were interested in were the ones that got the other team called for a penalty or elicited sympathy from the cheerleaders. Both helped them score.

"Football was the reason I started dancing. My father

thought dance classes would improve my footwork on the field. He was right. My senior year, our team won state. I also played Danny Zuko in our school's production of *Grease*."

"How did your dad feel about that?"

"He was in the front row for both."

I tried to imagine my father cheering my brother from the front row as he sang and danced around on stage. Nope. My imagination wasn't that good. "Your dad sounds nice."

Devlyn smiled. "He is. I was hoping to introduce you tonight, but you were too busy avoiding me."

Oops. "I wasn't avoiding you."

"Right. Just make sure you aren't avoiding me on Saturday night after the *Messiah*. My mother wants your autograph."

Now was probably not the time to tell him that Mike would be at the concert. Even if the police caught the killer by opening night, the lobby was going to be a very scary place. Something to look forward to.

Devlyn took the empty plates and mugs, loaded them into the dishwasher, and walked me down the hall to my room. "Remember to call your aunt and let her know where you are." He took my face in his hands, ran a thumb across my cheek, and placed a light kiss on my lips. "I'll see you in a couple hours."

Before I could sneak a peek inside his bedroom, he'd disappeared inside and shut the door. Drat.

Since Millie was likely to alert the National Guard if I didn't come home, I followed Devlyn's advice and got the machine. I left a message that I was spending the night at a friend's house, turned off the lights, and went to sleep.

My eyes flew open as I heard something move to my left. Not thinking, I grabbed a pillow and swung it.

"Oof."

Devlyn. My brain woke up along with the ache in the back of my head. "Sorry. I forgot where I was."

"I'm lucky you didn't go for the book on the nightstand." Devlyn took a seat on the bed next to me. "Well, I don't have to worry about testing your reflexes. But I am going to turn on the light and look at your eyes. If your vision is blurred, you'll need to see a doctor."

Yowzah. The shift from pitch-black to completely light had me seeing spots. When my vision cleared, I caught sight of Devlyn standing next to the bed in forest green boxers and felt faint. Devlyn in tight T-shirts was a sight to behold. Bare-chested Devlyn could illicit riots.

"How's your vision?" He leaned over and peered into my eyes. "Are you seeing double?"

"No. Although, seeing two of you wouldn't necessarily be a bad thing." Oops. I hadn't meant to say that aloud.

Devlyn smiled. "My parents are glad I wasn't a twin. I caused more than enough trouble on my own."

"Really? What kind of trouble."

"The kind you're going to get in if you don't stop looking at me like that." He touched his lips to mine in a kiss that was designed to be friendly but made me start to sweat. "The paramedics specifically said no strenuous activity."

"It doesn't have to be strenuous." It had been over a year since my last serious boyfriend, but I remembered that much.

"It's strenuous when it's done right." Devlyn's smile made everything inside me go limp. "We'd do it right." He gave me another light kiss before standing up and turning off the light.

"Get some more sleep. I'll be back in three hours to check on you." And out the door he went.

Until Devlyn's arrival, I'd had no trouble sleeping. Now I was wide awake and thinking about him lying shirtless across the hall. Since thinking about Devlyn wasn't helping me fall asleep, I changed gears and thought about the reason I was in Devlyn's guest bed. The killer clocking me in the school hallway told me he was getting more persistent. My investigation had to be getting too close for comfort. Too bad I hadn't a clue exactly what I was getting close to. Worse still was the knowledge that I had been hit by one person after being chased by someone else. Mike seemed to think my story about the second person was far-fetched. If Mike didn't believe me, the police would continue to focus on finding a solo killer. But if anything positive came from being whacked on the head, it was that I knew the cops should be looking for two people.

But which two? Most everyone in the *Messiah* cast knew one another from previous shows. Any two of them could have talked about their problems with David Richard and then conspired to do him in. Now those two were tag teaming me, and I needed to figure out how to stop them.

By the time Devlyn came back to do the *Sleeping Beauty* routine, I hadn't come up with any bright ideas as to how to track down the duo. I was stuck.

When I was struggling with playing a character, I always went back to the script to see what details might explain why the character behaved the way she did. Third-act melt-downs or unusually optimistic behavior were always explained somewhere in the show. If not by the character herself, then by the things other characters said in response to her. You just had to pay attention. And trust me, I had serious motivation to pay attention now. To solve the murders, I needed to go back to the beginning and figure out what details I'd missed.

So, what was the beginning? David's murder? No. That felt more like the end of Act One. This play had begun before the curtain came down on David's life. Since I couldn't count on anyone to tell me the truth about their experiences, I had to go by what I'd seen with my own two eyes. As far as I had witnessed, this melodrama began when a perfectly manicured hand collided with David Richard's face. A hand that belonged to Maestro Magdalena Tebar.

Chapter 18

Both my headache and Devlyn were gone when I woke for the last time. A note, a bottle of aspirin, and a key were on my bedside table. The note told me to stick around his place and take it easy. The key said that Devlyn knew there was no way in hell I'd sit around waiting for the police to resolve the situation and that Devlyn was asking me to lock up behind myself. I guess he wanted to come home to his flat-screen TV. Smart guy.

I showered, pulled my towel-dried hair into a ponytail, and shrugged into the oversized lilac sweater Devlyn had left by my bed. Then I called a cab to take me to the high school's faculty parking lot to retrieve my car. Both Millie and Aldo were out of the house when I arrived home. Too bad they hadn't taken Killer with them. I walked into the kitchen and heard a throaty rumble announce Killer's arrival. I did what any sane person would do—I raced to the fridge and grabbed the cream cheese and a soda. Killer turned toward the counter as I snagged a bagel out of the bakery box. The dog eyed my breakfast and gave a nasty growl. Killer didn't like being outsmarted.

Come to think of it, neither did I.

Killer guarded the fridge as I sat at the counter with my bagel and my cell phone. Magdalena wasn't answering her phone, so I placed a second call to her manager. In my best Texas twang, I said, "I'm looking to speak to Magdalena Tebar about a possible conducting appearance here in Houston. Not only would she direct a group of luminaries in a charity concert, but we'd like her to be the spokesperson for the event."

"This sounds interesting. If you'd give me more information, I'd be happy to discuss this with Magdalena." The manager didn't question my accent. When this was all over I would have to send my dialects teacher a thank-you note.

"The group holding the charity event would like to talk to Ms. Tebar personally. If she is to be the spokesperson, the organizers would like to be sure she believes in the cause and can speak passionately about it."

"What's the cause?"

Um . . . Killer barked and made a leap for my bagel. I whisked it out of reach of his teeth. "Animal starvation and cruelty. We plan on raising awareness with a national campaign, which is why the organizers would like to talk to Magdalena today if possible." I popped a piece of bagel in my mouth and gave Killer a big smile.

Killer whimpered. The manager sighed. He also told me Magdalena would be at the Lyric Opera all morning but free for a phone chat this afternoon. Eureka. Magdalena's hotel room was empty.

I made another call and then went upstairs for a costume

change. Ten minutes later, I was in my car decked out in black spandex pants, a tight purple spandex tank, and a workout jacket. First stop: Yoga instructor Dana Lucas's house for props.

Dana had short cropped hair, an aggressive personality, and a soft spot for my boss, Larry. I'd taken her Yoga class once and found it to be a more than a little scary, but somehow Dana and I had become friends. Which was good since I doubted she'd lend a perfect stranger two Yoga mats and a cotton candy–colored balance ball. I don't know if she bought my story of doing a photo shoot for a friend, but she didn't ask any questions as she passed the gear over and congratulated me on keeping my show choir coaching gig.

Next stop: Magdalena's Evanston hotel.

I just hoped this part of my plan worked. When a singer, actor, or conductor signed a contract, she got to add a rider asking for all sorts of cool stuff. The bigger the star, the bigger the demands: food, accommodations, a personal driver. At this point in my career, I was happy when the contract offered me enough money to pay the bills, but I dreamed of a time where I could make demands of my own. One of the most common demands was for a personal trainer, which was why I was impersonating Yoga Barbie. Now I just needed to find an employee gullible enough to let me into Magdalena's room so I could take a look around.

By the time I walked into the hotel's red, black, and white art deco lobby, I was beginning to have serious doubts about my plan. In movies, people sneak into hotel rooms all the time. But this wasn't a movie. This was real life. The way my luck was going, I'd more likely end up talking myself into a jail cell instead of into Magdalena's room.

The two people behind the check-in counter looked calm

and cool as a woman loudly complained about not getting whatever discount she was promised on the Internet. Nope. These people weren't going to hand over a key to Magdalena's suite just because I asked them to. I needed to go with plan B—getting out of here fast.

I was starting to put plan B into effect when a male voice asked, "Can I help you with something?"

I turned and smiled at a short, fresh-faced boy with a round, earnest face. Had he not been wearing a gray and white hotel uniform, I would have assumed he was a freshman in high school. His name tag read Harold Weddle.

Since Harold looked less intimidating than the folks behind the check-in counter, I decided plan A might still have a chance. If not, I was pretty sure I could outrun Harold before he could call the cops.

Getting into character, I bit my lip and gave him what I hoped was a vacant smile. The dumber I looked, the less likely he was to suspect me of any wrongdoing. Right?

"I just realized I forgot my key," I confided quietly.

The kid brightened. "No problem. Just tell me what room you're staying in and I'll get you another key."

Wow. That was easy.

"Do you have your driver's license with you?"

Okay, maybe it wasn't going to be that easy after all.

According to my acting teachers, the key to a convincing performance was actually believing what you were saying. If you believed it, everyone else would. Keeping that in mind, I said, "The key isn't for my room. I'm Magdalena Tebar's personal Yoga and fitness instructor. Or at least, I am today. My friend's been doing the job, but his mom fell down the stairs and broke her hip so he asked me to fill in. He gave me the key to her suite, but I think I left it on the kitchen counter when I was putting the Yoga mats in my bag."

I held up the bag with rolled-up pink and purple mats sticking out.

The kid peered into the bag with a frown. "That's a problem. What are you going to do?"

I did a mental eye roll and tried to conjure up some tears. Nope. No tears. Crying on command was something I'd never gotten the hang of. I needed better motivation for crying than a missed Yoga lesson. The best I could manage was a trembling lip. "I'm not sure. My friend said Magdalena is real particular about having everything set up before she arrives. I don't want him to get fired because I screwed up."

I managed to eke out one tear. Huzzah! The kid's eyes followed the lone tear as it streaked down my face. He then looked around to see if anyone was watching him before saying, "Wait right here."

For a slightly pudgy guy, Harold moved fast. The kid zipped behind one of the empty computers at the check-in counter and started typing. He stared at the screen as one of the hyperefficient employees resolved the problem with the complainer and walked over to him. She said something. He pointed at the screen and then at me. Eek. Every nerve in my body began to jangle as I pointed my feet toward the exit and prepared to run.

The woman said something back to Harold, shook her head, and walked away. Harold hit a few more keys, did a key card swipe thing, and came around the counter. "My manager isn't surprised that your friend didn't show up today. The staff has had some problems with Ms. Tebar. She has trouble restraining her emotions."

This wasn't a news flash. She *was* a conductor. Conductors were known for their controlling natures and frequent rehearsal meltdowns. Most attributed those emotional explosions to a conductor's passion for music. The press ate up the temper tantrums and ran stories about artistic natures, which is why some of the most level-headed conductors I knew staged their own artistic outbursts. They wanted to be certain their passion wasn't overlooked. Personally, I thought the whole thing was a crock. Just because you acted like a three-year-old didn't make you a musical genius. It just meant you needed a time-out.

Since telling that to Harold wasn't going to help, I put on my best worried face and said, "My friend never mentioned her temper problem."

"That might not be the only thing he lied about." Harold gave me a sad smile. "I'm going to bet his mom didn't break her hip."

"I guess I won't be sending flowers."

Harold said to follow him and escorted me up to the top floor and Magdalena's suite. "Technically, we aren't supposed to let you into the room, but none of us wants to cause Ms. Tebar any inconvenience. I'll give you five minutes to set up your equipment. Then you'll have to wait out here for Ms. Tebar to arrive."

He knocked and yelled, "Housekeeping." When no one answered, Harold slid the key card into the lock, opened the door, and held it open. "Five minutes. If Ms. Tebar returns before that, I'll let you know." Harold pulled the door closed behind me, and I walked into Magdalena's suite.

The suite's living room was enormous. White walls. Cream-colored carpet. Black conference table with eight black and red chairs. A long red couch. An art deco, uncomfortable-looking armchair. A kick-ass sound system and television. And papers. Lots and lots of papers. There were papers on the table. On the floor. Strewn across the couch and around the armchair. Some were crumpled into balls ready for a game of wastepaper basketball. Others were lying in piles. The place was an advertisement for the virtues of recycling.

The sheer amount of papers overwhelmed me. I had five minutes to find something incriminating in this mess, and I didn't know where to begin.

I glanced at the papers on the table and blinked. Staff paper. I unballed a sheet next to the DVD player. More staff paper. It was all staff paper. Some of the pages had lots of music notes written on the staves. Others had a couple notes with scratch-outs. Some even had Spanish lyrics and titles. While Spanish wasn't my best language, I had ordered enough burritos and guacamole to recognize it.

Setting aside the music, I took a peek at the clock. I had three minutes before Harold came knocking. I needed to hurry. I dumped my balance ball and bag on the floor and made a beeline for the bedroom. The king-size bed looked like it hadn't been straightened in days. Magdalena's temper and paper problem no doubt encouraged housekeeping to keep its distance.

Near the window stood an electronic travel piano. Strewn across the floor between the bed and the piano was at least a week's worth of pants, skirts, shirts, and lacy underwear. On the nightstand under a discarded hot pink bra was a hotel notepad filled with doodles and phone numbers.

I scribbled the phone numbers onto another piece of paper,

shoved it into my jacket pocket, and checked the end-table drawers. A Bible and some chewing gum. Moving on.

Back in the living room, I looked around for anything that might tell me whether Magdalena was guilty of more than being a slob. There was a computer buried under a stack of papers on an armchair. No doubt something interesting was stored on the hard drive, but I didn't have time to boot the sucker up, let alone dig through its contents. I was feeling stymied.

Wait.

A piece of paper on the table was a different color than the others. Only the corner was showing, but while the staff paper was a cream color, this paper was light blue. I pulled the blue paper out from the stack. It had handwriting on it. At the top of the list was the name David Richard—at least, I was pretty sure that's what it said under the red-pen slash marks. The rest of the names, however, were still intact. Placido Domingo and Juan Diego Florez topped the list of names. Most I recognized as operatic tenors, including the newest edition to the *Messiah* cast, Andre Napoletano. Next to their names were the words "full voice" and a series of letters and numbers. F2-E5. C2-D5. Next to that was the word "falsetto" and more numbers and letters to indicate the person's vocal range.

The door handle jangled. Yikes.

I slid the paper under a stack of others, grabbed my cell, and shoved the phone against my ear as Harold strolled in. I waved at him as I spoke to my phantom phone friend. "Yeah. I understand. Tell your mom I hope she feels better." Pretending to hang up, I sighed. "My friend called. Ms. Tebar rescheduled today's workout. I guess I won't need to wait around for her after all. Which is good because Yoga requires focus. I don't think I could focus in this mess."

———

Back in my car, I pulled the phone numbers I'd scribbled out of my pocket and studied them. Two had New York area codes. The third was definitely overseas. Since my cell plan covered calls in the States, I decided to give the New York numbers a whirl.

A perky girl answered at the first number. "Columbia Artists Management. How may I direct your call?"

I disconnected and dialed the next number. "IMG Artists."

Huh. I was guessing if I dialed the international number it, too, would be a high-ranking operatic talent agency. I was familiar with both companies I had just dialed. Their clients were a who's who of the operatic stage. While I was grateful to have a manager, I knew his connections were limited. I hoped to land more influential representation in the future. With that in mind, every month or so I Googled my dream management companies and read about the amazing gigs they'd landed for their clients. Come to think of it, several names on Magdalena's list of tenors were represented by these two agencies. That couldn't be a coincidence.

I found our assistant stage manager's number in my phone and dialed. Jenny's quiet voice came on the line. "I have a strange question. Was Maestro Tebar involved in casting for the *Messiah*?"

"Not that I'm aware of. Bill said she only agreed to the contract after she heard David Richard had accepted the job. I guess Magdalena and David were involved in some kind of project together."

"What kind of project?"

"I think it was some kind of recording project, but I'm not really sure. Bill knew more about it. Bill knew about everything."

There was a catch in Jenny's voice when she said Bill's name. My heart went out to her. Jenny sounded sad and overwhelmed.

"Bill would have been really proud of the job you're doing on this show."

Jenny sniffled. "Things are so confusing. The police are going to be at tonight's rehearsal, which upset Magdalena and her manager. I told them I'm doing my best to make it all work, but—"

"No buts," I said, trying to sound upbeat. "Everything is going to turn out great. You'll see."

I hoped I was right. The poor girl sounded wrecked. Losing her mentor and having the organization of the show dumped on her shoulders had to be stressful.

The good news was, talking to Jenny had helped me put the pieces together—the list of tenors, the keyboard and sheet music, the angry cross-out of David's name and the project they were working on, the mention of composition I'd seen on Magdalena's website. Now I just had to confirm my suspicion.

Unfortunately, for that I needed to talk to the maestro herself, and she was occupied. I could try her manager again, but I wasn't feeling confident in my ability to pull off another accent. There was one person, however, who might have his finger on the pulse of Magdalena's aspirations. The downside being that he was also one of the most likely suspects to team up with another cast member to off David and Bill. Jonathan McMann was friendly and inspired trust. If I was going to pick someone to murder with, he'd be at the top of my list.

Jonathan answered on the first ring. "How was the concert?"

Okay, last week I would have thought Jonathan McMann having my number programmed into his phone was cool as hell. Today, it rated high on the creep meter. "I still have a job," I answered honestly.

"That's good." He laughed. "Although after this weekend, you won't need it anymore. You'll be too busy singing around the world to coach show choir."

I wondered why that thought didn't make me do a happy dance. Probably because it was coming from a potential maniac. It was hard to take seriously compliments from possible killers no matter how sexy their phone voices. "I had a question about Magdalena Tebar and thought you might know the answer. Is Magdalena working on making a name for herself as a composer?"

Jonathan let out a sigh. "Why are you asking?"

"I saw something on her website that made me think she might be."

"Magdalena hasn't had her work publicly performed—yet. It's not common knowledge, but she was hoping to make a big splash by having David Richard record one of her songs and put it on his new CD."

"Let me guess, David said he would do it and then backed out of the deal." I was getting to know the man pretty well. The broken deal between David and Magdalena explained the slap I'd witnessed. It also explained Magdalena's fainting spell when David died. A dead David meant no chance of David releasing the song on his CD.

I did have one unanswered question. "If Magdalena didn't

want the recording to be public knowledge, how did you learn about it?"

Jonathan laughed. "David loved to brag. Everyone in the faculty lounge heard about his record deals, the roles he was offered, and his dates. He had no shame. He even bragged about the number of paternity suits naming him as a dead-beat father."

"Is that why Mark Krauss petitioned to keep David from a full-time faculty job?"

There was a pause. When Jonathan spoke there was an edge to his voice. "Why don't you ask Mark yourself? The two of us are meeting for lunch. We'd be happy to have you join us."

Eek.

"That sounds like fun, but I have some last-minute Christmas shopping to do. See you tonight."

I disconnected and put my car in gear. Jonathan had just let me know two things—that he and Mark were close enough to make lunch plans when school wasn't in session and that Mark was having lunch out. The first put the two of them much higher on my suspect list. The second told me Mark wasn't at home. While my discussion with LaVon had me thinking at least one of the murdering pair was female, her wishy-washy description left room for doubt. Maybe the knock on the head had totally taken away any sense I had because I was steering my car to Mark's house in the hopes I could talk Penelope the dog into letting me take a peek inside.

Chapter 19

There were lights on inside Mark's house. Had Mark left them on or was someone else in there? I parked my car at the curb and contemplated the question. Today's weather forecast had been for snow. So far none had fallen, but the sun had opted not to get out of bed. Due to the overcast sky, several houses on the block had their lights on. Maybe Mark had forgotten to turn the lights off on his way out the door. My brother used to do that all the time when we were growing up. The behavior was always rewarded with a lecture on responsibility. Something told me, if Mark caught me inside his house, responsibility was the last thing he'd want to discuss.

I jumped as my phone vibrated. I had a text message. *Forgot to mention earlier, Maestro Tebar would like everyone at the theater 45 minutes early. New call time: 5:45 p.m.—Jenny*

The text reminded me that I should be home preparing

for tonight's final rehearsal. Instead I was contemplating breaking and entering. How stupid was that?

Staring at the house, I considered my options. I could be smart and drive away or I could march up to the door and hope for the best. The silver car was gone. That made me feel mostly confident the place was empty. Too bad mostly confident wasn't good enough. The way my luck was going, mostly confident would get me killed.

Swallowing down a couple of ibuprofen, I put the car in gear and caught a glimpse of a woman inside Mark's house walking past the picture window.

Mark's wife. And since the car was gone, I could surmise she was inside alone.

Before I could second-guess myself, I pulled into the drive and hoofed it up to the front door. If Mrs. Mark could alibi her husband for last night, I could cross him off the list of suspects. A man curled up with his wife and dog couldn't have chased me down a hall or bashed me over the head.

Penelope's barking started the second my finger hit the doorbell. If I were a burglar, I wouldn't think twice. I'd hear that sound, turn tail, and run. Thank goodness I knew the dog was more mischievous than maniacal, so I wasn't worried about a canine attack when the door swung open.

An attractive woman with a cap of wavy red hair, a dusting of freckles on her cheeks, and a fabulous figure frowned at Penelope. Immediately, the dog stopped barking and plopped on its butt at her feet. "Can I help you?"

"My name is Paige Marshall. I'm performing in the *Messiah* with your husband this weekend."

The woman smiled. "I'm Nora, Mark's wife. I wish Mark was here, but he went out to do some Christmas shopping." Her green eyes sparkled with humor. "Mark normally waits until the last minute to get gifts, which means I end up with whatever sweaters or perfume no sane person would buy. I'm holding out hope that this year will be different."

Since Mark was currently stuffing his face instead of maxing out his credit cards, I was betting Mrs. Krauss was doomed to disappointment.

Since the woman was already being deceived, I opted to take the honest route. "I didn't come here to see Mark. I wanted to talk to you. Do you mind if I come in?" If not, my eyelashes and nose hairs were going to freeze during the time it took to have this conversation. It was that cold.

Nora pursed her lips and studied me for a moment then opened the door the rest of the way. I stepped into the warmth of a comfortable living room, albeit one laden with action figures and Matchbox cars. "I hope this won't take long. The kids will be home soon."

Penelope bumped her head against my hand for a pet and then trotted over to the corner and curled up in a massive pile of blankets. I waited for Mark's wife to offer me a seat. Nope. She just crossed her arms and waited. Her previous friendliness had been replaced by what I could only assume was suspicion.

Taking a deep breath, I said, "I don't know if your husband mentioned me to you. I'm one of the soloists."

"I know who you are."

The edge in her voice made me wonder whether Mark had made a disparaging remark about my singing. Pushing aside performer's paranoia, I forced myself to focus. "This show is important to me. If things go well, it could be the break I've been working for. Only things have been a little . . . scary."

"Because of the murders." Sympathy replaced the suspicion in her eyes.

"The murders are scary. The fact that someone tried to run me off the road on Wednesday and attacked me last night is even scarier."

"Someone attacked you?" Nora took a step forward. Penelope barked.

I nodded. "The police think whoever killed David and Bill also attacked me. Since I'm relatively new to the opera scene, I don't know the cast members very well. I don't know who I can trust. That's why I'm here. I heard Mark had problems with David Richard. I don't know what those problems are exactly . . ." And I didn't figure there was a shot in hell of Nora telling me about them now. "But I'm hoping you can tell me if Mark was home last night."

There was a moment's hesitation. A flush of the cheeks. A quickening of Nora's breath. Her jaw tensed, and her hands clenched for just a fraction of a second. Her eyes darted to the left, and she bit her lip before looking back at me. "Mark was here with me and the boys watching movies all night. I hope knowing that makes you feel better."

Right.

I got back in my car. Mark's wife watched me from the picture window while wringing her hands as I pulled away. She had lied to me. Mark was out of the house last night. Worse, she was worried about the lie. That meant Mark's wife thought not only that he had reason to kill David and Bill but also that he might actually have done it. Yikes.

Between the silver car, the lack of alibi, and a serious amount of dislike for the first victim, Mark had to be one of the killers. If this were a movie, I'd confront the guy, point my gun at him, and force him to confess. Since I wanted to keep breathing, I punched Mike's speed-dial number and waited for him to answer.

"I hope you're staying out of trouble."

Not exactly an auspicious opening. "No one's smacked me over the head today," I said.

"The day's still young."

Sad, but true.

"What's up? Dare I hope you're calling to tell me Millie has let me off the hook for tomorrow night?"

Yep, that was the sound of my ego deflating. Mike needed a serious course in tactfulness. "Hearing me sing isn't a fate worse than death, you know."

"No, but hearing a lecture on some dead guy and his music might be."

A valid point. Even I, who loved Handel's music, wouldn't be interested in sitting through a lecture on the subject. I'd done enough of that in college. "The restaurant is supposed to have excellent wine," I said. When Mike didn't answer, I caved. "Maybe I can convince my aunt to let you meet her and Aldo at the theater."

"I'm holding you to that." I could hear Mike's grin through the phone. "So, what did you call about?"

"I know who the killer is, and I want you to arrest him."

Everything went silent.

"Mike? Are you still there?"

A loud sigh told me the call hadn't been dropped. "I'll meet you at your aunt's house in twenty minutes. For God's sake, don't do anything until I get there."

I pulled into Millie's garage with six minutes to spare on Mike's deadline. Millie and Aldo were nowhere to be found. I nuked a cup of tea and took it with me to the living room to wait. The minute I sat down, I heard the telltale sound of Killer's claws against the hallway floor.

A puffy white head appeared in the living room doorway. Killer looked at me, glanced over at Millie's taxidermied canine carolers, and whined. I smiled and took a sip of my drink as Killer hovered in the doorway, too disturbed by a glimpse into his future life as a stuffed art piece to step foot across the threshold. Between the gun in my pocket and the dead dogs near my feet, I was as safe as I was going to get.

By the time the doorbell rang, Killer had abandoned his perch in the doorway. Mike walked through the front door with a frown and a large take-out bag. My nose twitched at the aroma of grilled meat and French fries.

"I figured you were probably too busy causing problems to eat lunch, so I got enough for two." Mike walked past me on his way to the kitchen. "We can eat while we talk."

Two double-decker burgers and two enormous orders of fries came out of the bag. Mike passed a wrapped sandwich to me, popped the top on his soda, and took a seat. "So, how did a woman who was home all day recovering from a concussion learn the identity of a multi-murderer?"

Why did I have the feeling this conversation wasn't going to go well?

Stalling, I unwrapped my burger and sighed with pleasure. Bacon, cheese, and lots of ketchup. Mike had earned a reprieve from opera lecture hell. I'd just have to find a way to convince Millie.

I took a bite of my sandwich for courage. Then, in between scarfing French fries, I gave a rundown of my day. Mike didn't say anything as I spoke. He took bites of his burger. He ate his fries. No yelling when I told him about my conversation with Jonathan and my decision to do a drive-by of Mark's house. Of course, that might have been because I skipped over the part where I posed as Magdalena's Yoga instructor and broke into her hotel room. No need to make Mike decide between eating and throwing his sandwich. Considerate was my middle name.

When I was done, Mike took a sip of soda and asked, "The working theory is whoever killed the tenor and the stage manager whacked you over the head last night?"

I shook extra salt on my fries and nodded.

"So whoever has an alibi for last night can be eliminated as a suspect?"

I nodded again.

Mike leaned forward. "You said Mark has an alibi."

"His wife was lying."

"And you know this how?"

"Before she answered, she looked to the side and bit her lip." Those were the signs of a liar caught in the act. It was Acting 101. "Mark's wife was worried. She thinks her husband might be a killer."

"For your sake, I hope you're wrong."

I stopped mid-chew. "Why?"

"Because believing someone is lying and proving it are two very different things. Cops need proof."

I knew that, but I'd been hoping Mike would be impressed by my reasoning and go find the proof that was needed.

"Let's put aside proof for the moment." Mike leaned back in his chair. "What's this Krauss guy's motive for killing the tenor and the stage manager?"

"Mark Krauss was campaigning to keep David Richard from getting a full-time job at Northwestern. The two of them got into a physical altercation not too long ago."

"Why?"

"Mark mentioned that David made a pass at his wife. That could have prompted the fight."

"So you think Mark offed David because the guy was a crappy teacher and flirted with Mark's wife? When do we get to the part where you convince me that your guy is the killer? I can't just go around throwing people behind bars because you have a feeling they *might* be guilty. Besides, I checked in with Detective Frewen today to tell him about last night's attack at the school. Mark Krauss is low on the suspect list. You're not going to convince anyone to arrest him. At least, not yet."

This wasn't what I wanted to hear.

I shoved the rest of my fries away and sat back in my chair. "So now what?"

Mike took another slurp of his soda, pushed back from the table, and shrugged into his coat. "Now you stay inside where you'll be safe and let the cops do their jobs."

No can do. "I have to go out later. I have rehearsal." I stood to emphasize my point.

Mike raked a hand though his hair. "Then get someone to drive with you." Tying his scarf, he stalked around to my side of the table. "I wish I could say that the killer will be arrested today and that you don't have a thing to worry about. But I can't. Investigations like this take time, and every time you go off investigating on your own, you give the perp a shot at hurting you." His fingers brushed the bump on the back of my head. "I don't have time to deal with you getting hurt again. Got it?"

The words were clipped, but his eyes were filled with tenderness and concern. The combination made my stomach flutter. Not good. Devlyn was the guy I was interested in. Not Mike.

Trying to keep it light, I quipped, "Watch out, Detective. If I didn't know you, I'd say you almost care what happens to me."

Mike's frowned. "I guess you don't know me as well as you think you do."

"Right." I wasn't insane enough to think Mike had real feelings toward me. Was he attracted? Yes. But emotional involvement was a whole different level. Assuring myself the hollow feeling in my stomach wasn't disappointment, I said, "I know you have to keep an emotional detachment from your cases."

"You're not one of my cases."

"Aren't you in charge of the assault from last night?"

"I passed the case to Detective Knight. You should be getting a call from Keith in the next couple of days."

Okay, that stung. Mike might be a jerk, but he was a jerk I trusted to find the person who attacked me. That he didn't care enough to do his job hurt. A lot.

"I look forward to talking to Detective Knight. You probably have a huge caseload. It's good you passed my case to someone who'll dedicate more time."

"Ha! Keith has a heavier caseload than I do. But he's got something I don't have."

"What?"

"Distance." Mike moved closer and ran a finger down my cheek. "A cop is a lot like a doctor. You can't think clearly enough to perform surgery when you think you might be falling in love with the person you're operating on."

The whole brain injury thing had me hallucinating. "Love?"

Mike gave me a cocky smile and moved closer. "I'm a

good enough cop to understand the real deal when I find it. You're it."

His mouth touched mine, and all thoughts of murder disappeared. Mike's lips were warm. One of his hands snaked down my back, pulling me closer. The other hand laced fingers with mine. My nerves jangled at his touch. Warmth spread through my body. I felt desired, protected, and scared as hell. Mike had kissed me before. Those kisses had had the fire of physical attraction and the skill of a man who'd kissed more than his fair share of women. This kiss had just as much passion, but there was something deeper. Kinder. More intimate than if we were both naked and doing the horizontal tarantella. This wasn't a kiss designed to maneuver me into bed. This kiss had the potential to steal my heart.

And it terrified me.

"Wait." I took a step back, caught my foot on the kitchen chair, and almost went flying. Mike's quick reflexes saved me. He then jammed his hands in his pockets and waited for me to speak.

Great. The one time he listened, I had no idea what to say. So I went with the most obvious. "You can't possibly think you're falling in love with me. We haven't even gone on a date." Wasn't there a rule that you had to date someone to fall in love? If not, there should be. At least then a person would be prepared for moments like these.

Mike laughed. "That's something I plan to remedy next week. And if you're good, I'll even buy you a Christmas present. That means stay inside and out of trouble. Got it?"

Without waiting for an answer, he turned and strolled out the door.

Why did the man always get the last word? I hated that. Next time, I'd be the one taking the last verbal shot. Maybe by then the shock would have worn off.

Detective Michael Kaiser had said he loved me. Strike that—he thought he might be in love with me. Which was almost the same thing. This was probably just some kind of reaction to my being in danger. Still, I was almost positive he meant what he said. How weird was that? Part of me was flattered. Another part was wigged out. Despite the strong jawline and the broad shoulders, Mike was not my type. He was loud, domineering, and hated classical music.

Okay, technically he'd never said he hated classical music, but he'd had to be cornered into coming to my performance tomorrow night. That didn't imply a love of all things theater. In his free time, Mike was the type who kicked back with a beer and the game of the week while I went to the theater or listened to music. A relationship between the two of us would be a train wreck. I knew that. Mike had to know that, too.

But Mike was right about one thing—staying home was the smart choice. I flipped the deadbolt on the front door, made sure the other doors were locked up tight, and went upstairs to change into clothes that didn't make me feel guilty for sitting on the couch instead of working up a sweat. I ignored Killer's growl from the middle of my bed as I pulled on a pair of charcoal pants, a white sweater, and the fuzziest socks I owned in preparation for a relaxing afternoon inside.

My phone buzzed. A text message from Devlyn asking if I wanted company. In its infinite wisdom, the school board had declared a half-day of school today. The thought was that teachers needed time to catch up on paperwork and meetings before the upcoming winter break. Most teachers I knew were using the time to finish their holiday shopping. An example of education at its finest.

My heart did a happy skip as I sent a "Join me at Millie's" text back. This was the guy I wanted to date. Devlyn was kind, fun, and understood theater and music. Not to mention the fact that he was sexy as hell. What more could a girl want?

The doorbell rang, and my heart skipped again. Devlyn couldn't have gotten here that fast, and I wasn't expecting anyone else. Clutching Millie's gun, I slowly walked to the door and peered through the peephole in time to watch the FedEx truck drive off.

I opened the door and smiled at the enormous box on the stoop. More Christmas presents. Millie didn't have kids or grandkids of her own, so she sent gifts to all of my cousins' families. In return, they sent her boxes of homemade fudge, cookies, brownies, and the occasional unfortunate fruitcake. The boxes had been arriving all week with instructions to open before Christmas.

Hoping for homemade caramels, I dropped the box on the kitchen table, opened the flaps, and fished through the packing peanuts for the tin of sweets. I froze as my fingers touched something sticky and wet. Ewww. A jar must have broken. Pulling my hand out, I almost fainted. The red substance on my fingers looked very much like blood.

Chapter 20

To my credit I didn't lose consciousness, and while on the inside I was screaming bloody murder, not a squeak passed my lips. Possibly I was just too terrified to make a sound. Or maybe I'd seen so many horrible things that I'd hit my saturation point. Hard to tell.

Since I wasn't in the mood to flip out, I took a closer look at the substance on my hand. It was red and gloppy and smelled like . . . ketchup.

Curiosity warred with caution as I took a step back and stared at the present. Curiosity won, and I pulled fistfuls of packing peanuts out of the box. Inside was a note and three items: a water bottle, a rope, and the source of the red substance—a satin gown-wearing Barbie stained with ketchup. Minus her head.

A water bottle had been used to poison David.

A rope had been used to kill Bill.

I could only guess that the headless Barbie represented whatever was planned for me.

Okay, *now* I was creeped out.

My fingers were unsteady as I reached into the envelope, pulled out the note, and gave myself a paper cut. Ow. Sucking on my index finger, I fumbled with the paper and read: *You're next.*

The bloody Barbie was juvenile, but I gave the killer points for brevity. And as silly as the gift from hell was, it had scored a direct hit. I was freaked. The killer had tailed me here, called the house, and now sent a direct threat to Millie's front door. According to Mike, Detective Frewen and company weren't planning on making an arrest anytime soon. Call me crazy, but I didn't want the killer to complete the Barbie portion of his little project. I wanted the lunatic caught—now.

First things first—I put the Barbie, noose, and water bottle back in the box and then got a Band-Aid and antibiotic ointment for my paper cut. The way things were going, an untreated cut would lead to the bubonic plague or worse.

Infection avoided, I grabbed my phone and tapped out a text to Mike. *Killer sent package to house via FedEx. Do you want to take a look?* I hit send and congratulated myself on how well I was handling all of this. That's when the sound of the doorbell made me jump. The phone crashed to the ground, sending the cover in one direction and the battery in another.

The doorbell rang again as I collected the pieces of my phone. Crap.

Killer started barking his head off, which for the first and probably only time made me happy. If the murderer was at the door, he'd think twice about coming in.

Fumbling to put my phone back together, I dodged a still-barking Killer and checked the peephole. Devlyn.

He walked through the door, took one look at my face, and opened his arms. I stepped into them and began to shake. Okay, maybe I wasn't taking the whole Barbie doll thing as well as I thought.

When the shaking subsided, Devlyn put his hands on my shoulders and asked, "What's wrong?"

Words wouldn't do the situation justice. I dragged Devlyn into the kitchen for show-and-tell and stopped in my tracks. Lying in the middle of the kitchen floor next to the overturned box was Killer. A smudge of ketchup was on his snout and a wet, slobbered-on Barbie rested in between his feet. Barbie had gone from American icon to headless rawhide in no time flat. Barbie was having a bad day.

Devlyn put the box back on the table, read the note, and took several deep breaths. "I really hate to ask this, but have you called Detective Kaiser?"

"I sent a text before I dropped my phone." I slid the pieces back together and waited for the phone to boot. When it did, a return text was waiting.

Out on a call. Will come by in a couple hours. Stay home. Don't do anything stupid.

Charming.

I flipped the phone shut. "Mike will be by later."

"And you're going to wait around for him to deal with this?"

That had been my plan until I got his most recent message. Mike's dictates made my common sense fly out the window. If he said stop, I felt morally obliged to hit the gas. But in this case, I still might have followed his instructions had the murderers' gift not given me a new lead.

After today, I was fairly certain Mark Krauss was one of the two people behind last night's attack. Since he and Jonathan were close friends, I'd assumed Jonathan was the other half of the murderous duo. Chew-toy Barbie had me rethinking that deduction. Jonathan's bio said he had two sons who lived with their mother somewhere in the burbs. And Mark had all boys in his house. I saw trucks and trains and action figures scattered around the living room. No Barbies.

While the feminist movement wanted Barbie to lose the unrealistic proportions and become a gender-neutral toy, Barbie was always going to be something mothers bought for their daughters. Girls understood Barbie. Boys— not so much. With male progeny, Mark or Jonathan wouldn't exactly have Barbie on his radar.

Put that information together with LaVon's description of the photograph buyer and I was almost certain Mark's partner was a woman. Since my gut eliminated Magdalena from the suspect list, I was left with two possible choices: Vanessa Moulton or Ruth Jordan.

Turning to Devlyn, I asked, "Do you think I should wait for the cops to figure out who's behind this?"

"Would you wait if I asked you to?"

Good question. I bit my lip as I considered the answer.

Devlyn laughed. "If I believed for one second that telling you to wait for the professionals to do their jobs would help, I would. But I know you. I figure the best I can do is make sure you don't get killed while doing whatever it is you're going to do."

"Well, it's a good thing I have you to keep me safe."

The light tone made it easier to ignore that we were both deadly serious. Good thing my goal was to avoid anything dangerous or illegal. I just needed to find information for the cops so I could step back and let them do the heavy lifting.

"So, what's the plan?" Devlyn asked as he put his arm around my shoulders.

"We're going on a scavenger hunt," I said. "For Barbie's head."

———

Devlyn removed Barbie from Killer's clutches, and I returned the doll to the box and placed it on top of the fridge where the dog couldn't reach it. Then we headed for the first stop on my scavenger hunt. A stop that was totally safe—my bedroom. I fired up the computer and took a seat at the desk while Devlyn perched on my bed.

First things first, I ran a search on the FedEx tracking number I'd copied off the top of the box. If I was lucky, the killer had shipped the box from a place down the street from her house.

Drat. The shipping location was right around the corner from the theater. Every one of my suspects had cause to be in that location. The tracking number was a bust.

On to the next search.

Before Killer had sharpened his teeth on Barbie's body, she'd been wearing a shiny hot pink dress with a lighter pink ruffle around the waist and hips. The look wasn't one of Barbie's better choices even without the ketchup stains. I clicked on the Barbie website and scrolled through the dolls until I found the one that matched Killer's snack. The doll was brand-new this holiday season, which meant the toy had to be a recent purchase.

A few keystrokes later and I had printouts of both women's photos as well as the names and addresses of the toy stores closest to Ruth's and Vanessa's apartments. I was betting neither woman was the type to overexert herself by shopping outside her known territory. If not—well, there was no way I could scope out all the toy stores in the Chicagoland area. I would visit these stores, flash Ruth's and Vanessa's photos at the sales clerks, and hope someone would remember one of them buying the doll. Was I smart or what?

I turned to reveal my brilliance to Devlyn, but the words died on my lips. Devlyn was stretched out on the bed. His eyes were filled with concern, which for some reason I found to be a huge turn on. Maybe the bedroom wasn't a safe place after all.

For a moment, I considered ditching the great Barbie hunt for some extracurricular getting-to-know-you time, but Devlyn was up and off the bed before I had a chance to put my plan into action. Which was good. Things were confused enough without adding an extra complication, no matter how desirable, to the mix.

"So," Devlyn asked, "where to?"

In a Hollywood action flick, the answer to that question would probably involve a darkened parking garage or a prison armed with snipers and barbed wire. My answer was, "Toys 'R' Us."

We took Devlyn's car. He drove while I made phone calls to the specialty toy stores in Vanessa's neighborhood. By the time we'd turned into the parking lot of the Toys 'R' Us closest to Ruth's address, I knew where I could purchase "Learn to dress" Kitty and "Fishes to Loaves" Jesus action figures. No Barbies were stocked at either specialty location. That meant Devlyn and I were currently walking into the Barbie-selling toy store closest to both Ruth and Vanessa. If they shopped at Target or Walmart, well, I was screwed.

I pulled the two women's headshots from my purse as we walked through the automated doors.

Devlyn dodged a woman with a blue shopping cart. "You do realize that even if Vanessa or Ruth bought the Barbie doll here, the chances of an employee recognizing them from a photo is slim to none, right?"

Devlyn was right. With Christmas less than two weeks away, the place had to be a zoo. My only hope was that the perp had bought Barbie sometime this week. And that, if the perp was Ruth or Vanessa, her artistic personality had made her stick out despite the sea of holiday shoppers.

The store looked as though the Tazmanian Devil had decided to help Santa shop. Shelves were half empty. Sale signs hung precariously from the walls. And boxes of whatever board games the store was featuring were scattered across the floor. Someone definitely needed to clean up Aisle Two.

The Barbie aisle was as bad if not worse. I pitied any girl whose parent hadn't shopped early. Something told me those kids were going to end up with the "Ken Goes to Hawaii" fashion accessory set. And unless something had changed since my day—aside from the stamped-on tighty whities—dressing up Ken was lame.

Next to the picked-through accessories, most of the shelf space where Barbie dolls normally stood was empty. But two Barbies with gowns resembling the one in the FedEx box remained. Since the store looked like it had last restocked around Easter, chances were good the dolls had also been available for purchase earlier this week.

Time to canvass the staff.

I handed one set of photographs to Devlyn. Then the two

of us headed to different parts of the store, looking for employees to show them to. I located my first potential eye-witness in the bicycle/skateboard and motorized car department. He had gray hair and glasses as thick as the jelly jars my mother used every summer. I showed him the photos and felt a burst of excitement as recognition dawned in the sales associate's eyes. Smiling, the man told me that the photo of Vanessa was of Marilyn Monroe and that Ruth was his ex-wife. According to him, neither had been in the store buying Barbie dolls on his watch.

The two other employees I found restocking shelves didn't recognize the women, either. Devlyn fared no better on his side of the store. That left the seven employees manning the check-out lanes, who in all probability were the most likely to recognize a past customer. Only something told me the customers waiting weren't going to let me cut in line. Good thing I still had Christmas shopping to do.

After standing in seven lines, I had purchased a fistful of videos, a set of Platypus walkie-talkies for my cousin's twins, two video games for my brother, and a disco light karaoke machine for Aunt Millie. In case Aldo and Millie got engaged before the holiday, I purchased a CD of love songs for them to perform together. If not, well, I had a CD of *Don't Worry, Be Happy* at the ready. Sadly, other than the gifts, I had nothing to show for my visit. Not a single clerk recognized either photograph.

Devlyn helped me stuff the bags into his trunk and asked, "Where to next?"

"I have no idea." In power shopping, I'd gotten an "A." In private detecting, I'd totally flunked. "If the killer does turn out to be the concert master or one of the soloists, the producers will have no choice but to cancel the show. I don't want to disappoint your mother. I did promise you I'd give her an autograph tomorrow night."

"About that." Devlyn shifted in his seat. "I'm thinking it would be better if you met Mom another day. Larry and a couple Music in Motion kids said they're planning on coming to tomorrow's performance. That might make things more difficult."

I was about to ask what one thing had to do with the other when the truth slammed home: Devlyn couldn't introduce me to his mother because she might reveal our almost-relationship to people from Prospect Glen High School. Devlyn's secret would be out.

Which made me wonder. "What happens if we actually start dating?"

"What do you mean?" His hands tensed on the wheel.

"Everyone thinks you date men. What's going to happen when they realize you and I are dating? We won't be able to hide a relationship for very long."

Especially since dating often lead to love, marriage, and all that jazz. People tend to notice when you start wearing a wedding ring.

Devlyn didn't seem concerned. "If we go places where students aren't likely to turn up, we should be okay."

I understood Devlyn wanted to protect his job, but his words made me queasy. They implied I wasn't good enough to be seen with him in public.

Was I being irrational? Maybe. Devlyn's desire to hide his true sexual preference was something I'd known about for months. But at this moment, his solution to unwanted attention from female students seemed like a huge problem. I was tired. The headache had returned. My emotions were churning from everything that had happened this week. Now was not the time to have a rational discussion about what might happen if we officially started dating.

I told myself to stay quiet, but found myself saying, "Do you ever plan on coming out of the closet? What happens if you fall in love? You'd have to tell people you were only pretending to be gay, right?"

Devlyn shrugged. "Gay men fall in love and get married to people of the opposite sex all the time. It just means they're more interested in the soul of the person than her sexual persuasion."

Better than being called a liar, liar pants on fire, but still . . .

"Look." Devlyn pulled into a parking lot and stopped the car. Reaching over, he laced his fingers through mine. Despite my annoyance, the contact made my body hum. "I know this isn't an ideal situation, and I wouldn't blame you for feeling put out or unhappy with the public limitations of a relationship with me. But I promise I'll make every moment we spend together in private worthwhile. Deal?"

The kiss Devlyn gave me then made me sure he would make good on that bargain. Hot and demanding, his lips made all my doubts vanish. Who needed public displays of affection? Private was good. We'd get to know each other better. No teasing from the students. No pressure from the outside world. Just me and Devlyn. What could possibly be wrong with that?

Of course, when the kiss ended and the haze of attraction dissipated, I had a hard time ignoring the flaws in his plan. I also had a hard time not comparing his kiss with the one I'd received from Mike earlier. Devlyn's was hot and sexy. Mike's was strangely sweet and filled with promises. Both made me feel safe and incredibly attractive. Both came with serious complications. No wonder I was off-balance.

My cell rang, cutting off any further comparisons of the two men. I answered my phone and was grateful I wasn't driving when I heard the voice on the other end say, "Paige, this is Ruth Jordan. The two of us need to talk. Now."

Chapter 21

Devlyn insisted on coming to my meeting with Ruth. Which was good. It saved me from begging him to tag along. Stupid I wasn't. The woman might have had a hand in killing David, Bill, and Barbie. I wasn't about to let her take me out, too.

Ruth insisted we meet at her condo in thirty minutes. Lucky for us, our search for witnesses put us only blocks away. We'd be at her place well before the appointed time. Ruth would have home turf advantage, but we'd have the element of surprise.

The principle violinist lived on the top floor of a gray stone building. I pushed the call button. Without inquiry as to who was waiting below, the door buzzed.

Devlyn gave me a tense smile as I knocked on Ruth's door.

"I told you to come alone." Ruth's lips pinched together,

and her nostrils flared. Flaring nostrils was not a good look for Ruth.

"You hung up before I could tell you that Devlyn and I were out shopping. Since the two of you met the other night, I assumed you wouldn't mind if he joined me." My wide-eyed smile was innocence personified.

The smile Ruth gave Devlyn tried for pleasant but came off pissed. "Paige must not have understood. The conversation she and I need to have is of a private nature. Would you mind waiting out here? I promise this won't take long."

Devlyn looked at me and raised his eyebrows, silently asking what I wanted him to do. The idea of talking to Ruth alone made me want to throw up. Not only was she potentially half of a killing duo, she hated vocalists. Neither personality trait made me think this conversation was going to be pleasant. But I couldn't see Ruth doing more than hurling snide comments with Devlyn stationed outside the door.

Knowing that one yelp from me would have him dialing 911, I told Devlyn to stay put and followed Ruth inside.

"I'd like this conversation to be quick since we both have rehearsal to get to." Ruth led me into a living room that could have come out of the pages of a magazine.

The walls were painted a warm brown. The carpet was a rich cream, as were the couch and chairs. Light blue and yellow accent pillows were propped on the couch. A deep blue vase filled with daisies sat on the coffee table. On the other side of the room was a perfectly polished ebony grand piano. A violin and bow were resting on a stand next to the piano. An open violin case sat on the floor nearby. No Barbie heads or ketchup bottles in sight.

"Can I get you something to drink?" she asked.

Hmmm . . . let me think about that. I had a flash of David drinking from his water bottle and said, "No, thanks."

Ruth frowned and settled on the sofa, indicating for me to do the same. Next to the cream-colored sofa her trim black sweater and tight black ski pants commanded attention. "Nora Krauss called. She said you'd been by to see her."

Huh. Whatever I'd expected Ruth to say, that wasn't it. I sat on the edge of the sofa and cautiously said, "There was a question I needed answered. Nora answered it for me."

"Nora told me that you implied her husband was behind David's and Bill's murders."

Nora had a big mouth. "Someone attacked me last night. The police believe the attacker was involved with our show. So I asked a couple of questions to make sure I'd be safe when I attended tonight's rehearsal."

Ruth's nostrils flared again. "So Nora wasn't wrong. You do think Mark is a killer."

The nasty edge to her voice had me scooting farther down the couch. "I think someone has sent me threatening messages, almost run me off the road, and given me a mild concussion. If I knew who it was, I'd have the cops arrest them. It could be Mark. Or maybe it's Vanessa or Jonathan or Maestro Tebar. It might even be you."

"Me?" Ruth's anger had been replaced by confusion. "What reason would I have to threaten you?"

"Whoever killed David and Bill is working to cover their tracks. I guess he or she thinks I know something that might lead the police to arrest them."

"What does that have to do with me?"

I wanted to believe Ruth's baffled reaction was an act, but my intuition told me it wasn't. Ruth was genuinely per-

plexed, which shot my Mark/Ruth tandem killer theory—
not to mention my investigative instincts—to hell.

I shifted on the couch and eased my hand out of my coat
pocket. "Two people were involved in the attack against me
last night. That means the murders were committed by two
people working together. You and Mark looked pretty friendly
when you came into the bar together on Wednesday night."

Ruth's mouth twitched into a half smile. "Nora and I are
second cousins. She met Mark at a concert that Mark and I
were both performing in."

"Do the police know you and Mark are related?"

She shrugged. "I didn't see a point in telling them, but I
assume they must. Detective Frewen seems competent. Of
course, they haven't arrested anyone yet, so I might be over-
stating that. Nora is going to be a wreck until they lock away
the killer."

"Because she thinks her husband might be involved in
the murders?"

Ruth's expression told me my instincts might not be so
far off target after all. "Nora thinks the stress of his work
at the university has made Mark a bit edgier than normal."

"By work stress, you mean the problems he had with
David Richard?" I asked. "I heard Mark was working to
keep Northwestern from offering David a full-time position."

"Mark took an immediate dislike to David, which is
understandable. Almost everyone disliked David."

"Including you."

"My dislike was based more on principle than personal
knowledge." Ruth shrugged. "Until this week I'd never met
the man."

"But you threatened to pull out of the show when they
offered David the tenor soloist role."

"I know. And that little stunt is why the police have me on their suspect list." She sighed and swiped a hand through her auburn hair. "Personally, I couldn't have cared less about David Richard being a part of this show, but Mark did. He thought if enough pressure were put on the producers they'd ask another tenor to take David's place. Since this production is being performed on Northwestern's campus, the dean of the music department would notice the casting change and perhaps rethink offering David a full-time faculty position. Mark asked me to talk to the producers, which I did, but he overestimated my clout. I'm one of the best violinists in the country, but next to a vocalist like David Richard— well, let's just say if the producers had to make a choice it wouldn't have been me."

Ouch. "Why did Mark have it in for David?"

Ruth frowned. "At first, Mark was annoyed with the way David canceled lessons and talked down to the students. He ranted a lot about David being a terrible educator. I thought it was typical university politics and didn't pay much attention until Nora told me about the fight. Mark isn't the type to use his fists. Something must have set him off."

"I heard that David hit on Nora and that was the reason Mark started the fight."

"David did make a pass at Nora, but according to her that had happened weeks before. To be honest, I don't think Nora knows what prompted Mark to hit David. Mark doesn't usually keep secrets, which is why she's concerned." Ruth straightened her shoulders. "But whatever Mark's secrets, both Nora and I know he isn't behind these murders. He's not the type."

I had to ask, "What type is he?"

"He's the type who'd throw himself in front of a bus to

protect his family and his students." Ruth smiled. "I think he might even do the same for me." She frowned at her watch and stood. "I hope you don't mind, but I'd like to practice a bit more before tonight's rehearsal."

I glanced at my own watch. Eek. It was really late. If I left now, I'd have just enough time to get home and grab my stuff before heading to rehearsal. If I was lucky, Devlyn would drive fast enough for me to have time to eat dinner.

I filled Devlyn in on the conversation as he pointed the car toward home. When I was done, he asked, "Do you still think Mark's one of the killers?"

I bit my lip and considered the question. Ruth thought her summation of Mark's personality vindicated him. I was more inclined to believe those same traits contributed to motive. Something had happened during David's time at Northwestern to make Mark's feelings go from annoyance to anger. I was betting whatever had outraged Mark into a public fistfight was the same thing that had gotten David Richard and Bill Walters killed. Of course, for that to do me any good, I needed to discover what that something was.

Snow started to fall as Devlyn pulled up in front of Millie's house. He gave me a short but sizzling kiss that kept me warm as I ran with my shopping bags from the car to the front door. My stomach growled as I stepped into the house. The aroma of garlic, basil, and tomato filled the air. Aldo was making pasta. There was a God.

I raced upstairs, stashed the gifts in my closet, and spotted a note sitting on the bed. Millie's friend Gayle had called with the names of three jewelry stores who used potassium cyanide. One was located only two blocks away from the Northwestern University campus. Huh. Promising myself

I'd check the stores out tomorrow, I hurried downstairs into the kitchen on a quest to mooch some garlic bread and almost plowed into Mike.

"Your car wasn't in the driveway," I said.

Mike's smile was anything but happy. "I parked on the street. I didn't want to block the garage."

"He's a nice boy." Aldo beamed as he stirred a bubbling pot of red sauce. "Detective Michael came to see you. When you were not here, he stayed and helped plan the perfect proposal for my Millie."

Uh-oh. Getting Millie to say "yes" was going to require finesse and romance. Those weren't exactly Mike's strengths. He was more the do-as-I-say-and-like-it kind of dude. If Aldo went with Mike's suggestions, things were going to go downhill—fast.

Before I could ask what Mike's idea of the perfect proposal was, Mike said, "Imagine my surprise when I dropped by and didn't find you at home. You told me you were going to stay put."

Yep—definitely upset I didn't do exactly as he said. "Something came up."

"Did that something have to do with the box delivered today?"

If I said yes, Mike would go through the roof. If I said no, I'd feel like a schmuck for lying. Neither option was appealing, so I went with door number three. "I needed to do some shopping. Since you didn't want me to go out alone, I took Devlyn with me."

Mike's hands clenched and unclenched and the vein on his neck began to pulsate. So much for door number three. Grabbing a piece of bread off a cookie sheet, I motioned for

Mike to follow me into the living room. With proposal planning, Aldo had enough excitement in his life.

I glanced at my watch. I didn't have much time to argue with Mike. Not if I wanted to make my rehearsal call time. Before Mike could start yelling, I planted a hand on my hip and said, "I planned to follow your suggestion, but then the box arrived. The thought of Aunt Millie or Aldo opening it wigged me out. I needed to do something. You were busy, so I went on a wild-goose chase to see if I could find the store where the doll in the box was purchased. The only thing I got for my efforts was a headache and a couple of Christmas gifts crossed off my list."

Mike's mouth twitched. "You canvassed toy stores less than two weeks before Christmas?"

I nodded and took a bite of garlic bread.

"While I'd like nothing better than to yell at you for taking an unnecessary risk, I've been shopping at a toy store this week and I know what a nightmare that is. You've been punished enough. Although I think I've earned this, since I gained at least a dozen gray hairs worrying about you."

Mike walked over and I waited for the kiss I was sure was coming. Not that I wanted him to kiss me, but . . . Mike reached out, snatched my bread, and took a bite. Disappointment snaked through me as I realized he wanted my food—not me. How twisted was that? I needed to get a grip.

Trying not to let Mike see that I was unnerved, I checked my watch and yelped. Whenever possible, I tried to get to the theater ten minutes before call time to give myself time to feel settled. Tonight I was going to be cutting that close. It was time to make tracks.

"Let me get the box for you before I leave."

Mike stopped chewing. "You're going out . . . alone?"

Exasperated, I walked down the hall to the kitchen. "I have to go out. Tonight's our final rehearsal."

"If the killer is part of the show, he or she will be there."

My gut twisted even as I explained, "A hundred other singers, instrumentalists, and crew will be there, too. Not to mention members of the Evanston Police Department." As long as I didn't allow my water bottle out of my sight or wander off alone for Mark or his accomplice to find me, I would be fine.

"I promise I'll have my phone ready to dial 911 at the sign of any trouble." I'd also have Millie's gun handy, but Mike didn't need to know that.

Aldo was draining pasta as we walked back into the kitchen. He assured me dinner would be ready in minutes. Too bad I didn't have time to eat it.

I grabbed the FedEx box off the top of the fridge and handed it to Mike. "I want to perform in the show this weekend. That means I have to go to rehearsal tonight."

Mike flipped the lid on the box and frowned at the contents. While he read the note, I shoved another piece of garlic bread in my mouth, shrugged into my winter gear, and grabbed my bag.

"You need to eat dinner." Aldo waved his wooden spoon at me.

I gave him an apologetic smile. "Tell Aunt Millie not to eat it all so I can have some later." Before Mike could protest, I grabbed a bottle of water from the fridge, opened the garage door, and ran out yelling, "Gotta run."

Snow was falling harder as I steered my car onto the street. The roads were slick, but traffic was moving. I finished my bread, drank some water, and periodically checked the rearview mirror for the silver car that had run me off the road. After I swallowed the last of the bread, I started to sing through some warm-ups.

Singing in the car wasn't the ideal way to prepare for tonight's rehearsal, but I didn't have time for much else. Besides, singing helped keep my mind off the churning in my gut. Part of it was the adrenaline rush that came with performing. The other part was fear.

Mike was right. Even with the crowd of performers and Detective Frewen and company in attendance, going to the theater tonight was a risk. But if I wanted a shot in this business, it was a risk I had to take.

Sitting at a red light, I glanced in the rearview mirror and frowned. I turned my head to get a better look and saw the person in the car behind me wave. Mike.

I put my phone on speaker and hit speed dial as the light turned green. "How did you get behind me?"

"I followed you."

"No, you didn't." If he had, I would have noticed. "How did you find me?"

Mike laughed. "I picked you up about a block back. This is the most direct route to the theater. I knew where you were going, so I took a chance."

Good to know I hadn't missed someone tailing me the entire time. That would have been disconcerting.

"And you're following me, why?" I asked.

"I called Detective Frewen. He confirmed he'll be at tonight's rehearsal."

"You didn't have to tail me to tell me that."

"You didn't think I was going to let the woman I might be in love with park God only knows how many blocks away and walk all alone into the theater, did you?"

Did I want him to act like my bodyguard? No. But I

couldn't help the shiver of pleasure that ran up my spine. Huh. Something to think about another time.

"You aren't planning on coming into the theater, are you?" Tall, dark, and ruggedly handsome, Mike would draw attention, which was the last thing I wanted.

"I plan on escorting you to the door. Frewen and his team will take over once you're inside."

I hung up and steered my car up and down the streets, looking for a parking spot. I was delighted to find street parking less than a block and a half away. Mike turned on his cop lights and waited as I collected my stuff and got out of the car. The passenger door of the squad car opened, and Mike motioned for me to get in. I was about to turn down the lift on principle, but the snow and wind had picked up. Freezing my butt off for the sake of proving my independence would be stupid.

Mike smiled as I climbed into his Mustang. I waited for him to drive and then saw him eye my seat belt. Oy. It was a block and a half.

When we arrived at the stage door, I unclicked the belt as Mike's hand grazed my cheek. I turned and his lips brushed mine in a light, feathery kiss that left me breathless.

"Have a great rehearsal," he said. "Make sure you take care of yourself and—"

"I know." I sighed. "Don't do anything stupid."

Mike watched from the warmth of the Mustang as I navigated the slippery sidewalk. Pulling the heavy stage door open, I waved and ducked inside. The wind whipped the door shut behind me with a resounding bang.

Both the stage and work lights were on. Shaking off the snow, I wrote my initials next to my name on the call-board and saw that Jonathan, Vanessa, and about a dozen chorus members had already signed in. Normally, I liked having a few minutes alone, but all things considered I was relieved so many others were around.

I stepped out of the wings onto the brightly lit stage. No one was seated on the chairs, but I did see someone moving around the light booth. Probably Jenny or our lighting designer. I waved to whoever was up there and turned to go back into the wings. I heard the stage door open and crash shut. Another cast member had arrived.

I walked into the wings and felt my smile of greeting fade. No one was there. I glanced at the call-board. No one new had signed in.

Yep, I was officially creeped out.

My pulse picked up steam as I walked toward the green-room stairs. By the time I'd reached the steps, I'd almost convinced myself that the person who just arrived had simply forgotten to sign in. It happened. Hell, I'd done it more than once in my career. Breathing easier, I put my hand on the staircase railing and stopped in my tracks as someone sneezed.

Chapter 22

My heart skipped and I held my breath as I waited for the sound to come again. Nothing, but I knew someone was close by. Someone who didn't want to be seen. That couldn't be good.

Achoo.

My fingers wrapped around the hilt of Millie's gun, and I considered my options. I could try to make it down the stairs to the greenroom. My feet itched to make a break for it, but doing so would leave my back exposed to whoever was up here. Running was a bad idea. Which left only one option.

"Who's there?" I yelled as I fished my cell phone out of my pocket with my other hand.

Silence.

"Come out now or I'll call the police." As though to prove my point, I hit Mike's number. I could call the Evanston PD, but the 911 dispatcher would want to ask me all sorts of questions. Questions I currently didn't have time to answer. Mike would show up at the door with guns blazing first and ask questions later.

"I'm calling."

More silence.

I put the phone up to my ear as Mike's amused voice came on the line. "Did you forget something in my car?"

"I need you to come back to the theater," I whispered. "It could be a false alarm, but I think there's someone hiding backstage."

All amusement disappeared. "Don't hang up. I'll be right there."

I slid the phone into my pocket and listened again for sounds of whoever was lurking in the shadows. "The cops are on their way. You can come out now or they'll drag you out. Your choice."

Something shuffled to my left. The curtain rustled. I held my breath, pulled the gun out of my pocket, and waited.

The curtain shifted again and I almost dropped the gun when Chessie appeared, followed by a sneezing Eric. "What are the two of you doing here?"

Chessie and Eric looked at each other. Finally, Chessie said, "I wanted to see what a professional dress rehearsal looked like."

I slid the gun back in my pocket and put a hand on my hip. "Really?"

Chessie nodded. Eric looked at the floor.

"Eric?"

His eyes rose to meet mine, and his cheeks turned bright red. "It was my idea to come tonight," he confessed. "I was worried."

Chessie elbowed Eric for ruining her cover and crossed her arms with a huff.

Maybe it was the concussion, but I was totally confused. "What were you worried about?"

"Well, there's a killer on the loose and you got hurt yesterday and I thought if I followed you . . ." Eric's voice trailed off and his face got even redder.

"You came here to protect me?"

Chessie snickered and Eric developed a keen interest in the floorboards, telling me I'd gotten it right in one try. Eric had braved the snow and snuck into the theater tonight to act as my bodyguard. I was stunned, amused, and incredibly touched. The kid's actions were misguided but very sweet.

Trying not to stomp on his sense of chivalry, I said, "I appreciate your concern, but it's the police department's job to catch the killer. Not yours."

It wasn't my job, either. But my life was at stake. I figured that gave me some wiggle room.

Speaking of cops . . .

I pulled the phone out of my pocket. "Hey, false alarm," I told Mike. "A couple of my students decided to play Perry Mason and scared the hell out of me."

The silence on the other end made me think the call had been dropped. Finally, Mike asked, "Are you sure?"

"I have Eric and Chessie standing right in front of me. Do you want me to have them say hello?" I smiled. Chessie scowled, which made me add, "Also, if you could pretend this call never happened, I'd appreciate it. I have a feeling their folks wouldn't approve of their extracurricular behavior."

Chessie let out a sigh of relief as I hung up the phone. "Thanks. My parents think I'm staying over at Kristen's house tonight. They'd panic if they knew I was driving around while it was snowing."

Something told me they'd do more than panic if they knew their kid had stalked a teacher and broken into the theater. Sweet or not, this wasn't the kind of behavior that got a kid into college, although Eric was planning on going into the criminal justice field. Who knows? Maybe they'd be impressed by his initiative.

Wait a minute . . .

I looked back at Eric. "What color is your car?"

He swallowed hard. "Silver."

Bingo. "Did you also follow me Wednesday night?"

Chessie took a step forward and jutted out her chin. "Eric was studying with me on Wednesday night. I had a trig test. So he couldn't have followed you Wednesday. Right, Eric?"

Eric winced. It was a good thing Eric was going into law enforcement, because he'd suck as a criminal.

The kid jammed his hands in his coat pockets and said, "I was at Chessie's house helping her study for trig. I left around nine. That's when I heard the news on the radio. They were talking about the two murders. They said how a member of the *Messiah* cast had found the second body, but that the cops were withholding the name of that person for safety reasons. With everything that happened earlier in the school year, I figured you must have been looking into the murder and stumbled across the other body. I was worried. If I could figure that out, then the killer could, too."

"So you came to the theater and followed me to the sports bar."

Eric nodded.

"And almost ran me off the road."

A much smaller nod. "I didn't mean to. The road was

slick, and I fishtailed into your lane. I was scared you were hurt so I drove around the block and came back to see if your car had moved. I would have called for help, but I saw you drive into your garage and knew you were okay."

Eric's face was devoid of color. His feet shuffled back and forth as he waited for whatever I would say next. The kid looked like he was waiting for the executioner. And I couldn't blame him. If I reported his behavior, Eric would probably get suspended, end up with a traffic violation, and piss off his parents when their insurance rates skyrocketed. And since Chessie's attempt to look innocent told me she knew all about Eric's adventures, she'd most likely get punished for being an accessory after the fact.

For the second time this semester, I had Chessie's future squarely in my hands. The glint of worry in her eyes said she was well aware of it and at this moment was remembering the veiled threats she'd made earlier in the week.

If it was only Chessie in this predicament, I might have made a report just to teach her the lesson she should have learned months ago. But I understood and appreciated Eric's good intentions if not his methods. While I wanted him to think about his actions, I wasn't about to let him blow his future over his concern for me.

"All right." I blew a strand of hair off my forehead. "I don't like what you've done, but I'm not going to report either of you to the principal, the police, or your parents." Chessie let out the breath she was holding and gave me a wide smile. "But I'm also not going to let you completely off the hook. Tomorrow morning, the two of you are going to report to my house at 7 A.M. to shovel my aunt's driveway."

The weather forecast was calling for at least five inches of snow between now and morning. Aunt Millie's driveway was wide and really long. It would take these two a lot of work to get the driveway cleared. While the punishment would be brief, I had no doubt it would make an impression.

Chessie's smile was less enthusiastic when she said, "We'll be there, Ms. Marshall, and we appreciate you not telling anyone about tonight. Neither of us meant any harm. Right, Eric?"

Eric looked ill. Chessie elbowed him. When he finally spoke it wasn't to agree. "The thing is . . ."

Oh no. "What else did you do, Eric?"

"You know how you were followed by someone in the hallway last night?"

I closed my eyes and rubbed my temples with my thumb and middle finger. "Yes?"

"I saw Detective Kaiser in the audience and figured you invited him to the concert because you were worried the killer might show up. So, when I saw you go out the side door of the theater alone, I got concerned." Now that Eric had started his confession, the guilt-laced words tumbled out in a rush.

"Why didn't you just let me know you were there? I wouldn't have thought you were doing anything wrong."

Eric gnawed on his bottom lip. "I've been reading a lot of books on law enforcement and private investigations that talked about the proper techniques for shadowing a subject. The methods didn't sound hard, so I decided to try them out."

Okay, I had to ask. "Why did you chase after me when I realized you were there?"

"I panicked." Another blush. "I guess law enforcement might not be the best field for me."

No offense to Eric, but his career-path dilemma wasn't my concern at the moment; the fact that he'd been following me was. Not because I was angry, but because I'd been wrong. The silver car used to tail me didn't belong to Mark Krauss. More important, there weren't two people lurking in the halls of Prospect Glen High School last night, waiting to do me harm. The killer wasn't acting in tandem. The killer was acting alone, and that changed everything.

Was Mark guilty of something? His wife and Ruth were worried about his behavior, but I had trouble believing he was the one who butchered Barbie and sent her to my house. The act felt feminine. As did David's murder. Poison could be used by a man, but everything I'd read told me it was most often used by women. And LaVon said it was a woman who bought her photograph.

My mind rapidly eliminated Mark and Jonathan from the suspect list and scrolled through the rest.

Based on my gut reaction, I didn't believe Ruth Jordan was the murderer. Her confusion today felt real.

Magdalena might be capable of killing someone, but I highly doubted she'd use a poison that might give her an allergic reaction and land her in the clink. And while David's decision not to record her music had to be a huge blow, there were lots of tenors out there. Lots of people who could record her songs. The list in her room suggested she'd already moved on to finding one. And face it: If I were Magdalena, I'd be looking forward to the day when David realized that the musical piece he'd dissed had racked up glowing reviews and a Grammy nomination. A dead David couldn't have his nose shoved in his stupidity or have his shortsightedness revealed to the media. In short, a dead David was zero fun for a person bent on humiliation and revenge.

That left Vanessa. I was petty enough to want it to be her. Her snotty treatment from day one rankled. But as much as

I tried to imagine it, I just couldn't see her killing David Richard. She hated her love for him, but from what I could see she hated her lack of fame more. This production wasn't just my big break. The *Messiah*, headlined by David Richard, had the potential to launch her into the limelight, too. When David died, there'd been no guarantee the show would continue. Killing David in hopes the producers could find another big name to headline the production was a huge risk. Vanessa's tactics to get to the top weren't the ones I employed, but they were tried and true. Murder—not so much.

I'd eliminated every single suspect on my list. Which meant there was someone I'd missed. Someone with a grudge against David Richard. Someone who was close enough to the show's stage manager to have drinks with him before stringing him up in his kitchen in hopes Bill would take the fall for poisoning David.

As my mind struggled to put the pieces together, I realized the theater was quiet. Chessie and Eric were standing silently next to the curtain leg. Without their chatter, the lack of sound was deafening. Which made no sense. The call-board showed more than a dozen singers had signed in. While the greenroom was on the level below, the doors to the greenroom had been removed long ago to ensure no one could close them during a performance. A performer running from one side of the stage to the other might not make her entrance if she had to struggle to open the door. And since this wasn't a show that required the ensemble to change into costume, there was no reason for the dressing room doors to be closed. With that many people downstairs, I should hear voices.

I looked back at the stage door. No one had come in since

Chessie and Eric's less-than-sneaky entrance. No singers. No orchestra members. None of Evanston's finest looking to keep us safe. Something was very, very wrong.

Fear must have flickered across my face, because Eric's contrite demeanor disappeared. He glanced around the wings of the theater and asked, "What's wrong?"

"We have to get up early on Saturday," Chessie hissed. "That's what's wrong."

I pulled out my phone as I walked to the stage door. Locked.

Ignoring Chessie's irritated glare and Eric's worried expression, I punched in Mike's number and waited for him to answer.

"What now?"

"Someone locked the stage door from the outside."

"Maybe it's frozen shut. The storm's getting pretty bad out here."

"I don't think so." I turned away from Chessie and Eric and lowered my voice. "The call-board says other cast members signed in, but no one is here and it's past our call time. I think we might be in trouble."

"I'm on my way. Have you seen anyone else in the building?"

I was going to say no, but then I remembered. "Someone was in the light booth when I first arrived. The booth lights were dim compared to the theater and stage, so I couldn't see who was inside."

But I knew.

There was only person who could have set this trap. The person who had sent the text with the new call time, knowing no cast member would ever question a message from a stage manager.

Jenny Grothe.

"Are the kids still with you?" Mike's voice was controlled, but I could hear the shimmer of concern.

"Eric and Chessie are right here."

"Good. Try to find another exit. Stay together. I'm going to call Detective Frewen now. He can probably get there faster than I can. I'll call you back as soon as I'm done. Got it?"

I swallowed a knot of fear and nodded. "Got it."

Switching the phone to vibrate, I turned back to Eric and Chessie. "The Evanston Police Department and Detective Kaiser are on their way. Detective Kaiser thinks the stage door is frozen shut. He wants us to check the other exits and see if we can't get out that way."

"You don't think the door is frozen shut, do you?" Eric stepped forward.

I debated how to answer the question. According to the handbook Larry had given me at the beginning of the year, my job as a teacher was to help provide a safe environment for students. Telling Eric and Chessie that a killer had lured me to an empty theater wasn't exactly following that edict. But I didn't see any other choice.

"I think there's a good chance the person who killed David Richard and Bill Walters is here in the theater with us."

Chessie's eyes widened, and she clamped her hand over her mouth. Eric swallowed hard, laced his fingers through Chessie's free hand, and said, "Tell us what you want us to do."

His calm demeanor was impressive. Maybe law enforcement was the right choice for Eric after all.

"There's an exit on the other side of the stage," I explained while I tried to remember the exact layout of the theater. "We're going to cross behind the risers and check that door. If it's locked, we'll go down the escape stairs to the doors in the lobby. As long as we stay together, we'll be just fine."

I hoped.

I walked behind one of the black velvet curtain legs designed to obstruct the audience's view off stage and peered out into the theater. No one was seated in the house. The lighting booth looked empty. I fingered the gun in my pocket and looked back at the faces of the two kids trusting me to get them to safety. Taking several deep breaths, I stepped onto the stage.

The lights were bright as we hurried across to the stage left wings. No Jenny. I let out the breath I was holding and pushed the bar on the exit door.

It didn't budge. Crap. Could one door get frozen shut? Sure. But two? No way in hell.

"We're going to the lobby," I whispered as I stepped back onto the stage. Still no one in the theater. Taking that as a good sign, I started to lead Eric and Chessie toward the escape stairs.

We got halfway there and the lights in the theater went black.

Chapter 23

Chessie screamed. I froze.

Someone had turned off the lights.

With no windows to the outside, the theater was pitch-black. Somewhere in front of me was the orchestra pit and the edge of the stage. Behind us were the risers and chairs. Moving forward, we'd risk falling either the four feet off the front of the stage or the ten feet into the fully lowered orchestra pit. Backing into the risers or a folding chair could injure us or, worse, make noise. Any sound would give away our position. And even if we could make it to the wings, there was no place for us to run. The doors were locked. In short, we were screwed.

Chessie's screams turned to whimpers. I could hear Eric whispering that everything would be fine even though I seriously doubted he believed that.

Adrenaline pumping, I gulped for air and willed myself

to stay calm. I was the adult—the teacher. Chessie and Eric needed me to get them through this.

Wrapping my fingers around Millie's gun, I whispered, "Keep quiet and get down on the floor. You'll be safer there."

If not from Jenny, then from me. I didn't want them in the line of fire if I was forced to start shooting.

I heard scuffling to my right as Eric and Chessie followed instructions. Taking slow, deep breaths, I pictured my exact location on the stage before the lights had been turned out. If I remembered correctly, the escape stairs were ten feet in front of my position. The pit was a couple of feet downstage and to the left.

Hoping my memory was intact, I took several steps to my left to put some distance between me and my students. Then, lifting my chin, I yelled into the darkness, "Jenny, I know you're there. You might as well give up. Everyone is going to be here soon for tonight's rehearsal. They're going to wonder why they can't get into the building and call the police."

No point in telling her the police had already been called. I hoped she'd find that out soon enough.

A loud *click* echoed through the empty theater. A moment later, a pool of white light appeared center stage. Someone had turned on the follow spot. I shoved my gun back into my pocket in an attempt to keep the element of surprise and watched the small pool of light shift to the left. When it reached the wings, it panned to the right, finally coming to a stop—right on me.

Squinting into the balcony, I could make out the outline of Jenny's small frame. I glanced down to my right, where Eric and Chessie were huddled on the floor. The blurred edge of the light was too close to them for my comfort. If by some miracle Jenny didn't know they were here with me, I wanted to keep it that way.

I took several more steps to my right. The tightly focused, four-foot patch of light followed me. The orchestra pit with its chairs, music stands, and timpani was three feet in front of my position.

"That's your mark," Jenny yelled. "If you move off your mark, you'll be sorry."

Sorry? I was already sorry.

"No one else is coming here tonight." Jenny's voice echoed in the theater. "As soon as you got here, I sent out a message canceling rehearsal because of the storm. You know, you should have stayed away tonight, Paige. I gave you a chance. I tried to warn you. If you'd stayed away, I was going to let you go. But you just couldn't resist the chance to be a star, could you?"

Jenny's voice sounded closer. I squinted into the light, trying to see whether she was still behind the follow spot. "What do you mean, you tried to warn me? I didn't get anything warning me not to come tonight."

"I sent you a Christmas gift warning you that you'd be next."

Jenny wasn't behind the spotlight. She must have locked the fixture in place before moving. Her voice was coming from somewhere farther to the right.

I took a step in that direction, trying to get a better look, and jumped as a *crack* filled the air. Chessie whimpered as something thudded into the stage at my feet. A bullet. Holy crap. Jenny had a gun.

"I told you not to leave your mark, Paige." Jenny's voice had relocated again. To the left? It was hard to tell.

"I wanted you to realize your life was more important than this show. But you're just like him. He loved the spotlight. He didn't have room for anything else."

Panic poured through me, making it hard to focus on Jenny's words. But I needed to. I had to find a way to give Mike and the Evanston PD cavalry a chance to get here while Eric, Chessie, and I were still in one piece. Talking seemed like the best option. Taking a shot in the dark, I asked, "Like you?"

I waited for her to answer, but there was only silence. I shielded my eyes from the light, trying to see beyond the orchestra pit and into the balcony. Where was she?

"Jenny?"

"You want to know what he said?" She'd moved. Her voice was no longer coming from the balcony. She was on the theater's main floor. "He told me I was a mistake. Just an impulse. A moment in time that wasn't supposed to go any further."

The tears in Jenny's voice would have elicited my sympathy if not for the threatening-me-with-a-gun thing. Remembering Vanessa's story, I said, "It isn't your fault. David seduced a lot of smart women."

"You think I slept with him?" Jenny shrieked. Her voice was closer. "Are you crazy? I wouldn't have slept with him." There was another crack and a clang far to my left.

Okay, Jenny was coming unhinged, and I was totally confused. This really wasn't good. I forced myself to breathe. To sound calm. "I want to understand what David did to you, Jenny. Please. Tell me."

Something shuffled on the stage floor. Another shot echoed through the theater. "Tell the kids to stay where they ‒re or I'll fire again."

I peered at the dimly lit side of the stage and watched Eric pull Chessie back to the ground. "They won't move again. They promise. Right, guys?"

"Right." Only Eric responded, making me think Chessie was too scared to talk.

I could empathize. I was scared out of my wits. But I knew I had to keep talking. "They aren't moving anymore. So tell me—what did David do to you? Why did you kill him?"

For several seconds, the only sounds were Chessie's soft sobs and the pounding of my heart. I slid my right hand into my pocket and wrapped my fingers tight around the hilt of the gun. How long would it take for me to get Millie's gun out of my pocket and fire *if* I located Jenny. Five seconds? Ten? An eternity, considering Jenny had her gun in hand and her finger on the trigger. I needed Mike, and I needed him now.

I was about to call out to Jenny again when she said, "You were right about David seducing lots of women. I didn't want to believe those stories. I thought that the media were exaggerating to sell papers and that he let them because getting press was good for his career."

"I didn't know you were such a big fan of David's," I said, trying to find Jenny in the dark.

"I'm not a fan, Paige."

The sound of feet climbing the stairs had me turning to my left. Jenny was coming onto the stage. Moments later, I spotted her in the dimness past the edges of my patch of light. It was too dark to see her expression, but there was more than enough light to make out the gun in her hand. She stopped walking and said, "I'm David Richard's daughter."

Yowzah. I'd considered a lot of motives for David Richard's murder, but death by daughter wasn't one of them. Probably because his bio said he didn't have any children. Either the bio was wrong or Jenny was, and since she was the one holding the gun, I was more than willing to hear her side of the story.

"You killed your father?"

"I didn't want to, but he left me no choice. I thought he'd be happy to know he had a daughter. My mother was in a show with him. As soon as the show ended, David left without saying good-bye or leaving his phone number or anything. She never told him about me."

"So you did."

"When I heard he was coming to Northwestern, I took it as a sign. I declared a music minor and registered for voice lessons with him. Every week I waited for him to notice how we have the same eyes. Since he couldn't make a lot of the lessons because he was so busy with his own career, I had to come up with another way to spend time with him."

"So, you convinced Bill to let you assistant stage manage this show."

She nodded. "Bill and my mom go way back. He said no at first because of my lack of experience. I've only stage managed student-directed shows here on campus. But I wasn't about to take no for an answer. I told him David was my father. That's why he gave me the job."

"And why you had to kill him."

"I didn't have any choice." The gun lowered a fraction of an inch. "We were supposed to meet at the theater to go over a few things, but Bill called and told me to come to his house instead. When I got there, Bill said he was going to explain my relationship with David to the police. He thought it would be better for me to have that information out in the open. That innocent secrets like mine and Magdalena's would make us look guilty if we hid them."

"He didn't realize you'd murdered David?" Wow, did that suck.

Jenny shook her head. "Not at first. It wasn't until he spotted the glass photograph Mom and I'd bought him for his birthday. He thought the photograph was made with potassium cyanide, but it wasn't. I mean, my mom and I got it when I was looking into the poison, but the photograph was made with something else. Only I couldn't tell him that without making him more suspicious. I knew he'd call the police the first chance he got. He didn't understand."

I didn't, either, and I was having it explained to me.

Jenny took a step closer. The gun in her hand trembled. "David was going to have me fired from this show, and threatened to go to the dean and have me expelled from Northwestern. He said I was stalking him, but I wasn't. I just wanted to be his daughter, and he wanted to ruin my life."

Sure, Jenny had the right to be upset. Having a father who didn't want to understand you and basically bowed out of your life was hard. I had firsthand experience with looking out into the audience only to find an empty seat where my father was supposed to be. But call me crazy—adding a body count to the mix didn't make things better. Too bad the girl didn't understand that.

"So now what?" I asked.

Jenny bit her lip. "I don't know. I thought framing Bill would fix everything. Do you know how much work it is to stage a hanging?"

Um. No. And I hoped I never had to learn.

"Bill is heavier than he looked. Between getting him up

on the table and then having to lift him while tying the rope . . ." Jenny sighed. "After all that work the cops didn't believe the suicide note. And Professor Krauss is starting to ask too many questions, just like you did."

Somewhere in the distance I heard something click. Jenny heard it, too. She swung toward the back of the theater and tightened her grip on the gun. Something shuffled. Mike and the cops had arrived. Unfortunately, I wasn't the only one who had figured out they were here.

Jenny swung back to me and aimed her gun. She had to believe the only way to escape was to take me out and race for the exit. I had to act.

I pulled the gun out of my pocket as Jenny's finger tightened on her trigger. Eric's or Chessie's gasp reminded me they were close by. They needed to get to safety. Now.

"Run," I yelled as I raced downstage out of the light. Jenny screamed and fired. A shot dinged off a music stand next to me. Yikes. To my right, the sound of footsteps told me Eric and Chessie had gotten off the stage. Knowing they were out of the line of fire, I turned and pulled the trigger.

Nothing happened. Oh no! The safety must be on. I hit the deck as Jenny raced forward and fired again.

My fingers fumbled with the gun as I frantically tried to flip the safety. I could find it in the light when I wasn't scared witless, but I couldn't find it now. And now was when I needed it, otherwise I was going to die.

I rolled to the left and smashed my shoulder into a chair as another gunshot split the air. The chair hit the ground with a clang, and I scampered to my feet and bolted toward the stage left wings.

Another shot. The bullet clanged against something

metal, sending up a spark. I spotted the outline of Jenny downstage left. Another shot. My heart skittered as the bullet lodged into the stage two feet in front of me. It was dark and Jenny wasn't a great shot, but she was getting close. Any closer and I was going to be really unhappy.

I shifted to my right. My foot caught on something, and I smashed into several music stands before landing half on the risers, half on the hardwood of the stage floor. Oh God. Millie's gun flew out of my hand. It hit the stage and skidded across the ground, away from me.

This was bad. This was very, very bad.

Crack. Crack.

Sparks flew inches from my head. Yikes. Yikes. Yikes.

Hands shaking, I grabbed a music stand and pulled it in front of me. The stands were sturdy black metal. I wasn't sure they would stop a bullet, but maybe they'd slow one down. Yes, I was grasping at straws, but at this point that was all I had.

Jenny came closer. Her gun shifted to take aim. I sucked in air and held my breath. That's when I heard footsteps. Someone was running toward us.

Hope lit through me as I squinted into the dim light. The footsteps came closer. Jenny heard them, too. She shifted her attention toward the sound as Eric raced on stage, illuminated by the spotlight. He clutched a large two-by-four in his hands.

Ice-cold fear raced up my spine.

"Run, Ms. Marshall," he yelled, brandishing the large block of wood.

Jenny pointed her gun at Eric.

Somewhere in the back of the theater I heard a door open

and close. Mike had to be here, but he was going to be too late.

Jenny straightened her arms. I pushed my music-stand shield off me, and it clanged to the ground. Jenny turned as I jumped to my feet and charged.

The houselights came up. The sudden brightness blinded me as I ran smack into Jenny. Her gun flew out of her hand. It crashed to the floor as the momentum of my leap carried the two of us toward the edge of the orchestra pit. Jenny's feet hit the last board of the stage, and her fingers dug into my arm. She teetered on the edge and then slid into nothingness.

Jenny screamed. I would have screamed, too, but I was too busy leaning backward, trying to break free of Jenny's hold and failing. My feet slid to the edge of the pit, and suddenly the ground was gone.

Oof.

Something grabbed me around the waist and yanked me back to safety as Jenny lost her grip and fell smack into the tympani drums with a resounding *thud*.

Chapter 24

The police charged down the theater's aisles. I spotted Mike near Detective Frewen. Our eyes locked. From here, I could see his relief and residual fear. Or maybe I was projecting, since I felt huge amounts of both.

Detective Frewen started shouting orders. The first of which was for the people on stage to get back from the edge of the pit. Considering what had just happened, both Eric and I were more than happy to comply. A team of uniformed cops wielding guns swarmed in front of the stage to ensure Jenny was unarmed. After a quick assessment, the paramedics were called in.

I was thankful Eric had saved me from needing that same emergency team. I turned to him and gave his hand a squeeze. "Thanks."

He looked more than a little green when he squeezed back.

Chessie started to run out on stage, but was waylaid by one of Evanston's finest. The minute the cop grabbed Chessie's arm, she started to scream. While Chessie might have the occasional pitch problem, she never had any trouble being heard. The restraining cop's ears were never going to be the same.

Detective Frewen continued to bark orders. A groaning Jenny was loaded onto a stretcher and rushed to the ambulance. Cops raced around taking pictures, marking bullet holes, and picking up guns. I felt a stab of regret as I watched Millie's pink gun get bagged and tagged. If my aunt ever got it back, I was going to practice unlatching the safety in the dark—just in case.

By the time the paramedics gave Eric, Chessie, and me the once-over and Detective Frewen took our statements, it was after eleven o'clock. Chessie's and Eric's parents had been called to the scene. Eric's parents looked terrified and relieved. Chessie's parents looked massively put out. From the dirty looks they gave me, I wondered if they'd use the events of this evening to prove my unfitness as a teacher.

Chessie argued with her parents and then raced across the lobby to me. Before I could react, the teen wrapped her arms around my waist and held tight. Her voice was muffled and shaky when she said, "I'm so sorry for everything."

I wrapped my arms around her, rested my head on top of hers, and let the tears that had been threatening fall. Another set of arms wrapped around the two of us. Eric. The three of us stood there for a long time. Tomorrow Chessie might hate me again or she and Eric might break up, but at this moment we were grateful to be together and alive.

I opened my eyes and stared up at the ceiling. My first thought was *I'm alive*. My next was today was supposed to be the day I took the singing world by storm. But while driving me home last night, Mike broke the news that my big break wasn't going to happen. The cops would need at least twenty-four hours to process the crime scene. Until the scene was processed and released, no one would be allowed inside. This meant that, despite theatrical tradition, the show wouldn't go on.

Killer whined from his spot next to me as I rolled out of bed. After a hot shower and several aspirin, I felt as ready as possible to face the day ahead.

"You are awake." Aldo stood up from the kitchen table and folded me into a big hug. "Good. Millie is in her office, answering the phone calls that have been coming in from reporters all morning."

"I haven't heard the phone ring." Which gave me hope that Aldo was exaggerating. While getting coverage from the press was something all performers coveted, we wanted glowing reviews for our singing, not stories about near-death experiences. One boosted calls from casting directors; the other meant stares in the grocery store check-out line.

Aldo smiled. "Millie turned off the ringers when the calls started coming. She didn't want you to wake up too early, although she was getting worried that you were sleeping so late. She wanted you to have time to get ready for your big day."

I winced. Last night, I'd been too tired and shaky to tell my aunt and Aldo the fate of the *Messiah*. Trying not to sound defeated, I said, "The theater's a crime scene. We can't use it for the concert, so the show's been canceled."

Aldo laughed. "The producer called to say your show has moved to a new theater. He also tell me he left a message on your cell phone."

I dove into my purse for my phone. Holy crap. Aldo was right. The show had been moved to the Merle Reskin Theatre in downtown Chicago. Patrons were being notified about the change of venue. The stories running on the news were boosting ticket sales like crazy. The show was going to go on as planned, albeit with a different stage manager.

I did a happy little dance and then felt the bottom drop out of my stomach as opening-day nerves set in. The show was going on, only this version would have a bigger audience. There would also be a large press corps somewhere in the crowd. Oh God! I was going to be sick.

Aldo brought me a cup of coffee already doctored with copious amounts of cream and sugar. Next to the mug of coffee he'd placed a plate of cinnamon toast and fresh fruit. Aldo was a saint.

"Devlyn called to check on you, and Detective Michael called, too. Michael said he would drop by and take you to retrieve your car." Aldo waited until I started eating my toast before going off to tell Millie I was conscious.

I tried to relax and enjoy my food, but nerves had set in. All I could think about was flubbing my notes or making a fool of myself in front of tonight's audience. Which I supposed was better than the nightmares that had plagued me throughout the night. Falling flat on my face as I crossed the stage was far preferable to being gunned down in the spotlight.

Since the only thing that would banish the fears was practice, I decided to take the toast, coffee, and rehearsal bag to the living room, where Aldo had installed his baby grand piano. I was halfway through my second aria when I noticed Mike standing in the doorway of the living room. He had a strange look on his face. Did he like my singing? I couldn't tell, and I was annoyed with myself for caring. Pushing him and his opinions out of my mind, I forced myself to concentrate as I finished the song. When I stopped singing, I turned back to him and said hello.

"Your aunt told me how good you were." He jammed his hands in his pant pockets and leaned against the doorway. "I don't know anything about the kind of music you were just singing, but I think she might have undersold you."

"Thanks." I think. As compliments went, it was one of the best I'd received, but the tone was disgruntled. Strange.

"Come on." Mike pushed away from the wall. "Let's go get your car."

Settled in the comfort of Mike's Mustang, I waited for him to talk about last night. Only, Mike wasn't chatty. Drat. Once I'd gotten home yesterday and climbed into bed, I'd realized I had lots of unanswered questions. Detective Frewen could answer them, but I seriously doubted he would. Driving me home, Mike had mentioned he'd been invited to sit in on the interviews. Being a part of the take-down got him a seat at the table. That meant he could fill in some of the blanks for me.

"I haven't heard any news reports," I said. "Is Jenny going to be all right?"

Mike shrugged. "Physically, yes. The girl caught a break when she landed on those big drums. A dislocated shoulder and a couple of bruises. But mentally—well, the lawyers her mother hired are already talking diminished capacity. From what Detective Frewen can tell, the lawyers aren't too far off the mark."

I remembered the singsong quality of Jenny's voice before she started firing and agreed. Jenny wasn't playing with a full deck.

"How did she get the potassium cyanide?" I asked. "I know she gave Bill Walters a wet-plate photograph that he thought had been created with the stuff. But the artist doesn't use cyanide for her work. So, where did the poison come from?"

Mike raised an eyebrow but didn't bother to ask how I knew about the wet-plate photograph or the gallery. I guess Mike didn't want to fight. "Jenny was dating a jewelry store clerk. He gave her a tour of the vault and other rooms in the back of the store. While he was in the bathroom, she put on a hospital mask she brought and put the powder in a Ziploc bag. Since it doesn't take much cyanide to kill someone, the jewelry store owner never noticed any was missing."

Scary.

"Jenny had some cyanide left, so she slipped a smaller dose into Bill's wine. Once he was dead, she moved the kitchen table under the light and used it to stand on while she strung him up. Cyanide is a popular suicide drug. Jenny assumed it would lend credibility to the suicide confession scene she set."

I pictured David Richard taking a drink and falling to the ground. "There wouldn't be time to hang yourself after taking the poison."

Mike's smile was grim. "Logic isn't the overwhelming force in Jenny's life. The interviews Frewen did this week say Jenny's behavior deteriorated around the time David

Richard stepped on campus. A lot of people, including her mother, were concerned, but everyone thought it was just the typical college senior stress."

If only one of those people had reported Jenny's behavior to health services or to a faculty member . . .

"What about Mark Krauss?" I asked.

"What about him?"

I sighed. "What was his part in all of this?"

Mike's eyes flicked to me. "As far as I know, Mark Krauss isn't involved. You told me the silver car that followed you belonged to Eric Metz." His rolled eyes spoke volumes about my plea to keep that information to himself. I'd also asked whether Mike could get Millie her gun back. He said he'd try, but I was pretty sure I would be buying my aunt a new Beretta for her birthday next year.

"Mark's wife and Ruth suggested that he was involved in something," I explained. "They both said he's been acting strange."

"Maybe he's having an affair." Mike shrugged. "If it makes you feel better, I'll have Frewen ask Jenny about Mark Krauss. But I don't expect it'll turn up anything. Once Frewen got the girl talking, she was more than happy to share her secrets."

Another check mark in the insanity column.

Mike pulled up next to my car, and I waited for him to go for a kiss. Instead, he patted my hand, pecked me on the cheek, and said, "Drive safe. The roads are still a little slick. I'll see you at the concert tonight."

Huh. Maybe Mike thought I needed to be treated with kid gloves after almost dying. Sweet, but unnecessary. I was fine. Or I would be after I had a couple more answers.

Since the show had moved locations, the call time had also been changed. That meant I had just enough time to let Millie do my hair and makeup, grab my garment bag, accessories, and dress shoes, and head downtown to the theater. My heart skipped several beats as I walked through the stage door and signed my initials on the call-board. Once again, there were a dozen or more people signed in—only this time the theater wasn't quiet. There were crew members shouting to one another as they moved risers and stands into position on stage. Someone—I was guessing our new stage manager—was waving his arms while barking into a phone. It was business as usual in show business. Tonight, the only danger I would face would come from the critics.

A list on the board told me my dressing room was on the second floor. I headed toward the stairs, trying hard not to notice the number of stagehand conversations that stopped as I walked past.

The larger theater had more dressing rooms, which meant I no longer had to share. I found the door with my name on it, pushed it open, and was hit by the smell of flowers. Lots and lots of flowers.

I hung up my dress and bag and checked out the cards on the nearly dozen bouquets crammed into the small space. Aunt Millie. Aldo. Devlyn. The Prospect Glen School Board. My manager. The producers of the show. Bill Walters's family. Mike. There was even one from Jonathan.

Trying hard not to notice the lack of flowers or note from my parents, I closed the door and changed into my red silk gown. The dress had one shoulder strap and hugged my body from the chest to just past my hips, where it gently flared away from my legs. Tiny red beads were sewn down the side of the dress. While the gown showed very little skin, it was sexy, eye-catching, and a perfect color for the holiday season.

I stepped into my sparkly silver shoes, added the dangly diamond earrings I'd borrowed from Aunt Millie, and turned to examine my appearance in the full-length mirror. The eyes staring back at me were filled with excitement and nerves. This was my chance. A chance that had almost been taken away. A chance that might not come again. Which meant I'd better not screw it up.

Taking deep breaths, I grabbed my water bottle and black music folder, stepped out of my dressing room, and just about smacked into Mark Krauss. He looked striking in his black tuxedo—albeit a bit off-balance since I'd caught him preparing to knock.

He gave me a forced smile. "I know we have to walk the stage soon, but I was hoping you could spare a few minutes to talk."

We had ten minutes until the stage manager would ask us to come downstairs. Plenty of time to get some answers. Stepping back, I waited for Mark to enter the dressing room before closing the door.

Mark adjusted his bow tie and cleared his throat. "I'm sorry for what happened to you yesterday. If you'd been hurt . . ."

"You'd have felt responsible?"

Mark sighed. "Nora told me you came by the house. She said you suspected I might be involved with David's and Bill's murders."

It was my turn to look uncomfortable. "I was wrong," I admitted.

"I didn't have anything to do with the murders, but I still

take some responsibility for them. Jenny was my student. I ran into her outside of David's studio one day. She was crying. Her hair and clothes looked disheveled. Knowing David's reputation, I immediately assumed he'd made an attempt to seduce her and tried to get her to file a report. She wouldn't. When I saw David later that night, I accused him of sleeping with his students. He didn't deny it, and we ended up in an argument that got a little out of hand."

The fistfight.

"Jenny heard about the fight and came to my office. That's when she told me about David being her father. She was so upset when he died. It never occurred to me that she could have had anything to do with his murder. At least, not at first."

"When did you start to suspect her?"

"After Bill was killed. She said she never saw him that night, but I saw a note she had on her rehearsal schedule about a meeting with him."

"Why didn't you go to the police?"

He ran a hand through his sandy hair and started to pace the small space. "I didn't want to believe she did it. She trusted me with her secret. If I went to the police with my concerns and was proven wrong, my betrayal would have sent her over the edge."

A neat trick considering she was already there.

"So you did nothing?"

"No. I kept an eye on her. She trusted me, so she didn't question when I called every couple of hours to ask how she was doing. I even called all the main cast members in this production to make sure no one had arranged to meet her one-on-one."

A light bulb went on. "You called my house pretending to be a reporter."

"The guy I talked to swore your high school choir concert would be packed with people. I never dreamed Jenny would risk going there."

"Your wife said you were home on Thursday night, but you weren't. She's not very good at lying."

Mark laughed. "She loses at blackjack every time we go to Vegas." His smile faded. "I sat in my car outside Jenny's apartment building. If she left I was going to follow her, only she never came out the front door. When I heard about your attack, I thought that proved Jenny was innocent."

I guess Mark had never heard of the back door.

But I didn't doubt his sincerity when he raised his eyes to mine and said, "I was wrong and you could have died because of it. You have no idea how sorry I am. I doubt you can ever forgive me, but if I can ever—"

"You're forgiven." I held out my hand.

Mark took my hand in his with obvious surprise, but I meant what I said. I might not have liked the outcome of his actions, but I was starting to understand a teacher wanting to do right by the students who were entrusted into his or her care. He wanted to protect Jenny. The purpose behind his actions was just, even if Jenny ultimately didn't deserve his aid.

The monitor crackled to life, and the voice of the new stage manager asked the cast to walk the stage. The house doors would open in thirty minutes.

Yikes.

My legs shook as I walked next to Mark down the stairs.

The minutes until curtain flew by. I checked to make sure my water and chair were exactly as I wanted them set on stage. My cheeks were kissed in greeting by our new tenor, the incredible Andre Napoletano. There was a conversation with Vanessa, who was jealous she hadn't been shot at last night. ("Think of the press I would have received.") Than a chat with Magdalena about a recording project I might be perfect for and a good-luck wish with a suggestion for a post-show celebration from Jonathan.

I didn't have time to think about my nerves until the chorus walked onto the stage. Butterflies tickled the lining of my stomach as Ruth's violin played and the orchestra began to tune. The stage manager cued us soloists. My heart thundered. My fingers clutched my black binder. My legs were weak, but my shoulders were straight as I followed Vanessa onto the stage accompanied by thunderous applause from a packed house.

Smiling, I scanned the audience as we waited for Maestro Magdalena Tebar to take the podium in the pit. I spotted Millie, Aldo, and Mike directly in front of my position three rows from the stage. Millie was beaming as she poked Aldo's arm. Devlyn was ten rows back in the center, holding the hand of an older blonde woman I guessed was his mother. I don't think I imagined the pride in his smile as he winked at me.

The audience applauded again as Maestro Tebar strutted to her podium. She bowed to the audience, picked up her baton, and indicated for the chorus and soloists to sit. I was halfway into my seat when another group of familiar faces caught my eye: Larry, Eric, Chessie, and members of the Music in Motion cast.

They were here. My eyes skipped from face to face to face. All fourteen of my students had come—for me.

Magdalena raised her baton. My pulse jumped as the first notes of the overture resonated through the theater. My heart soared as our new star tenor, Jonathan and Vanessa, the chorus, and the audience sang their hearts out. And when it was finally my turn to stand, I no longer was scared. I was ready for this performance and whatever tomorrow might bring.

Someone wants to bake a killing.

FROM *NEW YORK TIMES* BESTSELLING AUTHOR

JENN MCKINLAY

RED VELVET REVENGE

A Cupcake Bakery Mystery

It may be summertime, but sales at Fairy Tale Cupcakes are below zero—and owners Melanie Cooper and Angie DeLaura are willing to try anything to heat things up. So when local legend Slim Hazard offers them the chance to sell cupcakes at the annual Juniper Pass Rodeo, they're determined to rope in a pretty payday!

But not everyone at Juniper Pass is as sweet for Fairy Tale Cupcakes as Slim—including star bull-rider Ty Stokes. Mel and Angie try to steer clear of the cowboy's short fuse, but when his dead body is found facedown in the hay, it's a whole different rodeo…

INCLUDES SCRUMPTIOUS RECIPES!

"I gobbled it up."
—Julie Hyzy, bestselling author of the
White House Chef Mysteries

facebook.com/TheCrimeSceneBooks
penguin.com

Becca Robbins is happy to help research a farmers' market and tourist trading post—until she has to switch her focus to finding a killer…

AN ALL-NEW ESPECIAL
FROM NATIONAL BESTSELLING AUTHOR

PAIGE SHELTON

Red Hot Deadly Peppers

A Farmers' Market Mini Mystery

Becca is in Arizona, spending some time at Chief Buffalo's trading post and its neighboring farmers' market to check out how the two operate together. She's paired with Nera, a Native American woman who sells the most delicious pecans—right next to a booth with the hottest peppers money can buy.

When Nera asks her to deliver some beads to Graham, a talented jewelry maker inside Chief Buffalo's, Becca is grateful to get a break from the heat. Little does she realize that the heat's about to get cranked up even more—because Graham has been murdered, and she's the one who finds his body. She soon discovers that Graham was Nera's cousin, and that her uncle was recently killed, too, after receiving a threatening note. Becca begins to think the murders may have something to do with the family's hot pepper business. Now she must find the killer, before she's the one in the hot seat…

Includes a bonus recipe!

paigeshelton.com
facebook.com/TheCrimeSceneBooks
penguin.com

M1144T0712